# A High
# and Beautiful Wave

*Enjoy the ride!*

*John M White*

*wythewhite@gmail.com*

# A High
# and Beautiful Wave

A novel by
John Wythe White

Mutual Publishing

ISBN-10: 1-56647-880-4
ISBN-13: 978-1-56647-880-9

Library of Congress Cataloging-in-Publication Data

White, John Wythe.
  A high and beautiful wave : a novel / by John Wythe White.
      p. cm.
  ISBN-13: 978-1-56647-880-9 (pbk. : alk. paper)
  ISBN-10: 1-56647-880-4 (pbk. : alk. paper)
  1. College teachers--Fiction. 2. Middle-aged men--Fiction. 3. Hawaii--Fiction. I.
Title.
  PS3623.H5767H54 2008
  813'.6--dc22
                                    2008024659


Design by Daphne Chu, Merriam Fontanilla
Cover Design by Daphne Chu, Merriam Fontanilla
Cover Illustration © Carlo Carbajal

First Printing, September 2008

Mutual Publishing, LLC
1215 Center Street, Suite 210
Honolulu, Hawaii 96816
Ph: (808) 732-1709
Fax: (808) 734-4094
e-mail: info@mutualpublishing.com
www.mutualpublishing.com

Printed in Korea

## ACKNOWLEDGEMENTS

Excerpts from "Taylor Camp, Hawaii: The life and death of a hippie community" by Thomas J. Riley and Karma Ibsen-Riley (Field Museum of Natural History Bulletin 50[6], 1979) reproduced with permission of the authors.

Excerpts from *101 Things To Do: Kauai* reproduced with permission from 101 Inc.

Excerpts from *Beaches of Kaua'i and Ni'ihau* by John Clark (© 1989 The University of Hawaii Press) reproduced with permission from the publisher.

Excerpt from *Lonely Planet Guide Hawaii* reproduced with permission from Hawaii 5th Edition © 2000 Lonely Planet Publications.

Excerpts from *A High and Beautiful Wave* appeared in two issues of Bamboo Ridge, a Hawaii literary journal. One was a runner-up in the journal's fiction competition.

Thanks to Daphne Chu, Merriam Fontanilla, Arikka Johnson, Renee Tamanaha and Hiromi Zimmerman of Ostrander-Chu for their cover and book design, and to Carlo Carbajal for his cover illustration.

Thanks to everyone who helped with the vision and revision of this book, including Ian MacMillan, Steve Shrader, Victoria Kneubuhl, Jim Kraus, and Dawn Sueoka. Thanks also to my wife, Victoria Gail-White, and my sister, Sue White, for their encouragement.

ACKNOWLEDGMENTS

For everyone who came of age in the 1960s and was part of that decade's extraordinary cultural and political changes, and for all those who are keeping the spirit alive.

*The new generation...discovered the environment, and the damage we were doing to it in our ignorance about the workings of nature...Ecology became the new word, and "Earth Days" the new celebrations. There was great sincerity and honesty among these new nature-lovers. They leaped oceans and continents and are appearing in all the grand beachcombing sites this plundered planet can still provide. So many appeared in Hawaii...that authorities began speaking of them as The Problem...I suggest that what they are calling The Problem may well be the solution to the real problems.*

Euell Gibbons, *Beachcomber's Handbook* (Preface to New Edition, 1972)

*My generation left the country better in some ways, not least by destroying the letter of the laws of racism and sexual discrimination. We were one of the generations to which the word "Romantic" might be applied—the offspring of a period inclined by history to highly value the Dionysian and the spontaneous, to exalt freedom over order, to demand more of the world than it may reasonably provide. We saw—may we be not the last to see—this country as blessed in its most generous hopes.*

Robert Stone, *Prime Green: Remembering the Sixties* (2007)

*Every now and then the energy of a whole generation comes to a head in a long fine flash, for reasons that nobody really understands at the time—and which never explain, in retrospect, what actually happened...There was a fantastic universal sense that whatever we were doing was right, that we were winning...Our energy would simply prevail...We had all the momentum; we were riding the crest of a high and beautiful wave.*

Hunter S. Thompson, *Fear and Loathing in Las Vegas* (1971)

*He floats on a surfboard, offshore in the moonlight. He sees so clearly that it could be daytime, except that the light is silver and the things it illuminates have no other color. A full moon silverplates the shoreline, a strand of beach walled by vertical cliffs. Beyond, in shadow, rise volcanic mountains. A second moon floats like a label sewn to the billowing fabric of the sea. The black water is unruffled in the still air, its surface smooth and thick as glass.*

*Fish swim beneath him, impossibly visible. A manta ray flaps by. Sea turtles come close, curious, gliding back and forth beneath his surfboard. On the horizon dolphins jump and spin; their splashes spread glistening shards of metallic light.*

*Shapes float past in the day-like darkness. An old Chevrolet. A vinyl sofa. The peaked roof of a treehouse. A picnic table. A camera. A desk.*

*A swell appears, a watery hump lifting the horizon. He points his board toward shore and feels the wave take over. He stands, turning into the curling crest, crouching as it surrounds him with whirling silver glass.*

## INTERNET CONNECTION

A few miles inland from this cold, gray ocean, up through the morning cloud banks and over the coastal range, a warm summer sun is surely shining. I hang my parka on the hook behind the door. From the large window overlooking the seacliff at the campus's edge, the edge of the continent, I can see the swell pushing through the kelp beds.

When I started teaching here, I faced my desk to the window. But I was mesmerized by parading clouds, sunlight rheostating up and down, ocean colors shifting, glittering wind-generated textures on the water. I couldn't concentrate. So I turned the desk around.

Twenty years ago. Just before Sage and I got married.

A knock on the door and in comes Wendy Furumoto, a frequent visitor, petite, smart, and serious. She's in English 105, a core course that I teach primarily to non-majors. She takes off her daypack and gets down to business.

"I think I've got 'The Song Bird' figured out except for one line. The bird sings in the middle of the summer, the song warns us that fall is on the way, that we're not gonna be young forever."

She tilts her head slightly, a request for a response. I offer none. She sighs.

"OK. Then Frost says that what's also on the way is 'that other fall we name the fall.'" She stares out the window at the gray ocean. "I think of surfers falling off of their boards. They get back up, paddle back out, catch another wave, fall off again. One day comes that last time. Surfers and everybody, you and me, slowly getting old and one day falling over dead." She retilts her head. "What does 'that other fall' mean to you?"

"Well, I went to church when I was a kid, and if you were raised a Christian, you've heard the story of Adam and Eve getting kicked out of the Garden of Eden..."

"The Fall!"

"...from grace."

She smiles. "So we have two falls in the poem, but three possibilities. Which is right?"

"It's your favorite two out of three. Or all three on an alternating basis."

"It's sad, that last line, when it says 'what to make of a diminished thing.'"

"Why sad?"

She shrugs. "That's what must happen when you get old. How old are you, fifty?"

"Fifty-six." I'm not sensitive about my age. What can I do about it? Why should I hide it?

"It's like in those sped-up nature movies," she says suddenly, "when they show a sprout popping out of the ground and the stem shooting straight up and the buds flowering to full bloom in a couple of seconds. I think they should show us the rest of the story, the flower withering and the stem stooping over and finally the whole thing returning to dust."

She gets up to leave, hoists her pack over a shoulder, and is halfway out the door when she stops and turns around.

"I almost forgot." she says, "I think I saw you on the Internet."

"You mean something I wrote?"

"No. Your picture. I saw it on PeopleSeeker.com. Have you seen that site? You can post pictures of people you're looking for. If you see your photo there and want to respond, you can."

"And you saw a picture of me."

"My roommates and I were scrolling through some of the missing person photos, and I saw one that looks like you. A lot younger, but I'm pretty sure it's you."

"Which would mean someone is looking for me."

She shrugs. "There's a banana tree in the picture. Maybe Hawaii. You ever go there?"

Wendy Furumoto shuts the door quietly behind her. With my key I open the drawer on the upper right hand side of my desk. Inside is a pewter flask. I keep it filled from a bottle of vodka in my knapsack. I take a pull, replace it and relock the drawer. Absolutely delicious. It's only 10 AM but the sky is dark and the cocktail lamp is lit. I'm drinking too much, too early in the day, but I don't give a flying fuck.

I take a swig of bottled water. As a colleague in environmental engineering says, "The solution to pollution is dilution."

I boot up my computer and find PeopleSeeker.com. I've never seen the photo before, but there's no question about it: That's me, on Kauai, back in 1970, standing on a muddy road, pointing at a bunch of sun-dappled bananas. Beneath the photo is a caption, a quote attributed to Joni Mitchell:

"We've got to get ourselves back to the Garden."

## PHOTO OPPORTUNITY KNOCKOUT

Norm and Fleur were waiting for Oakley at the baggage claim at Lihue Airport. Norm was clearly happy to see him, all smiles and hugs and welcomes. Fleur smiled her own smile, the private one that took him back to their time together. The three of them walked in the stifling afternoon heat to a faded red '55 Chevy with rust holes all over it. He stashed his backpack in the trunk, keeping only his camera for the ride. Norm drove, Fleur rode shotgun, Oakley sat in the back.

"Good news," Norm said. "Surly Steve went back to New Mexico a week ago. He was living in a tent on a plywood platform. The platform's still there, so we reserved it for you."

"That's great. Thanks."

"You can pitch your tent on it like Steve did," Fleur said, "or if you decide to stay, you can build yourself a treehouse."

"How high up is it?"

"Only a couple of feet, actually," Fleur said. "The platform's on tree stumps."

"So I guess it would be more of a stumphouse than a treehouse," Oakley said.

"At Taylor Camp, what we call 'treehouses' aren't necessarily up in the trees," Norm said. "They're attached to trees, but you don't necessarily climb up to them. You just walk in."

"Did you bring any weed?" Fleur asked.

"You told me not to."

"Oh yeah, I guess I did. How about acid?"

"Nope."

"You still doing it?"

"Nope."

"When was the last time?"

"About three years ago."

"Bum trip?"

"Not really. What happened was, reality got so weird I didn't need it anymore."

"Right on," Norm said. "Or, in Kesey's words, 'How many times can you walk through the same door?'"

Just outside Lihue town they drove down a wet dirt road and stopped beside a jungle full of bananas.

"What's happening?" Oakley asked.

"We're gonna pick us some delicious bananas."

"Just rip 'em off?"

"I have the owner's permission. All I can take is bunches that are almost too far gone."

Before they left the car, they shared a joint.

"You grow this?" Oakley asked.

"Can't grow at Taylor Camp. The man would love any excuse to bust us."

"But you can grow if you want to, Oakley," Fleur said. "I mean, in a spiritual way. That is, if you can handle it."

"Don't let her give you any shit," Norm said.

Oakley wondered: *Is that what she's doing, giving me shit?* and then *What a strange saying, to 'give shit.' To 'take shit.'* He was glad he had stopped after two hits. One would have been enough. He wondered what he was thinking about before he went off on the shit metaphor, and then remembered: Fleur. When did she pick up this new habit of mockery?

Oakley took Norm and Fleur's picture, Norm holding a machete, Fleur vamping. Then Fleur took a picture of Oakley, pointing to a bunch of green bananas dangling over his head. His first two photographs taken in Hawaii, with his new Mamiya Sekor single lens reflex, bought for this trip and all the trips to come. He intended to keep a pictorial record of his travels.

He wanted to lock his camera in the trunk, but Fleur said not to bother; she'd wait in the car.

Walking into the jungle, stoned, introspective, Oakley considered the promise he had made to himself, to fill his life with travel. Not just visiting places but living in them, making them home, wherever he chose to hang out for a while. In his pack was an open-ended return ticket to Los Angeles and six hundred dollars in traveler's checks. When the money ran out, he'd get a job and work until he saved enough to go somewhere else. He could always get another teaching job. All he needed to do was forge some papers and create a new identity.

When they returned to the car, each hoisting a fat bunch of bananas, Fleur was gone and so was Oakley's camera. He assumed that she had taken it with her, but when she appeared a few minutes later, strolling dreamily up the road, all she was holding was a yellow, waxy, ridged object the size and shape of a toy football.

"Star fruit," she said. "Wait'll you taste it."

"Where's my camera?"

"Where you left it."

"No it isn't."

"Then I don't know where it is."

Oakley was pissed. "You left it on the seat with the car unlocked and the windows open?"

"Did anybody drive by when you were down the road?" Norm asked.

"Just a pickup truck."

"You said you were going to stay in the car."

"It was too hot." She punctuated this pronouncement with a fart.

"At least they didn't bust in here," Norm said, opening the trunk. "Your backpack is safe."

They reported the theft. An officer met them at the scene, expressed doubt that Oakley would recover his camera, then began his own line of questioning.

"What you folks doing here?"

Norm explained the banana situation. The officer looked dubious.

"What's your name?"

"Why?" Norm asked. "I'm under suspicion for something?"

The officer tried another approach.

"Who told you you could help yourself to these bananas?

"Mister Souza."

The officer seemed satisfied.

"Where you folks stay?"

"Ke'e."

"Taylor Camp?"

Norm nodded.

"I nevah woulda guessed."

"Would you like a hand of bananas, officer?" Fleur asked.

"Nah."

They drove from south shore to north shore on Kuhio Highway, counterclockwise on the map, with the mountains on their left and ocean on the right. The perimeter road first hugged the coastline, passing through the occasional small town, and then moved inland a mile or two, through vast expanses of grassy green open lands. Some of it was fenced for farming, some seemed to be uninhabited wilderness. Only a few homes were set beside the highway, but several connecting dirt roads indicated a population out of sight in both directions.

The ocean was a vast blanket of blue in the distance. Oakley kept his head out the window to take in the sights and the smells and the warm air, and to avoid breathing the exhaust fumes rising from a hole in the floor between his feet.

He tried to overcome his irritation with Fleur by focusing on the cosmic significance of the event, contemplating why he had been separated from his camera at this particular moment in his life.

After three-quarters of an hour, they passed a small airport and a sign that read, "Future site of Princeville Resort and Golf Course. Groundbreaking 1968."

"The first big tourist development on the north shore of Kauai," Norm said. "The locals are pissed off, but there's nothing they can do about it. At least this won't happen anywhere past this point."

"Why?"

"You'll see."

Behind the airport, in the distance, rose a massive range of jagged mountains. Norm pulled off the road at a scenic vista. Below them, a thin river disappeared around a turn in a vast valley enclosed by the steep, deeply ridged mountains, which were lined with thin waterfalls. On both river banks were wetlands and square fields of green plants. The land was all green. Light green in the valley, dark green in the mountains.

"Kauai has a nickname," Norm said. He and Oakley stood at the edge of the lookout. Fleur stayed in the car.

"I know. I read it on the plane."

"So now you know what they mean."

"Is that rice?"

"Taro. The Hawaiian staple food. They use the whole plant. They beat the roots into poi."

Princeville turned out to be at the top of a hill. Past the nascent development, they began a steep descent into the valley. Norm stopped at another lookout where they could see the river mouth open into a beautiful semicircular bay. A faint double rainbow arced across the sky above the light blue waters, against the mountains to the west. Oakley wished he had his camera.

"Hanalei Bay," Norm said. "Also Hanalei Valley, Hanalei River, and Hanalei town. To moviegoers this area is more familiar as Bali Hai. This, however, is the *north* Pacific, not the south."

Near the valley bottom they stopped at a one-lane bridge, waited for an oncoming car to pass, then drove over the wooden-planked, steel-girdered bridge. The road followed the river into Hanalei, which was nothing more than a few homes, a school, a couple of churches, a restaurant, a gas station, a real estate office and a small general store named Ching Young Store.

"Ching Young owns a lot of land around here," Fleur said. "Nobody knows how much."

Norm drove slowly around a large black Labrador stretched out comfortably in the middle of the road. The dog raised its head, then put it back down.

"This must be what they mean when they call a town 'sleepy,'" Oakley said.

Outside of Hanalei they crossed several more one-lane bridges, some of them paved with asphalt, others planked with wood.

"I see your point," Oakley said. "It would be pretty hard to build a hotel out here. These bridges couldn't support heavy trucks."

"And they're too narrow for fat tour buses," Fleur said.

After Hanalei, homes were few and far between. Of the houses that were visible from the road, many were built high off the ground, some as high as fifteen feet, propped on cinder-block legs.

"Why the stilts?" Oakley asked.

"Two tidal waves, 1946 and '57," Norm said, "wiped out most of the houses. Guess they don't want it to happen again."

After passing countless golden photo opportunities, Oakley worked it out in his head: On this adventure, he wasn't supposed to take pictures.

## PHOTO I.D.

No way I can't go down this fork in the road. In response to my email claiming I'm the one in the picture, "kalana@hawaii.rr.com" emails back twenty-four hours later, *Send me a current photo of yourself.*

*Why?* I reply.

*Can't say until I know it's you.*

With a scanned-in snapshot attached, I write: *You might not recognize me in this one. The other was taken thirty years ago.*

*I know. There's another that looks like it was shot in the same place, at the same time. Tell me who or what's in it, and I'll know you're the person I'm looking for.*

*Why are you looking?*

*I'll tell after you tell me about the other photo.*

I can't see any harm in the game. I write back: *As I recall, it was a photo of the two people who picked me up at the airport. A woman and a man. The woman is slender, with dark hair cut short. I don't remember what she's wearing. The man is slightly shorter than the woman, with brown hair tied into a pony tail and a long, curly beard. He's holding a machete.*

It's two days before I get this reply:

*OK. One more question: Are you the owner of a camera that was stolen, in 1970, from an empty car on a dirt road in Lihue?*

*What if I am?*

*I'm the one who stole it. I still have it. I want to return it and ask for your forgiveness. Would this be possible?*

*Tell you what: You're forgiven, but I don't want the camera back. I've owned at least three other cameras since then. I don't need it anymore.*

*You don't understand,* comes the reply. *I need to give it back. It's a spiritual*

PHOTO I.D.

*thing. This church I belong to, they want us to make up for our past wrongdoings whenever we can. The only way I can do that is by actually returning your camera.*

*How do I know you're not bullshitting me? If I give you my mailing address, how do I know you're not going to steal my identity?*

*I don't want to send you the camera. I want to give it to you in person.*

*I'm in California. You're going to fly over?*

*I'd like you to come to Hawaii.*

*No way I'm going to pay for round-trip airfare to Hawaii just to pick up a thirty-year-old camera I don't want, from a repentant thief.*

*You don't understand. The trip's on me.*

## MOMENTARILY POSSESSED BY A YOUNGER SELF

*I'm walking alone down a Paris boulevard, wearing Frye boots, Levi's, a white T-shirt, a blue wool navy surplus pea coat, and a smile. I have a Beatle mop top. It's the summer of 1966, I've just graduated from college, and I'm farther away from home than I've ever been.*

This is not a dream, but a visitation. I'm in bed, but not asleep. With the visual image comes a surge of phantom energy that floods me with the way I felt back then: independent, carefree, bright and eager, alive with laughter and determination.

For a joyous instant, a rush of elation, these feelings are mine again.

A moment later they're gone, drawn away like a wave washing up on the shore and disappearing into the sand.

Afterwards, all that remains is a mental snapshot of a soft-faced young man, still a boy really, smiling to himself on the streets of Paris.

No point in dwelling on it. The feeling is already losing intensity; by the morning it will be gone. Regret and remorse are useless; the past is passed. No more joy, only bitterness. My life has turned to shit, the world has turned to shit, what's to be done about either one?

# FISH ESCAPES BOWL

Oakley flew to Europe in the middle of May, after final exams. He missed graduation but didn't care. He stayed until early September. His intention was to travel alone, randomly, impulsively, cheaply. To make his money last. The airfare was a graduation present from his parents. The rest was up to him.

He went to Paris, where he stayed for a month. He walked all over the city—to monuments, museums, galleries, movies, and plays. He found it easy to meet people his own age, mostly students or drop-out intellectuals. They helped him replace his classroom French with the real thing.

In college his teachers had told him he would never need to use the second person singular address, "tu," as opposed to the more formal and polite "vous," second person plural. The familiar form of the pronoun, they told him, was only for addressing family members or intimate acquaintances.

It turned out that his teachers were behind the times. People his own age, male and female, addressed him as "tu" and "toi" from the moment they met him. Those who remained "vous" were older adults, especially parents. The youth of France, like those in America, were flouting established conventions.

On the other hand, adults still seemed to be observing tradition, as evidenced by a fight that broke out between two men in a bar where Oakley was playing pinball. When bystanders separated them, one of them angrily told the bartender, "Il m'a tutoyé!"— "He called me 'tu'!"

Oakley went to the May 24th Bob Dylan concert at the Olympia Theater. Dylan was in the process of merging folk-style lyrics with rock-and-roll arrangements, rewriting the rules of popular music. The night of the Paris concert was Dylan's twenty-fifth birthday, but it wasn't a happy one. The audience booed him, and save for a few, the reviews in the next morning's newspapers were unfavorable.

Why was the audience so hostile? What had Dylan done to offend them? Oakley figured it had something to do with the language barrier, Dylan's lack of stage presence, the irritating intervals of guitar-tuning and the mumbled, cryptic small talk between songs. And then coming back after the break with an electric guitar and the Hawks. The French wanted the folksinger Bob Dylan, solo, guitar and harmonica only, not a rock band.

Another thing: the audience liked Dylan the artist but not Dylan the American. Behind him and the Hawks, filling the entire backdrop, was a huge American flag. Thanks to Vietnam, Americans weren't very popular in Europe. Oakley took to telling people he was Canadian.

The longer he stayed away from home, the more Europeans he met and spoke with, the more he saw how they lived, and the better he could see America. He adopted an outsider's perspective.

His French friends told him that Americans had unnecessarily large cars, bathrooms, and food markets. That they were wasteful, irresponsible, and obsessed with owning things they didn't need. That they had no sense of proportion or moderation. They were consuming far more than their share of the world's resources. Worst of all, they were hell-bent on imposing their bad habits and shallow cultural values on the rest of the world.

Jean-Patrique, skinny, pale, animated, reeking of Gauloise and BO, spoke English and read Marshall McLuhan. He called Oakley *un poisson dans un reservoir de l'eau*, a fish in a tank, à la McLuhan: contemporary man immersed in media, with no true understanding of his environment.

Oakley had to agree. But he was learning fast.

## VISION STILL VIVID

It's 2 AM and I'm awake, French connection reverberating in my head. The past is passed, but it has asserted itself in the present. I gulp from a bottle beside my bed. Helps me get back to sleep. Pot doesn't work, it's all anxiety and paranoia. Booze numbs.

Why? Why did this vision arrive, at this particular time? How does it connect to now, my current circumstances, Sage gone for two months, gone for good, living with another man? Me behaving this way, drinking, doing nothing new with my life. It's like sitting on a surfboard in the lineup and letting all the waves pass by.

I know why. It's why the vision was so vivid. And now, hours later, remains so disturbing.

It's not her I miss, it's me. Me with my bright future; me in a wide-open world, a world beginning to change for the better, full of people beginning to wake up, and understand, and change.

## WELCOME TO TAYLOR CAMP

Five miles or so past Hanalei, the world seemed to constrict. A low, thick cover of gray cloud sealed off the sky. A wall of wet rock rose from the roadside; on the right, the thick jungle closed in. They drove into a pot-holed dip in the road; a stream crossed under their tires. They passed a gaping cavern that must have once been a sea cave.

"That's the dry cave on your left," Norm said. "On your right is Haena Beach Park, where you can pitch a tent and spend the night, or a few weeks if you like. Second-class accommodations compared to Taylor Camp, however. Look back over your shoulder and you'll see Tunnels. In a few weeks, when the north swells begin to hit, Tunnels will become your favorite surf spot, guaranteed."

"I need a board."

"I know. I've got a couple of possibilities, both used, good condition. Seven-four and seven-eight. Ready to ride."

"How much?"

"Fifty bucks for the one you choose."

"Can I try them out?"

"Sure."

A tiny bridge crossed a foot or two above another stream. On the left was a small parking area occupied by a couple of cars.

"About a hundred yards up the mountain is the Waikapalae wet cave. Nice place to cool off," Norm said. "There's another one right beside the road up here, called Waikanaloa. But the other one's the best. It's bigger and less populated."

"How do you remember all these names?" Oakley asked. "They all sound the same to me."

"Just keep repeating them," Norm said, "and after a while you don't have to think about it anymore."

He pulled into a muddy clearing occupied by a half-dozen rusty cars. "This is it. Welcome to Taylor Camp."

Outside the car, the afternoon air was still and humid, reeking of rotted fruit, filled with flies and mosquitoes.

"You picked the worst time of the year to come," Norm told Oakley. "At the end of August, the trade winds die, these condensation clouds come over the mountains and just stick there, and the humidity goes through the roof. It doesn't rain much, but you're wet all the time."

"How long does this weather last?"

"Maybe a month. More or less."

Oakley's brain had inflated inside his skull, and the expanded mass throbbed in sharp, painful surges. His reward for inhaling carbon monoxide through the hole in Norm's car floor.

Oakley, Norm, and Fleur walked from the helter-skelter parking area into a forest of vines, bushes, and ferns, and beige-trunked trees of varying thickness and height. They walked single file on a thin muddy trail, pushing aside cobwebs, hanging roots, and thin saplings, stepping on live roots, dead logs, and oblong seed pods as hard as peach pits, but bigger, that had fallen from the giant, broad-leafed trees that blocked out light but not heat.

"Kamani," Norm said, in the lead, pointing as he walked. "Also called Indian almond, although those seeds don't taste like almonds. Java plum. Pandanus. Guava. Staghorn fern."

Fleur picked up a small, round, yellow fruit and tore away its thin skin to reveal a pinkish seedy mush inside. She shoved it under Oakley's nose. Oakley recoiled, not from the fruit but the abruptness of Fleur's gesture. His head throbbed from the motion. Fleur laughed.

"Lots of vitamin C in guavas. And they fucking literally grow on trees!" she shouted and laughed again.

Oakley was puzzled by Fleur's behavior—so loud, so abrasive. She had never been like this before. She used to be more reserved, deferential, self-contained. The quiet, mysterious type. That was one of the things he had always liked best about her.

She also used to be less careless. Today she hadn't apologized, or even accepted responsibility for her role in the theft of his camera. Apparently, in her mind, it had nothing to do with her.

And then there was the farting. She never used to do that, at least audibly, in the presence of others.

The trail began branching, Oakley caught glimpses of structures concealed in the dense jungle growth. Thin walkways along the branch trails led into small clearings, each containing a stone-circled firepit, a makeshift porch with chairs or wooden boxes, and a dwelling of some type. Camping tents of different colors and sizes were outnumbered by more permanent structures, from tiny A-frames a foot off the ground to more elaborate buildings with platforms rising into the trees or stretching back into the jungle. On some of the structures the frames were cut branches, on others milled lumber. The exterior wall of choice was thick, transparent polyethylene plastic sheeting—the kind you bought on a roll at hardware stores. Oakley could see inside the walls that weren't hung with material—usually those thin cotton bedspreads from India. The interiors looked elaborate, with shelves and tables and beds and other furniture, most of it homemade. The structures looked well-built, functional, and comfortable. These weren't campsites; they were homes.

Most complex and impressive of all the dwellings was a two-story structure grafted into a massive, strange-looking tree that grew upward and outward farther than Oakley could see. Its horizontal branches were supported by walls of trunk-like roots that spread out in all directions.

"That's Fred the Zen's place," Norm said. "He lives in a banyan with his many companions. You'll meet him soon enough."

"Fred the Zen?"

"A so-called Zen Master with a handful of female disciples. He sleeps with them all, of course. He's a horny bastard."

"Is it some kind of Manson-family arrangement?"

"No, they're not a problem. Fred can be irritating, but he's harmless."

"Nobody knows his last name," Fleur said. "Nobody even knows if Fred's his real first name. At Taylor Camp, everybody has an alias."

"What's yours?"

"Blur. Because I'm too quick for everybody."

"Tell the truth," Norm said. "Blur as in crazy, blur as in speed freak."

Fleur adopted an exaggerated pout. "Ask Norm his alias, then."

"Well?"

"Ab-Norman," he said with a smile. "Shortened to Ab-norm. You pronounce it like Costello used to call Abbott: 'Hey, Ab-norm!'"

"Let's give Oakley an alias now," Fleur said.

"No, thanks," Oakley said.

## ALTer-egO

Alternate-Oakley lives in a parallel world. It's a better world, in which (among other things) JFK and RFK and Martin Luther King and Malcolm X were never assassinated. Ronald Reagan was never president. Bill and Hillary Clinton masterminded a brilliant plan for universal health care in America, and it's working fine. Monica Lewinsky never existed. George W. Bush is not president. The ozone hole is shrinking and the environment is next to dandy. Education in America is at an all-time quality high.

It's a wonderful world, but Alternate-O isn't necessarily a wonderful guy.

He's a parallel me, different in ways I'm not too sure about and don't always enjoy. He comes to visit whenever he pleases, unannounced, uninvited. We have conversations, but Alternate-Oakley also has more powerful, trickier, more sinister methods of communicating with me.

When he shows up this time, I'm at my computer. I enter the Alt-o command, which I have reprogrammed to bring up not the format menu but a slide show of waves. Waves of all shapes and sizes, with or without surfers. To get him out of my head. But it doesn't work. He has some unfinished business. The France thing, that was him. Wendy connecting me to the Internet photo? Alt-O.

"What's your point?" I ask.

"That Furumoto girl. Not bad."

"Don't even go there."

"Her and about two dozen others. How can you keep your hands off 'em?"

"Why are you pushing the past into the present?"

"France in 1966, Hawaii in 1970. I wonder what they had in common."

"I spent a couple of months in both places, when I was in my twenties."

"Duh. Besides that."

"Distance from home."

"Keep going."

"Displacement. The ordinary replaced by the extraordinary."

"More."

"OK. What I used to do was deliberately remove myself from my comfortable context, relocate myself, drop myself into unfamiliar places, meet new people, learn to cope with the situation. I lived simply, spontaneously, in the moment, day to day, no plans or schedules, responsibilities or goals."

"There's something else," Alternate Oakley says.

"I give up."

"How did we begin this conversation?"

"Women."

"Bingo."

## COUP DE FOUDRE

After a month, Oakley left Paris for the countryside. He was traveling around the Loire Valley, visiting the châteaux. He met Flora at Azay-Le-Rideau.

She, too, had been traveling alone. She, too, spoke some French—had spoken it growing up in Montreal, before her Hungarian immigrant parents moved to Toronto and the family switched to English.

The night they met, at a campground near the château, they talked for three hours in front of a campfire. Flora's hair was black and her eyes dark. She was big-boned and looked strong, but she was slender and her skin was smooth. Even more than her physical beauty, however, it was her unpredictable responses that pleased Oakley, and her soft-spoken intelligence that sent him over the edge.

They sat there, a point of light inside the night. Two bright, eager faces flickering in the fire. They smoked a joint and stopped talking, looking into each other's eyes, in silence, for about ten minutes. Then they went into Oakley's blue nylon tent, made love, and spent the night together.

The next morning they decided to stay together, at least for the time being. No commitments. No obligations.

"Coup de foudre," she whispered in his ear, and pulled away to face him with an insouciant smile.

"I don't know what that means," he said.

"Lightning bolt. French for love at first sight."

## 10. Kauai 1970

## LIZ'S BROTHER'S PLACE

His carbon-monoxide headache relieved by a handful of aspirin, Oakley pitched his tent— the same one he had taken to France—on the plywood platform he had inherited. From the platform, it was just a few steps up a rise to small ridge where the jungle ended and the beach began, a curved stretch of clean white sand sloping gently to the ocean about a hundred yards away. Waves broke on a reef close to the shore.

The platform rested on the stumps of four trees that Norm said were ironwoods, already dead when they were cut down, he assured Oakley, killed by salt water that had invaded the jungle last year during a huge winter swell. A row of live ironwoods lined the ridge at the beach's edge.

Oakley accepted Fleur's invitation to dinner at their treehouse, a bamboo-framed, two-story structure that showcased Norm's skills as a handyman. One wall of the main room, taken *in toto* from on old shed, contained a wood-framed glass window. In one corner, covered by a suspended mosquito net, was a queen-sized mattress and box spring on the floor. Beside it was a bookcase filled with paperbacks, magazines, and cassette tapes.

After a meal of brown rice, roasted macadamia nuts, collard greens, bananas, and cheap red wine, Norm lit a joint and filled Oakley in on the story of Taylor Camp.

"The road ends here; you can't drive all the way around the island. If you want to go any further, you have to hike in on the Na Pali cliff trail. It's not an easy trail, and sometimes it can be scary, but it leads to some beautiful places. Two miles in, you come to Hanakapiai Beach, where there's a waterfall. Nine miles beyond that is Kalalau Valley, where thousands of Hawaiians used to live."

"A bunch of hippies are living in both places now," Fleur said. "They come out only to stock up on provisions."

"The beach in front of us is called Ke'e," Norm continued. "The word means 'avoidance.' Apparently, for the old-time Hawaiians, this place was too far away and too much trouble to bother with. The name Taylor Camp came from the man who owns it, Howard Taylor, brother of the movie star, Elizabeth."

"No shit," Oakley said. "She was great in *Virginia Woolf*. I loved her opening line, 'What a dump.' Does she ever come to visit?"

"Nobody around here's ever seen her," Fleur said.

"Howard owns and lives in a big beachfront house back down the road a couple of miles at Haena," Norm said. "He bought the land we live on, where he wants to build another house. But the state of Hawaii won't let him, because they rezoned the land for a future park.

"Possibly in a gesture of retaliation, Howard has abandoned this prime beachfront acreage to anyone who wants to crash here, which at present includes you, me, Fleur, and about forty others, not including transient backpackers, surf bums, and tourists."

Norm filled the wine glasses, inserted what was left of the joint into a tubular, wormlike piece of white seashell, and lighted it.

"Nice roach pipe," Oakley said.

"Nature's gift," Norm said. "They're all over the beach."

"How long has the camp been around?" Oakley asked.

"About three years," Norm said. "It started out as a commune, but that arrangement fizzled after a year. Now it's sort of a semi-commune. You can keep to yourself if you please, or you can join the community in our efforts to grow food."

"And to keep the Health Department from closing us down," Fleur added.

"Different people live here for different reasons," Norm said. "Hippies seeking alternate lifestyles. Disillusioned ex-hippies trying to escape the insanity. And assorted other political and cultural fugitives from mainland America. We have in our midst a talented songwriter, an authority on the more humorous and mind-blowing aspects of Zen Buddhism, someone we suspect is a U.S. Army deserter and—now that you've arrived, Oakley—a bona fide draft dodger."

## WHY GO THERE?

Am I losing my mind? Am I like the homeless guy I see staring at his reflection in storefront windows, and having a conversation with himself?

"That image of Paris won't go away," I tell him.

Alt-O says, "It's not supposed to. I worked hard on that one."

"And then there's the existential dread."

"I can feel it across the dimensions. You poor boy. 'Le pauvre,' as they say."

"You won't stop bringing up France, will you?"

"You know what was different about you back then? You didn't have a lot of baggage."

"Actually, I did. I had my backpack, which weighed about sixty pounds, including food."

"I'm not talking about that kind of baggage."

"And I brought along my guitar. I don't know why I lugged a guitar around for three months."

"You weren't bad on the guitar. Not gifted, but not bad. But you're changing the subject."

"I need to get away."

"That doesn't always work." Alt-O is a truth-teller.

"But it might. I'm not teaching the second summer session, so I could go for a week in September before the fall quarter. It would be the same time of year I was in Hawaii before, back in 1970."

"You want to remove yourself from your context, the way you used to do. You assume the travel will be therapeutic."

"That's the idea," I say.

"Bullshit. You just want to escape. You can't handle your life, which you now realize is meaningless. Sage is now an empty space, but that's not the big thing. The big thing is the empty space in your soul. So what'll it be, Hawaii or France?"

"Hawaii's closer, and the airfare's free."

"Plus you get to surf. How long has it been?"

"I haven't gone once this year. In the last ten years, I've been out there maybe a hundred times. I used to surf that many times a year."

"You still remember how?"

"It always comes back," I say. "I'm having this recurring dream about riding waves. At night."

"That's when people tend to dream."

"No. I mean I'm *surfing* at night."

"Yeah, I know. I did a good job on that one, too. You know, there's a third alternative. Something that will really do the job, context-removal-wise."

"I know."

"Pack up your sorrows and ship out for good. No more pain. Just sweet oblivion."

## 12. New York 1945

## SHOOTING THE BREEZE

Oakley was born on the island of Manhattan at 8:45 AM on the last Saturday in July, one hour before an airplane flew into the seventy-ninth floor of the Empire State Building, starting a fire and killing fourteen people. At first everyone thought it was a Japanese kamikaze attack on New York, but it turned out that the plane was one of our own—a ten-ton, twin-engine B-25 Mitchell bomber flown by a Lt. Col. William Smith, veteran of thirty-four bombing missions, en route to New Jersey from Massachusetts, in a thick fog, flying off course and too low. Two dozen fire companies rushed to the scene and put the blaze out in less than an hour. One of the plane's engines had crashed through the building and out the other side; the other went into an elevator shaft and ended up in the basement.

One week later, on August 5, at 7:15 PM, the U.S. dropped an atomic bomb on Hiroshima, following in four days with a second on Nagasaki.

Years later, because he had been born too early to be included in the "baby boomer" demographic group, Oakley labeled himself a "baby bomber."

Almost as soon as he could walk, he had been drawn to the ocean. In a home movie, made in 1947 at his parents' beach house at Point Breeze, near Coney Island, Oakley is waddling in the shallows, thrilled by the shorebreak that knocks him gently onto the wet sand. Every time he falls, he jumps back up, turns around and runs back out, eager for more. Wave after wave until the cameraman has had enough. The cameraman, his father, an advertising executive, shot the footage just before he left New York with his wife and two-year-old son for Southern California, Westwood Village, a college town just three miles from the Pacific Ocean.

## WHOOPS

I met Sage in the mid-sixties in Los Angeles; she and her boyfriend Mark and I became close friends. We went to foreign films and rock concerts together. We smoked pot and dropped acid together.

After I came back from Hawaii, I didn't see them. I moved to San Francisco with Sandy, taught school and tried to deal with her chronic manic depression. I couldn't handle it. It was a kind of insanity. The longer I stayed around it, the more I was sucked into it.

She was hurting us both and I didn't know how to help, so I had to bail. She needed professional help, not my feeble, half-hearted attempts at cheering-up.

For a while I was alone, except for some short affairs. Then I ran into Sage again.

She had left Mark, moved to Berkeley, and opened a shop on Telegraph selling clothing and accessories imported from China. I was wandering around one day and chanced into the shop out of curiosity.

There she was. We hugged, laughing. Made a date for dinner and talked over old times, especially a memorable night ten years before camping in Tahquitz Canyon. Found we still enjoyed one another's company. Started dating, became lovers, decided to live together. Four years later we were married. Sage sold the shop (it wasn't for me; she hated retail) and we moved to the north coast when I had been hired to teach at the college.

The night I stumbled into the discovery that ended our life together, it was like the explosion that sends astronauts into outer space, a Cape

Canaveral launching like the ones I watched on TV in the sixties. First comes a preliminary blast that's followed by a massive lurch in the rocket, which doesn't take off right away. The flaming noise intensifies and the rocket lifts up, slowly at first, as the surrounding scaffold breaks away and disintegrates in the molten air. With a final push, the searing fires disconnect the rocket from planet Earth and it shoots into the cosmos.

A phone call from Sage's mother in LA triggered the countdown. Eight-thirty on a Wednesday night. I was reading.

She wanted Sage, but Sage was at work, on the night shift at the North Coast Bistro.

"I don't have that number, can you give it to me please?" She didn't sound too happy.

"I can call the restaurant and tell her to phone you. It's the rules over there."

"I'm going to have a mastectomy," she told me. "I have breast cancer. I need to talk to her."

"Oh, geez, Evelyn. I'm sorry."

When I called the restaurant, I was told that Sage wasn't there.

"Is this Ted?" The night manager. "It's an emergency."

"Oh, yeah, Oakley? She's not here, man. It's her night off."

"Sunday is her night off."

"Yeah, right. Sundays and Wednesdays."

That was the moment of the preliminary blast.

"Aw, shit, I forgot. Sorry to bother you, Ted."

I hung up, sat back, closed my eyes, and clenched my teeth against the rushing pressure as I felt the flimsy scaffold fall away, the structure of my marriage that had seemed so sturdy, so permanent. I felt myself disengage from everything I had taken for granted. I had lift-off.

Where the fuck was Sage? What the fuck had she been doing on all those Wednesday nights?

## 14. Kauai 1970

### FIRST DAWN

After a long night's sleep, Oakley woke up feeling fine. Outside his tent, the air was cool and crisp. Beyond the jungle canopy, the sky was bright.

He heard the sound of a guitar, not far away, the player fingerpicking a simple folk-song chord progression with an alternating bass. He pulled on shorts and a T-shirt and walked toward the source of the music. It was coming from the banyan tree.

Oakley stayed concealed in the jungle as he approached and spotted the musician—white-skinned, round-shouldered, in his early twenties, with straight black hair down to his shoulders, sitting on a stump stool in Fred the Zen's open-air ground floor kitchen and dining room. Not wanting to interrupt, Oakley kept out of sight.

## GOODBYE, CALIFORNIA

     C        Em
Goodbye, California
 C         Em
We won't stay to mourn ya
     G
Look at LA slipping away
   C        Em
Eureka we found it
   C      Em
Eureka we drowned it
     G          C
California who took you away?
          F
    The mountains are smoking
        C
    The valleys are choking
        C       G
    The foothills are filling up fast
        F
    The rivers are crying
        C
    The oceans are dying
        G            C
    California, how long can you last?

The coastline is built up

The cities are filled up

But people keep moving out West

Beware for God's sake

Who knows, it might take

An earthquake to clean up this mess.

    The mountains are smoking

    The valleys are choking

    The foothills are filling up fast

    The rivers are crying

    The oceans are dying

    California, how long can you last?

## 16. Europe 1966

## HOTEL VOLTAIRE

Flora and Oakley traveled together for two months, spending their nights in campsites and cheap hotels. They rode trains, took taxis, and hiked with their backpacks. They hitched a ride into the Swiss Alps and stayed in a youth hostel, climbing a nearby hill to watch the sun set and smoke the hashish that their hostel-mates had smuggled in from Turkey and Afghanistan.

They rode the train to Barcelona where they rented a tiny car, two weeks with unlimited mileage, and drove down the Mediterranean coast, camping on hot beaches beside the still, dead sea. They watched a bullfight in Valencia and ate a six-course dinner in a Cartagena restaurant that cost them five dollars each, including wine. They drove for hundreds of miles through arid, rocky hills until they encountered civilization again in the South Coast vacation resorts of Torremolinos and Málaga.

In Algeciras, a fellow wanderer advised them not to take their car, or themselves, on the ferry to Morocco because of their appearance. He told them that hippies were no longer welcome in Tangier, and that they could run into trouble with the local authorities even if they had their passports and rental papers in proper order.

So they drove instead across the southern tip of Spain, parallel to the Straits of Gibraltar, to the Atlantic Ocean, which to Oakley felt cool, fresh, and alive after the heat and stillness of the Mediterranean Sea.

For almost a week they camped out on a broad, empty stretch of coast near Cádiz, a few miles from a village called Zahara, which appeared to be populated solely by the families of fishermen. The villagers left them alone, except to stare at them rudely from the street as Oakley drove Flora through the town to the beach where they pitched their tent and built driftwood fires in the sand.

All day and all night long, they had nothing to do but be together. They were completely alone on the beach. They watched the fishing boats head out at dawn and return with the setting sun. In the village, they bought wine, bread, salami, cheese, and sweets. They smoked hash and Gauloise cigarettes. They made love day and night. They gazed at the moon and a million stars. They slept in Oakley's rainproof, bugproof tent, protected and undisturbed. They read each other's books and talked about them. They exchanged their life stories. They talked about everything but tomorrow.

They washed the salt out of their hair and the sweat off their skin with fresh water from big plastic jugs they refilled at a well in the village, self-conscious but determined to ignore the stares of the villagers.

Oakley bodysurfed in small green waves while Flora walked for miles, for hours at a time, up and down the endless strand, more content to be by herself than was Oakley. When she smiled her broad, unfathomable smile, it was only to herself and only for herself. She collected firewood. She watched the shorebirds. She hummed softly to herself. She gathered hundreds of tiny, red-flecked spiral seashells, then left them all behind.

Further north, in Portugal, the pine trees and long lines of breaking waves reminded Oakley of Northern California. They drove up the coast of Portugal back into Spain, then cut across the mountains to Barcelona and returned the rental car.

An overnight train took them to Paris. They found the Hotel Voltaire, a reasonably priced, semi-clean establishment in a skinny old three-story building on a tiny avenue off the Place des Invalides, not far from Napoleon's tomb. They rode the Métro to museums and movie theaters. They walked the arrondissements of the circular city, holding hands and kissing in public.

Oakley was hopelessly in love with this mysterious beauty, who had chosen, at least for the time being, to love him back, who clung to him in bed and softly wept after their lovemaking. She professed to love him so dearly that he never really acknowledged what he vaguely understood about the two of them: that his need was greater than hers. That she loved him only to the extent that she was happy not to be alone anymore on her European adventure. That she didn't even know what love was. Or that, even though she used the word and meant it, she didn't mean it the way he did.

Back in Paris Flora decided to change her name.

"What's wrong with Flora?" Oakley wanted to know. "It's pretty. It means flowers."

"I know what it means," Flora said. "It just sounds so clunky. Like a name you'd give a cow."

"It doesn't sound that way to me. It sounds beautiful, like the way you look."

But Flora wasn't listening.

"I'm doing this in Paris," she said. "So, from now on, my name is Fleur."

"That'll give me lots of opportunities to work on the pronunciation of my r's."

"I wonder what Ian will think."

"Who's Ian?"

"My boyfriend in Toronto."

## SAGE STEW

Where was Sage? Where had she been on all those Wednesday nights? I called some friends, gave up on it, then called her mother and admitted I didn't know where she was. It was obviously a miscommunication, I told her. I would call her back as soon as I located Sage.

I waited five hours for her to come home. Waiting to confront her, I cooked up a stew of invented scenarios. How long had she been lying to me? What was I going to do, what was I going to say, how was she going to respond, what could she possibly say?

How bad was the truth?

When she finally returned, it was a bad scene, thanks to me. I was drunk and angry and reality-challenged. I shouted, I stomped around, I broke some things.

She told me the obvious: There was another man, someone I didn't know. Yes, she met him at the Bistro, yes, it had been going on for a while—two years. Yes, she only had Sunday off at the Bistro and she'd been seeing him every Wednesday. Yes she had been cheating on me, yes she had been deceiving me, yes she had broken our trust.

As shocked as I might be, she said, this was sudden only for me. For her, it was merely the final step in a process that had been ongoing for years—like a disease that drains an infinitesimal amount of your life, day after day, until you're finally tapped out, on your back, and though you are now certain you're dying, you didn't even feel sick until you found out you were almost dead. As if the discovery was all your death had been waiting for.

"I'm a disease?" I asked.

"Not really. It's like we've been frozen in place. We did it to ourselves and to each other. Built a cage of expectations that we both agreed to live in."

"So let's fix it together."

"Too late. I've already broken off from us."

Sage had been changing before my eyes. I should have seen it coming. That I didn't was due to no extraordinary subterfuge on her part, but a great deal of blindness on mine. I had been looking at her but not seeing her. I had been looking at an image, a photograph taken a long time ago, and she was no longer the person in the picture.

## 18. Kauai 1970

# ZEN IS NOW

From his concealed vantage point Oakley continued to observe the activity in Fred the Zen's treehouse, which was walled on two sides by solid wedges of root emanating from the trunk of the banyan. Various found materials had been used in building and furnishing the structure: odd pieces of driftwood, recycled boards, crates, bamboo, and assorted junk.

The ground floor was a kitchen and dining area. Several tables held dishes, drinking glasses, and cooking equipment. Shelves contained tin cans of food, condiments in glass jars, and large plastic water jugs. The fire pit was rigged with a spit; a pot hung over the burning embers. Furniture included a picnic table with benches and an assortment of chairs and stools.

The second floor, which merged into the banyan tree, was supported from beneath by several poles of thick bamboo seated in half-buried clumps of concrete fortified with river rocks—in effect, the cornerstones of the structure. Three wooden ladders provided access to the rooms above.

The wiry, pale-skinned musician had finished singing his song, but he continued to play the tune.

A man who looked to be in his late forties climbed down one of the ladders. He was wearing only khaki shorts. His skin was wrinkled, but his body was muscular and agile. He had a long face, a large mouth, and bright eyes. As Oakley watched, his face kept changing expressions, as if he were exercising his facial muscles by running them through an exaggerated range of emotions: grief, joy, astonishment, fear, incomprehension, madness. Oakley thought, *Fred the Zen.*

The man took a large coffee mug from a makeshift counter, scooped in a spoonful of instant coffee from a jar, and poured some hot water into it from the pot hanging over the fire.

"What a way to start the day, Soundtrack. 'The rivers are crying the oceans are dying.' How 'bout something more positive, more optimistic? You know any show tunes? 'Oh, What a Beautiful Morning'? 'The Hills Are Alive With the Sound of Music'?"

Soundtrack stopped playing but did not respond.

"Coffee?" the man asked.

Soundtrack shook his head.

"If you want tea, you'll have to wait. I make coffee."

Soundtrack nodded.

"Two monks come to a muddy intersection," the man said, as if starting to tell Soundtrack a joke. "A beautiful woman is standing there, all dressed up, afraid to cross. One of the monks goes over and speaks with her, then carries her across, piggy-back. He puts her down on the other side and she goes on her way.

"A couple of miles down the road, the second monk tells the first monk he's not sure it was a good idea to carry that woman across the street; after all, she was a geisha, a courtesan, and monks are supposed to stay away from such women.

"The first monk says to his friend, 'I dropped her off an hour ago. But you're still carrying her.'"

The man stared at Soundtrack, his head tilted. Soundtrack did not respond.

The man took a plastic bottle of dry creamer and a tin of sugar and added a spoonful of each to his mug. Soundtrack began to pluck the melody of "Oh, What a Beautiful Morning." The man stoked the fire, adding a few sticks from a woodpile, then sat down to drink his coffee.

A woman descended the same ladder the man had used before. She had an angular face, short black hair, and milk chocolate skin.

She was wearing blue jeans and a T-shirt. She could have been in her late teens. Her posture was poor, shoulders round, head always looking down at the ground. She moved cautiously, looking as if the slightest disturbance could frighten her away. In spite of this timidity, or possibly because of it, he found her attractive.

She walked over to the man and hugged him.

He told her, "I promised Soundtrack you'd make him a cup of tea if he stopped bringing us all down."

"He's lucky" she said. "He knows how to stop."

"So do you," the man said. "You just forgot."

"No," she said with a hint of desperation. "Forget is what I'm trying to do."

She got a pot and a tin of loose leaves, and began to make tea.

He said to her, gently, "Oblivion is not the only alternative to pain."

## SURFER IN THE RYE

When Oakley's behavior began to displease his parents in the late sixties, they blamed their son's estrangement on "liberal college professors." But the process was more philosophical than political, and its roots were older and deeper.

One morning in 1957 at Henry David Thoreau Junior High School in West LA, crossing the asphalt playground between the gym and the administration building, Oakley's best friend loaned him a paperback copy of *The Catcher in the Rye*, passing it furtively like a nudie magazine.

"This," his friend said, "is the best book you'll ever read."

For twelve-year-old Oakley, it was an eye-opener. Holden Caulfield didn't make Oakley angry or depressed, not even gloomy; he assimilated the character's perspective without suffering any attendant angst. It made him think about things in an entirely new way.

Over time, Oakley changed his behavior. He stopped trying so hard to fit in, to be popular with his classmates, to seek companionship with people he didn't necessarily like. He spent more time reading. He spent more time talking to girls. He stopped playing and watching team sports (Holden's words in his head: "You're supposed to kill yourself if the football team loses or something.") and was pleased to discover that the girls he liked best didn't even care.

J. D. Salinger and Holden Caulfield did Oakley the favor of undermining the automatic authority of elders. For the first time, he realized that he didn't need to accept or believe everything his teachers taught him, or want for himself everything his parents and relatives wanted for him.

At the age of thirteen, Oakley told his parents he wanted to stop going to church. His mother, the disciplinarian of the family, refused to honor the request.

"Don't you want to know why I don't want to go to church?" Oakley was defiant.

"It doesn't matter," his mother said. "You're going to church with us every Sunday."

"It has no meaning for me, and for you and Dad either. You just go because you think it's good for me."

"That's not true!"

"And you like to parade me around the courtyard after the service, all dressed up in my suit and tie, and show me off to all your friends."

"Not true!"

"Then why can't I leave right after the service? I told you I want to walk home, but you always make me hang around for an hour while you and Dad blab with everybody."

"We're just socializing, and we want you to be there."

"I don't want to be there. I don't think I believe in God."

"Well, you'd better think again."

"All I know is, if there is a God, and he's the kind of God that sends you to hell if you don't show up in church, then I'm not sure I want to pray to him."

Oakley loved bodysurfing. It was something he could do alone, without competing. He would get to the beach any way he could—usually by bus, with his Churchill fins wrapped up in a beach towel.

He started out bodysurfing because he wasn't sixteen yet, and couldn't drive. Surfboards in those days were nine or ten feet long and weighed at least twenty-five pounds. There was no way to get one to the coast without a car, and rides weren't easy to get. So Oakley, sometimes alone, sometimes with a friend, took the Sunset Boulevard westbound bus to Will Rogers State Beach with enough spare change for lunch and bus fare secure in the snap-down pocket of his swimming trunks.

In the eyes of his parents, surfing was a meaningless pursuit. It had no social purpose, no finish line, no linear progression, no path to verifiable success. You swim out to where the waves break, catch one and ride it back to shore. Then you turn around, swim back out, and catch another wave. You're in motion, but ultimately going nowhere. In some people's eyes, you're not making any progress. You're like a dog chasing a stick.

But for Oakley, riding waves existed somewhere outside of meaning. It was enjoyable, it was thrilling, but neither of those was the best thing about it. The best thing was that he was in another world, a world of lunar rhythms, shifting currents, the sight and force of waves, of floating on clouds of foam, flying toward shore, bursting through yielding surfaces, and of silence underwater.

# TAKEOFF

I shuffle past a young girl, maybe seven or eight, in the aisle seat, and take my window seat. I smile at her and say hello. Just because I'm child-free doesn't mean I don't enjoy the company of children. Alternate-O has children. He's always telling me I left a big hole in my life.

I want to offer the girl my seat, but before I can do it she's gone. Apparently the two older girls in the row in front of us are her sisters, and their parents are in center seats across the aisle. A muffled family discussion begins. The seat beside me remains empty.

The family appears to be part of a larger tour group. Across the aisles, kids and adults are signaling excitedly, visiting, trading seats, stuffing bags into the overhead compartments, videotaping one another, and making it difficult for the remaining passengers to settle in. The plane is full even though it's after the Labor Day weekend, and summer has officially ended. Vacation travel is supposed to drop, yielding to school and business. So what are all these tourists and tourist kids doing here?

Just before takeoff, the father of the three girls settles in beside me without a glance. He removes a laptop from his carry-on. He looks young for a man who has fathered three children. He's blond-haired like all the females in his family.

After takeoff, the father sets up the computer on his tray and begins to work on a document containing artwork and photographs. From the corner of my eye, I can see photos of kids on a playing field. The document is titled "Dixon Kids Soccer Pics." The father replaces it with "Our Trip To Hawaii." Then he inserts clip-art cartoon images of paradise: a sunset, a surfer on a wave, a bearded man sitting alone on a tiny island with a single coconut tree.

One by one, the father recaptions the soccer photos: "The Dixons in Paradise," "Tammy tries to surf," "Helen on the hotel balcony—ocean view!" His oldest daughter comes up beside him and stands in the aisle.

"What are you doing?"

"Working on our website."

"How come you say it's Tammy surfing when it's a cartoon?"

"Once we get home, I'll put our pictures in."

"How do you know what the pictures are going to look like?"

"Well, I don't, really. I'm just guessing."

"Can I have another game?"

The father takes some kind of module from his bag and gives it to his daughter, who disappears up the aisle.

Later in the flight, after a couple of screwdrivers surreptitiously strengthened by the contents of my pocket flask, during the movie I'm not interested in watching (*Spy Kids*), I tilt my seat back and close my eyes, and guess who comes to visit?

"Maybe your plane will crash and you won't have to do it yourself," he says.

"Leave me alone."

"What happened?" he asks me. "When you were twenty, you had big dreams. You were going to become a traveler, a wanderer, live everywhere, no permanent home."

"I was going to be a lover of many women, a man of vast experience, a wise man, a man who would make a difference in the world."

"Instead you became a teacher, got married, bought a home and settled down."

"Ordinary. Nondescript."

"Unremarkable. Commonplace. And then there's the old George Bernard Shaw saying, 'Those who can, do. Those who can't, teach.'"

"Thanks for reminding me."

"If you can't make a living playing the violin, you teach music. If you can't cut it in the major leagues, you coach baseball or teach PE. But what can't you do that makes you end up teaching English? You can't make a living as a writer?"

"Asshole," I tell him. "It's not about teaching, and it's not about me. The times are different. The sixties were a great time to be young in America. Good things were happening: civil rights and women's rights and the peace movement and the new environmental consciousness, when people finally took a look at the havoc we were wreaking on what was left of nature. But it all went bad."

"That didn't happen over here," says Alternate-O.

"Tell me about it."

"In my world, there's lots to be optimistic about and very little, if anything, to worry about. No greedy, exploitative multinational corporations. No overpopulation."

"What about global warming?"

"Not happening."

"No plundering the environment or poisoning your natural resources?"

"We're not that stupid."

"Do you watch television?"

"We had television, but we banned it because it was hypnotizing us, making us buy things we didn't need."

"Don't you care about the private lives of celebrities?"

"Nope."

"We used to drive sensible small cars, but they've been replaced by gigantic gas-guzzling SUVs."

"We don't have those."

"Who's president, Al Gore?"

"Ramsey Clark."

"No shit!"

"We didn't back out of the Kyoto Protocol or break the ABM treaty. And we went along with international resolutions on land mines and AIDS drugs."

"In your world, do Americans get fat on Big Macs and Whoppers?"

"Our fast-food restaurants serve wok-fired vegetables."

"Is the U.S. the planet's largest consumer of resources, polluter of the atmosphere, and arms dealer?"

"Not over here. No fucking way."

"How do you protect America's financial interests around the world?"

"Let's just say we've found better ways than supporting military juntas and totalitarian regimes that repress their citizens and keep them in poverty."

"Go away," I tell him.

"Hang it up," he says. "Take the leap. Hose from the exhaust pipe. Head in the oven. Barrel in the mouth. You'll be gone, but part of you will survive. Me and all of your other selves in all the other alternate worlds."

He's beginning to make sense. I'm beginning to feel tired.

*I'm the teacher, a rock in a river, immovable, with my students flowing past me, splashing against me only for a second, then gone in the rushing current. They will absorb in passing a few molecules of educational minerals. The rock of a teacher that is me never budges, the river of students never stops moving. They leave, I stay. They take, I give. They grow larger, I grow smaller.*

I wake up feeling low. What happened to the joy? What happened to the hope?

I live and work under gray clouds in a northern California coastal region whose coves and beaches, for miles to the north and south, shape beautiful waves to ride, but the ocean is so cold that I don't care to.

## FRED & COMPANY

"It's not nice to spy on people." Norm had snuck up behind Oakley. He was carrying something in a paper grocery bag.

"I heard some music and I was just—"

"Come on. Let's meet the troops." Norm let out a piercing jungle call and escorted Oakley into the big open kitchen. The black girl disappeared up the ladder.

"Good morning, Campers! Hey, Sandy, come back! Meet the new guy."

"You scared her off, Tarzan," the older man said, giving Oakley a long look. An expression of intense redneck hatred appeared on his face. "Fuckin' hippie! If you don't like this country, why don't you move to Russia?"

"Don't be misled by the long hair, Fred," Norm said. "He's not a hippie. Hippies don't surf. This here is Oakley, a good friend and a straight-up guy, come to live with us for who knows how long? He's going to set up shop on the platform Surly Steve left behind. Oakley, meet Fred the Zen—guru or con man, or both, depending on your point of view."

Fred greeted Oakley with a crushing handshake and a broad, exaggerated smile. He looked into Oakley's eyes for an uncomfortably long time before loosening his grip.

"And this is Soundtrack, Taylor Camp's resident minstrel poet. Soundtrack, Oakley. Oakley, Soundtrack."

Soundtrack stood to shake Oakley's hand, then sat back down with his guitar and resumed tentatively picking out the melody of "Oh, What a Beautiful Morning."

"I liked that song you just played. Did you write it?"

Soundtrack nodded.

"You from California?"

Soundtrack nodded again.

"What part?"

Soundtrack just sat there.

"He won't speak to us, Oakley," Norm said. "The only time he uses words is when he's singing songs." Norm stood in front of him, as if cross-examining a witness. "So we know for a fact that he is physically capable of human speech. And he doesn't appear to be mentally or psychologically damaged in any way. Which leads me to conclude that he has made a voluntary decision not to speak. Am I getting warm, man?"

Soundtrack nodded, smiling.

Fred had been sitting at a bench, head in arms on the picnic table, looking dejected. He rose from his slump and hoisted his coffee mug.

"What have you done to the booze, Oakley?" he asked, eyes riveted on Oakley. "We can't get drunk anymore."

"You got the wrong name," he told Fred, pleased to catch the literary allusion. "The iceman's name was Hickey, not Oakley."

As if electrically shocked, Fred's body stiffened and his face froze, aghast. Then, instantly, he shifted into a demeanor of childish delight, as if he had just discovered Oakley behind a shrub in a game of hide-and-seek.

"Look what I found!" he shouted. "Another college graduate!"

"Right on, Fred," Norm said. "Maybe the only resident of Taylor Camp with a Master's degree in literature."

"You sure you're not a hippie?" Fred asked. "Why do you want to go around looking like that?"

"The word never meant anything anyway," Oakley said. "It's just a catch-all invented by the media to describe young people they're criticizing. A big overgeneralization."

"Nobody in Hawaii knows that yet," Norm said. "We're a little behind the times. Hippies are still a relatively new phenomenon in the islands. There's an expression here: 'If you liked 1960, you'll love Hawaii.'"

A young woman climbed down another of the ladders. She was short, slightly plump but nicely shaped, wearing cut-off jeans and a flower-printed blouse. She had short, spiky red hair and lots of freckles. Her body made her look about sixteen; her attitude added a couple of years.

"Yeah, Fred," she said, not looking at him but walking straight up to Oakley. "Everybody's got long hair now." She smiled warmly at Oakley. "Besides, I think it looks good on him."

"You're just horny for some new dick," Fred said.

"Oakley, please disregard Fred and meet Marsha," Norm said. "Marsha, Oakley."

"Hello," Oakley said.

"Hello to you."

"Egomania!" Fred shouted, slamming his fist onto the table, startling everyone present. He turned to Oakley and said, calmly, reasonably, "On the surface, an enlightened man looks pretty much the same as any other man. He doesn't want to look different; he has no need to call attention to himself. But it's a disguise. Because underneath, he's like nobody else in the world. He's free of illusions. Have you ever stumbled onto any Zen?"

"Zen? No. In college I guess they kept me pretty busy with Western religion."

"Oh *they* did, did *they*?" Fred spoke in an amazed, appreciative tone, as if Oakley had just uttered a wonderful observation that only the two of them understood. It made Oakley uneasy. He didn't respond.

"Whatever happens to you," Fred said, with a forced smile, "be sure to blame it on *them*."

Oakley got the point, acknowledging his understanding with a weak laugh.

Norm broke the mood. "I brought you folks some vegetables," he told Fred. "Picked 'em just now. How about a cup of coffee for me and Oakley?"

"Help yourself," Fred said, still glaring at Oakley.

Oakley declined. Norm made himself a cup of coffee while Fred looked into the grocery bag.

"What's this stuff? Some kind of spinach?"

"Collard greens," Norm said. "They're good for you. And they grow like weeds. There's summer squash in there, too. And check out the Manoa lettuce! Before you steam those collard greens, Marsha, pull out the stringy part. "

"Why are you telling me, Norm?" Marsha asked. "I'm not the little housewife around here."

"No offense, I just want to make sure that this healthy food is properly prepared and enjoyed by everyone."

"Yeah, well, Fred does most of the cooking."

Norm rolled a number, lit up, took a deep hit, then passed it around. Everybody toked but Fred.

A tall, thin young man with a black beard and long, stringy black hair walked past on the trail, hesitated, then decided to pay a visit. He was wearing blue jeans heavily embroidered on the pockets with floral motifs, peace signs and colorful, seam-reinforcing stitching. His T-shirt was tie-dyed and looked old. Around his neck was a string of beads.

"Patrick!" Fred shouted, his mouth spreading into a gigantic smile. "Bet you smelled the pakalolo!"

Norm offered Patrick a hit; Patrick accepted.

Fred held up a two-fingered V. "Peace, brother! Everything's groovy! Isn't it?" Then the smile disappeared, the brow fretted. "Or is it?"

"What's your problem, Fred?" Patrick asked.

"No problem at all, brother Patrick," Fred replied. "I just feel privileged to know one of the last surviving examples of a dying breed. Oakley may deny being a hippie, but Patrick's proud to claim the title."

"Hippies are far from extinct," Norm said. "Thousands of 'em are living on reservations in California, Vermont, and Tennessee. Thousands more are mutating into new socio-economic profiles. The rest are hiding out in the mountains, pretending it's 1870."

"Patrick, meet Oakley," Fred said.

Patrick barely nodded at Oakley. "I don't know what you've got against me and Heather. We're not bothering you or anybody else."

"I never said you were bothering me," Fred said with apparent sincerity.

"Then why didn't you give us a ride into Lihue yesterday? You had plenty of room, but you just passed us by."

"Yeah, we had plenty of room," Fred said. "Yes, I saw you and Heather with your thumbs sticking out. But there *we* were—me at the wheel, Sandy sitting peacefully beside me in the front seat, lean legs and green eyes, lean and green, Marsha stretched out in the back, popping up and down, being loud, singing songs, enjoying the view, digging the drive in our good old comfortable Buick, in our happy little family group. You might say we were *having a nice day*. And there *you* were, looking so *adamant, waiting* for charity and *expecting* it because, after all, you ain't heavy, you're my brother. So we all decided, with that kind of attitude, you deserved to be passed by and left behind." Fred smiled sweetly at Patrick. "Does that answer your question?"

"In a way. It tells me a lot about you."

"The way you keep your wife hidden away from everybody, like a prisoner, tells me a lot about you," Fred said. "But we're still friends, aren't we?" He made the peace sign again. "Peace, brother?"

"Yeah, what's the story, Patrick?" Norm asked. "Don't you and Heather believe in women's lib?"

"We believe in being free to define our own relationship, rather than have you define it for us."

"I see," Norm said. "I guess Heather just never wants to walk around by herself, then. She's too shy to be seen in public."

Patrick disregarded Norm and said to Fred, "By the way, she's not my wife. We don't believe in conventional marriage."

"But you have an old-fashioned relationship. You're the boss and she obeys. Is she over eighteen?"

"None of your business. At least I'm being faithful to her."

"At least," Norm said, "he's being fearful of her."

"What I mean is, at least I'm not living with two women like Fred."

Fred said, "I thought hippies were supposed to believe in sexual freedom."

"Some of us believe in monogamy."

Fred said, "The word you want is monopoly."

"Or monotony," Marsha chimed in.

"If you ever change your mind," Fred said, "I think Sandy likes you. Sometimes she's not so shy in the dark. You know what they say: 'Once you've had it black, you'll never go back to white meat again.'"

"Jesus."

"Maybe it's *Marsha* you want! I don't blame you—she's a tiger!"

"I don't fuck male chauvinist pigs," Marsha said. "Except for you, Fred."

"Come on over tonight, and don't forget to bring Heather," Fred said. "Then all five of us can get together for one of those love-ins or whatever you call 'em!"

"You're perverted!" Patrick said and headed off down the trail.

Sandy climbed down a ladder, fetched the mug of tea that she left behind on the picnic table, and started back up. She paused, glared at Fred, and said softly, "Honky asshole."

"Oh, boy," Fred said. "She's coming back to life."

"Before you disappear again, Sandy," Norm said, "meet the new kid on the block. Sandy, Oakley. Oakley, Sandy."

"Hi," Oakley said, trying to get a look at her face. She kept her head down and her short, straight hair fell to conceal it. For a moment she looked up to acknowledge Oakley. Her eyes were emerald green and shiny, an amazing contrast to her short-cropped ebony hair and creamy chocolate skin. Her face was sculpted into facets, like a polished wood statue of an Ethiopian princess. Except for the posture. Her posture was terrible.

"'Lo," she mumbled, then turned to take her mug up the ladder and disappear from view. He heard her footsteps on the ceiling above his head. Then he heard the sound of classical music, a harpsichord concerto.

"Please excuse Sandy," Norm said. "She's a little skittish sometimes."

"How come?"

"You ask a lot of questions, don't ya, stranger?" Fred said in a high, crackly voice, flapping his arms like chicken wings, impersonating Walter Brennan playing a gimpy sidekick in an old Western movie. "Maybe we should ask *you* a couple of questions, like what brings you to these parts, nosin' into peaceable folks' business? You one of them big-city newspaper reporters?"

Fred backed off suspiciously, then limped over to the ladder and hauled himself up on his one "good" leg.

"Don't mind Fred, either," Norm said. "Think of him as therapy. As for Sandy, who knows why she's so weird? One day she just showed up in camp that way, and Fred glommed onto her. Something bad must have happened to her. Maybe she was an abused child. Maybe it was drugs. Maybe rape. I think Fred knows, but he's not discussing it with anyone but her."

"Shouldn't she see a psychiatrist?"

"Fred's taking care of her," Marsha said. "She's coming along fine. You should have seen her two months ago."

"Time to get to work," Norm said. "Want to help, Marsha?"

She ignored him. "She says she's from Iowa. Black people, in Iowa?"

"How 'bout you, Oakley? We're going to dig a hole for a brand-new shitter. Right, Soundtrack?"

Soundtrack nodded. He fingerpicked "Whistle While You Work."

"Hey, Oakley," Marsha said. "Need a place to crash? The more the merrier in our spacious three-bedroom home."

"Thanks for the offer, but I've already got a place."

"Have it your way. But be sure to stop by and see me sometime. We like to play musical bedrooms." Marsha disappeared up a ladder.

"That reminds me," Norm shouted after her. "You never returned my Black Flag."

"It's right here," she yelled from above, dropping the red aerosol can to bounce on the packed-dirt floor.

"Mahalo, Marshmallow!" Norm shouted. "Want to see the garden?" he asked Oakley. "We've cleared about a half acre so far. Let's check it out, then we'll go dig the hole."

"I was planning to take a walk on the beach."

"Plenty of time for everything. We could use some help."

"That's Marsha's nickname, Marshmallow?"

"Soft and white."

"She doesn't mind. She's a liberated woman, comfortable with her roly-poly body type even if it doesn't correspond to the male-oriented ideal media image of a beautiful babe."

"How come you're building an outhouse? Can't everybody just take care of their own shit?"

"That's what we used to do until the Department of Health stopped by last month. They told us if we don't build a legitimate pooper, and if it isn't at least a hundred yards from a place where people cooked and ate, they'll close us down. They gave us thirty days to comply. They're looking for any excuse to get rid of us vermin."

"What's the Black Flag for? You got ants?"

"Crabs. The cheapest, most effective cure available without a prescription. Just spray it on your crotch and they're gone."

"Ow."

They headed for the garden, Soundtrack strolling and strumming the dwarves' happy tune.

"This one's just a temporary shitter. I've got plans for another one, with a septic tank, a raised platform, and a panoramic mountain view. But after this comes the shower."

"Why a shower?"

"Why not? It's easy enough to build. Just elevate a big tub of water and gravity does all the work. Then we don't have to bathe in the stream all the time."

The garden was in a clearing hacked out of the jungle. Several machetes stuck out of the dirt nearby.

"Wow," Oakley said. "Looks like a lot of work."

"Couple of hours a day for about three months. Mostly me and Soundtrack, but some others help now and then. Marsha, Fred, Patrick. I hope you'll be a regular."

"Why not?"

Later, shoveling dirt from a hole, Oakley said, "Fred sure knows how to pin a guy down. I mean, the college graduate thing."

"You were embarrassed because he caught you showing a little ego," Norm said, "feeling proud because you knew what he was talking about."

"But he called me on it, and in a way he was right. I was displaying my knowledge. I could have simply appreciated what he was doing without talking about it."

"It's not like you were bragging or anything. Forget about it."

"Hey, Norm," Oakley said. "Before today, did Fred know about my education or being an English teacher?"

"I never told him."

"He sure zeroed in on me. It was weird. That stuff about blaming 'them,' too. He's right about that."

"Some people think Fred's psychic, but to me there's nothing supernatural about it. He just watches people and figures them out. He's really perceptive. He learns who you are so well that he can guess at what you're thinking. But that doesn't mean he can read your mind."

## 22. Europe 1966

## PARIS DISSOLVES IN ACID

One summer evening in late August, a rainstorm darkened the city of light. Gray skies, an unseasonal chill, and unfriendly wet streets kept Oakley and Fleur in their third-floor room at the Hotel Voltaire.

Who cared? They had food to eat, big bolsters in bed to prop themselves up on, books to read, stories to tell, love to make. They also had two hits of acid to drop, which Oakley had scored from a fellow Californian in the Métro.

Neither of them had taken LSD before, but both knew what to expect. They believed, along with many of their peers, that acid was an automatic consciousness expander, a substance that spurred incredible insights into one's self and environment, that turned off the socially-embedded mental machinery to allow a glimpse of the eternal reality behind the temporal mask. LSD was a gift from God, designed to help mankind evolve more quickly and save itself from its own stupidity.

Oakley had read William Burroughs, and kept some of the man's words in a notebook he carried with him, filled with quotes from books he had read:

> The hallucinogen drugs shift the scanning pattern of "reality" so that we see a different "reality"—"Reality" is simply a more or less constant scanning pattern—The scanning pattern we accept as "reality" has been imposed by the controlling power on this planet, a power primarily oriented towards total control. In order to retain control they have moved to monopolize and deactivate the hallucinogen drugs.

Along with a quote from Timothy Leary:

> The most efficient way to cut through the game structure of
> Western life is the use of drugs. Drug-induced satori. In three
> hours under the right circumstances the cortex can be cleared.

If, on their first acid trip, Fleur and Oakley didn't quite attain
cosmic consciousness, they had a wonderful time. With their sensory
receptors jacked up to maximum input, all filters and regulators
disabled, they experienced a rush of feeling and perception that kept
them busy for hours. When they made love, the boundaries of their
bodies dissolved and merged. When they took turns reading from
Fleur's slim volume of Leonard Cohen poems, they admired his
wisdom. The cheese and pâté and baguettes were incredibly flavorful.
The *vin ordinaire* was extraordinary.

They laughed and cried, whispered and shouted, sang songs and
tried to speak without using words. They stared into one another's
souls and studied their own faces in the mirror above the dresser. For
the time being, Fleur's enigmatic smile was no longer a mystery. Her
hair looked like ink to Oakley, and his teeth looked like piano keys
to her. They wondered what clocks were for, and why the floor held
them up. They marveled at the resilience of skin and the fluidity of
water. They went through each other's backpacks, examining every
item inside, considering its size, shape, and function.

After an indeterminate time, Oakley looked out the window. The rain
had stopped, the sky had cleared, and the moon had risen. He saw his
reflection in a puddle of water on the street below, realizing that this was
an impossibility. He urged Fleur to get dressed and go outside with him.

The night air was clean and fresh. The streets were practically
empty. They walked in silence, listening to the echoes of their
footsteps, surrounded by pools of collected rainwater reflecting the
night sky and streetlights. They had no idea what time it was, and
didn't care to know.

They followed the distant sound of melodic voices into a small, illuminated park beside a church. To their amazement, a choir was singing, as if for them alone. The park benches were wet, so they stood and listened until the singers went into the church. The leaves of trees glistened with raindrops. A spider's web, beaded with water, looked a like a silver necklace.

## WORKING FEVERISHLY

During his first weeks at Taylor Camp, Oakley was a busy man. He helped Norm in the garden. He got to know the camp residents. He hitched rides into Hanalei, the little town seven miles back in the direction of civilization, where he bought necessities, wine, and snacks at the Ching Young General Store, and did his laundry at Ching Young's laundromat.

Understandably, Ching Young was one of the few people in Hanalei who didn't object to the presence of hippies on the island.

The first north swell of the season had brought four-foot waves, and Oakley surfed almost every day for a couple of hours, usually at Tunnels, the break two miles up the road at Haena Point. He hitched rides with Norm and his surfer friends, or else walked along Kuhio Highway, not actually a highway but a two-lane country road. He kept to the left-hand side, the ocean side, board under his left arm, right arm stuck out straight, thumb thrust forward toward the waves he wanted to ride.

But Oakley's biggest project during this time was building himself a shelter on the platform he had inherited from Surly Steve, a tiny house to replace his hot tent.

Unlike the majority of dwellings at Taylor Camp, Oakley's homesite was located on the east side of Limahuli Stream. He liked the privacy and quiet.

Over the plywood platform set on its four ironwood cornerstumps, he erected an A-frame three times the interior surface square footage of his three- by five-foot tent. He scavenged or purchased materials.

All the tools he needed were in Taylor Camp, and their owners were willing to lend them out.

The diagonals of the "A" were larger at the back than the front, so the ceiling tapered down toward the entrance.

For the two-piece end diagonals and the top beam connecting them, he used long branches sawn from dead ironwoods nearby, lashed together with fishing line. Enclosing this framework were stacked crosspieces of bamboo, similarly lashed to the ironwood. Oakley had harvested the bamboo from a nearby forest where the State allowed people to cut it for building, or making fishing poles and mango pickers.

When he had been in Taylor Camp only slightly more than a week, something in the water or his food had made Oakley sick. He suffered chills and fever. He didn't know what it was, the onset of dysentery or maybe just the flu. At night he thrashed in the grip of feverish, repetitive dreams. During the day he was driven by an equally feverish desire to finish building his home.

Once he had completed the framework, he added the roof-walls. In the traditional Taylor Camp style, they consisted of thick, clear vinyl sheeting cut from a large roll at the hardware store in Lihue. The sheets were staple-gunned to the cross-pieces of the frame. To seal and waterproof the stapled areas, he applied criss-crosses of elastic tape. He bought cheap orange cotton yardage to apply to the inside walls of the back half of the A-frame, his bedroom, to a height of three feet. His bedroom was separated from the anteroom by a wall of stacked crates, which contained his clothing, tools, supplies, and books. His sleeping bag, cushioned by a plastic air mattress, was covered by a tent-shaped mosquito net suspended from above.

At the threshold it was three steps down to ground level, each step a circular slice cut from the stump of another dead ironwood. The ground level was covered for another ten feet by a canopied walkway, an extension of the vinyl-covered A-frame that continued to taper, narrowing and lowering so that when Oakley exited under the final pointy hood, he had to duck under it.

This was intentional, because it required him (and guests) to bow upon departure, delivering a forced tribute not to his abode but to the scene ahead: As he walked up a short incline, through a thin band of jungle, a huge horizontal span of seashore, ocean and sky appeared. The sight was deserving of the brief homage.

The wall-free outside canopy contained Oakley's front porch and cooking/dining area. He installed cinder block and wood-plank shelves for pots and pans, plates and bowls and cups, knives and forks and spoons, and canned, bagged, and boxed food. Just out from under the canopy was a fire pit lined with round black stones collected from a nearby stream bed.

He bought a cracked vinyl, three-cushion sofa for five dollars from a resident who was replacing it, and strategically set it outside the canopy in front of the structure, at the top of the rise, under the ironwood trees at the edge of the jungle, where he had a panoramic view of the sandy stretch of beach, the reef beyond, the ocean's horizon, and the infinite sky.

It took Oakley two weeks to finish his new home, running on virus-driven energy. When he was done, he collapsed and slept for fourteen hours, two nights in a row. After that, he spent a dreamless night and woke up the next day recovered.

## 24. Southern California 1961

### SURFING IS BAD FOR YOU

Oakley started board surfing the year he turned sixteen and got his first car, a turquoise '58 Chevy Impala convertible. Even with the top up he could carry his surfboard, inserted through the zipped-open plastic back window, the nose securely wedged behind the front seat. Oakley thought it looked pretty cool, that nine-foot-two Dave Sweet, not strapped down on a surf rack like Little Nell tied to the railroad tracks, but sticking up into the Southern California sky at a jaunty forty-five degree angle.

His parents gave him a car at that age because they understood that living in Los Angeles and depriving your offspring of this basic form of teenage transportation and freedom, even for a day after their sixteenth birthday, would expose them to peer ridicule and seriously cripple their social growth. In LA, if you don't let your kids have their own cars, you lose their love forever.

People in LA drive seventy miles across town just to try a new restaurant. Oakley and his friends, high school juniors out looking for waves, would drive up or down the coast, a hundred miles in either direction. They would leave home at five in the morning under dark, chilly skies. They would cruise the Pacific Coast Highway from Santa Barbara to San Diego, even drive into Baja below the border, in search of waves. Not roadmaps but surf reports and tide charts were their guides. They knew every surf spot on the Southern California coast: Rincon, Point Dume, Malibu, Redondo Breakwater, Lunada Bay, The Wedge, Salt Creek, Trestles, Tamarack, Moonlight Beach, Swami's, Osprey Reefs, Cardiff By the Sea, K-49, San Miguel.

Oakley's parents couldn't hold him back. He was an A student; he had earned the right to surf. And so he went surfing. A lot.

Worried that it was becoming an obsession and would eventually interfere with his grades at school, Oakley's mother did her best to discourage him from surfing, and she had a special way of going about it. She was articulate and opinionated, had a master's degree in Library Science from a women's college in Ohio, and was the medical librarian at a hospital in Santa Monica.

She spoke with doctors and researched medical journals, taking detailed notes on the many perils of surfing, from shark attacks to skin cancer, surfboard-inflicted concussions and lacerations, sore necks, dislocated rotator cuffs, hypothermia, and calcium deposits—the "surf bumps" that grew below the knees and on the tops of feet, caused by these four pressure points rubbing against the deck of a surfboard while a surfer is knee-paddling.

Even though it was easier and faster to do it prone, Oakley and his friends knee-paddled all the time, partly because they believed the rumor that surf bumps could get you declared 4-F, physically ineligible for military service. It turned out to be false.

The books Oakley's mother would check out of the UCLA School of Medicine's library for her doctors were gruesome, filled with photos of people with grotesquely swollen necks, festering sores, and decomposing flesh. She would leave copies of the most sensational surfing disaster stories on top of his bed, where she also deposited her scribbled reminders of all the duties, appointments, and social engagements which required his attention or attendance.

To be fair, she was just trying to protect him. She didn't want her son to get hurt. But she had a weak argument, and they both knew it. Based on comparative statistics of accidents, injuries and fatalities, driving on an LA freeway was hundreds of times more dangerous than surfing.

But that didn't faze her. She kept on clipping articles and leaving them on his bed. She dropped comments at the dinner table, such as "Did you see the paper this morning? Another drowning at Malibu."

Oakley always did his best to defuse whatever she said, with comments like, "I guess I'm pretty lucky—in all the time I've been surfing, I've only drowned once."

One day a friend came over at 4 AM, the time they had agreed on but not informed their parents about, to pick Oakley up for a trip to Huntington Beach, Newport, and points south.

His mother, whose hearing was as sharp as her tongue, caught him trying to sneak out of the house and cornered him at the door.

"Where do you think you're going?" she demanded.

"Surfing."

"It's still dark outside!"

"It won't be when we get there."

"Where?"

"We don't know. We check out a lot of different spots."

"You're going to stay right here and leave at a respectable hour!"

"Mom, what's not respectable about 4 am as opposed to 5 or 6?"

"Don't you get smart with me. At least stay and have a decent breakfast."

Grumbling, shaking her head, she turned away and let him go. He hurried to load his board onto Lee's car, but before they could escape she stepped outside and fired a parting shot:

"Surfing breeds disease!"

It became an instant mantra: everything there was to be said about surfing in three words, to be uttered anytime and anywhere, for years to come.

"Hey, Lee, let's go up to Rincon tomorrow."

"Don't think so, Oakley. Like to, but, you know...*surfing breeds disease.*"

## AU REVOIR

Oakley flew home to Los Angeles, Fleur to Toronto. She left from Heathrow, he from Orly two days later. They had spent a week in London exploring the city, living in a cheap rooming house in Russell Square with one bathroom per floor, no hot water and a lecherous landlord.

Oakley couldn't blame him, or anyone else for that matter, who lusted after Fleur. His need for her was physical, emotional, and intellectual. He understood the futility. Part of the reason he wanted her so much was that she needed him so little.

But none of that mattered. Oakley was with Fleur, in the moment, even if it was the final moment. The landlord was disgusting but harmless, Fleur found him funny, and the room was cheap and just a block from the underground, which they rode to the British Museum, the Tate, and all the other galleries, and plays and movies, parks and restaurants.

London was colder than Paris, even in early September, and Fleur was reminded of Toronto winters. She told Oakley she didn't want to go back, but she was not behaving accordingly. He could see the part of her that was relieved to be returning home, whether to the ease of routines or the arms of Ian, or both, Oakley couldn't tell. But in an unarticulated place, he perceived that she lacked any desire for a permanent attachment to him, maybe to anyone, including Ian. She was an independent, or at least someone whose dependencies were only temporary and easily discarded.

At the airport he couldn't help himself. He asked Fleur if she wanted to get married.

"I hope you're kidding," she said. "I'm not going to be anybody's wife. Now or ever." She leaned over and kissed him. "Nothing personal, Oakley. You know I love you."

"Whatever that means."

"What are you saying?"

"I guess I don't know what love means to you. To me it means I don't want this to end, I want to be with you longer, maybe for life. What does it mean to you?"

"You're too serious, Oakley. We have this wonderful connection. Maybe it's ending, maybe it's not. We should laugh and celebrate, be grateful we found each other."

"When some people find each other, they want to keep each other."

"I don't want to keep anybody, and I won't let anybody keep me."

"I don't mean 'keep' like 'possess.'"

"Yes you do. Everybody does. They just won't admit it."

## PURE FLEUR

One October afternoon, Oakley was stretched out on his bed—
the cheap plastic air mattress, two white sheets and his zipped-open
sleeping bag for a blanket—reading. Earlier he had surfed at Tunnels,
worked in the garden, and helped Norm haul garbage halfway to
Hanalei, to the nearest dump. He heard soft footsteps, someone
approaching.

"Anybody home?"

The voice was Fleur's. Book in hand, Oakley went out to greet her.
She was wearing a black bikini. Her big-boned, slender body hadn't
changed in four years.

"Did I wake you up?" Her smile was the same, too—not projected
outward, but private, a response to the world that she shared with no
one.

"I was reading." He showed her the thin paperback. "Fred loaned
it to me."

She grabbed it from him and read the title. "'The Gospel According
to Zen.' Religion."

"If this is religion, give me more." He took the book back,
flipped through the pages. "Listen to this: 'We sleep with both legs
outstretched, free of the true, free of the false.'"

"Words to live by."

"You've gone sarcastic since we were together."

"We were 'together'?"

Oakley shook his head. They sat on his couch, legs outstretched,
looking at the beach where Taylor Campers were drying laundry on

the sand, sunbathing naked, and swimming in the calm waters inside the reef. Small waves were breaking outside.

Fleur looked back at Oakley's treehouse. "Not too shabby. Beachfront, ocean view. You know what you're doing. It might even hold up through the winter."

"'Hold up'? What's going to prevent it from holding up?"

"Weather."

"You mean rain? No problem. It's waterproof. Already been tested."

"Not really. Not yet."

"Jesus, Fleur, would you stop being so fucking mysterious and get to the point?"

She looked at him for a few seconds. "The point is, it hasn't really begun to rain. You'll see what I mean."

"You're saying it'll get worse?"

"It will rain more. And harder. The trails turn into rivers. Your clothes and your bedsheets stay damp all the time. They begin to mildew, and stink, and turn black. Then the storms come, and the winds pick up, and the rain starts to blow in sideways, against the walls. And the surf gets so big it shakes the ground under your feet. You can feel it all the way up to the road. Sometimes the waves eat away a big chunk of the shoreline. In fact, you might have built too close to the water."

"Nice of you to mention it two weeks after I finish. But I've been checking it out. I'm a hundred yards from the high tide line. The ocean's never going to come up here."

"It did at least once before, when it killed the trees your platform is built on."

"Oh, yeah. Norm mentioned that."

"It doesn't matter anyway. One tsunami would wipe out all of us in a minute."

"When do these torrential rains begin?"

"Maybe in a month, maybe two. Maybe they'll give us a break this year and never come at all."

Fleur produced a joint and a wooden match from her bikini top, lighted up, and passed it to Oakley.

"Did you hear about Janis Joplin?"

"What about her?"

"She died. Two days ago. Heroin overdose."

"That was two weeks ago, Fleur. And it was Jimi Hendrix, not Janis Joplin. I heard all about it."

"You're right, Oakley." She paused to take a hit. "But so am I. They're both dead. Jimi two weeks ago and Janis two days ago. It was in yesterday's paper. Didn't you see it? Her picture was on the front page."

"I don't read the news anymore."

"I always buy a paper when I'm in Hanalei. Just to let the locals know I can read."

They finished the joint in silence. The beach looked hot, but Oakley's home was shaded by the thick canopy of kamani trees fifty feet above their heads. A light breeze blew through the ironwoods lower down.

"Are you glad you came here, Oakley?"

"Yeah, sure. Why?"

"I was just wondering. You don't seem very happy."

"I suppose I'm not. I think it's finally sinking in that I burned all my bridges, and I can't go home without being arrested."

"Why did you come here? Why not Canada? Toronto has thousands of draft evaders."

"They can't go home, either," Oakley said.

"But in two years they can become Canadian citizens. After two years here, assuming you're not caught, you'll still be an outlaw."

"I don't know anybody in Canada except you. And you're not there now, are you?"

"I could have given you some names. You could have stayed with Ian."

"No, thanks."

"Maybe you came here because of me."

Oakley looked away and let out a long sigh. "I gave up on that a long time ago."

"Maybe you shouldn't have."

"Oh, Jesus, give me a break. You come to see me in LA, get bored and go back to Ian. Then you show up in LA a year later, this time with Ian. Then you break up with Ian and run off with one of my best friends. And you're telling me I shouldn't give up?"

"If you really loved me, you would have kept trying."

"Fuck that shit. You can only get burned so many times."

"By the way, it wasn't boredom that sent me back to Ian."

"What was it, then?"

"You always talked about how much you loved me, but you never acted like it."

"You picked a lousy time to show up."

"I didn't pick a time. The time picked me. I wanted to see you. I wanted to be with you."

"A feeling that lasted for about two weeks."

"Ian was calling me up from Toronto, crying over the phone, begging me to come back. You were in class all day. You didn't care about me."

"You're wrong about that. I cared about you a lot."

"Not enough."

"I had responsibilities."

"You were so fucking responsible it made me want to puke."

"Gee, I apologize for that. What a nightmare bummer."

"You were being responsible to yourself. Not to me. You left me all alone, all day long."

"Like I said, it was bad timing."

"You made it bad. You could have cut classes. When Ian and I were in college, we almost never went to class."

"I'm supposed to admire you for that?" Oakley stood up, ready to leave. "This is going nowhere."

"Please sit down. I'm sorry. I didn't come here to argue with you."

"Why did you, then?"

"To ask why you've been avoiding me."

"I haven't been avoiding you."

"Yes, you have. You spend all your time with Norm. And Soundtrack. And Fred. You haven't spent hardly any time with me at all. You hardly even talk to me."

Oakley sat back down.

"You're right. It's not that I've been avoiding you, though. It's that— well, I don't feel that comfortable around you since I got here."

"Is it Norm?"

"No. It's you. You're different now. Kind of…mocking. You give everybody a hard time, and you think it's funny."

"I don't mock people."

"Yes, you do. I hear you've been calling me 'Acorn' because you think I'm immature."

"You *are* immature. I was telling you the truth, not giving you a hard time."

"In what way am I immature, then?"

"You haven't accepted the basic fact that the only thing that's going to give your life meaning or purpose is yourself."

"I think I accept that."

"No, you don't. You think your stupid college degree is going to give your life meaning. Or some job you work at. Or some relationship you're in. You expected me to give your life meaning. You wanted to marry me because you thought our marriage would make everything fall into place, give you some purpose that you were lacking. But that's not the way it works."

"I guess you're right. Us getting married would have been meaningless."

"Oh, now he's hurt." Fleur sat up, turned to Oakley and put a hand on his shoulder. "It's OK, you'll figure it out sooner or later. You give your life meaning by the actions you take."

She kissed him on the cheek, and nuzzled her face into his neck. A knife stabbed his heart from the inside out. A surge of desire made him hard.

"What's this all about?"

She kissed him on the lips. "I miss fucking you." She pressed her body against him, moaning softly. Surprised and thrilled, Oakley embraced her. Bliss. That wonderful intimacy Oakley had not felt for a long while, the fondly remembered scent of Fleur, the physical joy of touch and fondle. He loved it.

He pulled away.

"One thing I don't miss," he said, "is you fucking with my head. But here you are, doing it again."

"Did someone say 'head'?" She pushed her forehead against his chest, pressed it slowly downward, and began to chew on his erection through the material of his jeans.

This was the Fleur, the Flora, that Oakley wanted to come back to him again, the playful and erotic one. The one with the strange gypsy smile. The one who had seemed to need and want him. He could have just let go and enjoyed it. He wanted to be able to just let go and enjoy it.

She was undoing his fly when he pushed her away.

"You know something? I don't want to do this."

"Is it because of Norm? Don't worry. He knows."

"Knows what?"

"I told him I wanted to make love to you, I asked him if he could handle it. He said he could."

"Yeah, well, just because *he* can handle it, doesn't mean I can."

"Come on, Oakley."

He slid out from under her and got up from the couch.

"I give my life meaning by the actions I take."

She said disgustedly: "Oh, now—"

Without looking back, he walked out of the jungle onto the beach, took off his clothes and jumped in the ocean.

## 27. Northern California 1962-1966

# EXISTENTIALISM BREEDS DIS-EASE

Oakley's parents wanted him to go back East to college, to Harvard or an Ivy League school. But for fear of going stir-crazy in an icy, landlocked city, Oakley insisted on Stanford, an hour away from the fogbound but surf-laden coast of Santa Cruz.

For four years, whenever he could work a free morning into his course schedule, he would head south on Highway 101 to San Jose, then west on 17 to the ocean where he would ride Steamer Lane, Cowell's, River Mouth, Pleasure Point, and Wild Hook. In the foggy mornings, the water and air were both cold. He wore a full wet suit, three-quarters of an inch thick, a black rubber outfit he had to powder with cornstarch to get his arms and legs in. He had to file the leading edge of the skeg on his surfboard to cut through the kelp, the thick beds of kelp that depended on undulations of waves for their existence. Just like Oakley.

Because he liked to read, Oakley chose to become an English major. It was in a sophomore course called "Theology in Contemporary Literature" that he read another book that shaped his mind: *Existentialism from Doestoevsky to Sartre*, in which he discovered, to his surprise, a religion without a God.

In the book were the ideas of both Christian and atheist existentialists; Oakley preferred the latter, especially Sartre, who posited a meaningless universe in which it was nevertheless necessary to behave unselfishly and even morally, without depending on a deity (or organized religion) for instructions. He kept a quote in his notebook:

> I say that man is condemned to be free. Condemned, because he did not create himself, yet is nevertheless at liberty, and from the moment that he is thrown into this world he is responsible for everything he does.

Man was alone in the universe, said Sartre, and free to create his own meaning, his own purpose in life, his own code of behavior. Anything was possible, but there was a catch. By your actions, you defined who you were. Not only that, you defined all of humanity as well. Therefore, if you chose to steal, you were defining yourself as a thief, and all of your fellow men as thieves. You could expect no more from them, if you could expect no more from yourself. On the other hand, whenever you did something to help someone else, you defined yourself as a helpful person, and human beings as people who help one another.

For Oakley existentialism was simply an elaboration of the Golden Rule: Do unto others as you would have them do unto you. He felt that existentialism provided all the guidance he needed to live a decent life—and yet the only instruction it offered was that there were no rules.

And then there were Albert Camus and Sisyphus. When Oakley read the story of the man who was condemned to roll a rock to the top of a hill, watch it roll back down, and roll it up again, for all of eternity, it made him think about surfing. Paddle out, catch a wave, paddle back out again. Camus wrote, "We must imagine Sisyphus happy."

In Oakley's senior year he took a course in twentieth century English lit from a professor who applied existentialist interpretations to everyone from Charles Dickens to Virginia Woolf. The professor asked the class, a small seminar, "What does an existentialist do for a living?"

"He's a doctor," Oakley said, "or a teacher."

"Why?"

"Because it's an occupation that helps other people."

"Is he required to help others?"

"There are no requirements."

"So?"

"However, man defines himself and others by his actions, so he should choose to help others rather than hurt them."

"What if he were to live as a hermit, helping no one but himself, yet harming no one else?"

"I guess that would be acceptable."

The professor told the class the story of a friend of his, a man who constantly traveled around the planet, his quest to visit as many of the world's major cities as possible in his lifetime.

"He hires a cab at the airport," the professor said, "and has the driver take him around the city for an hour or two, then goes back to the airport and catches the next flight out."

"That's fine for him," Oakley said. "But he's defining all the rest of us as travelers without any particular purpose."

"How is that definition inaccurate?"

## BACK TO THE GARDEN

At Honolulu International Airport I change planes for Kauai, as I did thirty-one years ago, having no desire then or now to explore Waikiki and the Big Pineapple. The airport has grown considerably. So has the interisland terminal. Snazzy graphics cover the high walls above the check-in counter: Hawaiian warriors, surfers, musicians, and flowers. The new tropiganda.

As I board the plane, the line in front of me stops moving down the aisle as a dark-skinned, buzzcut teenager takes his time removing several items from a bag he has stuffed into an overhead bin. His friend, wearing a black tank top bearing the message "Locals Rule!" mocks him in a friendly way, loud enough for all to hear.

"Suckeen Grant, dis wan twenny minute flight, you gotta stop the line fo' get da stuff you need. Twenny minute flight!"

Grant shoots his friend a hostile glance. I remember the local term for it: stink eye.

At my seat, I look out over the wing, trying to remember if my earlier flight was on a propeller plane. This aircraft, according to the folder in the pouch, is a DC-950 jet. Outside and in, it looks brand new.

In 1970, all I had to do was show my round-trip ticket to the local airlines and I could fly to any other island, one-way, for seven dollars.

The magazine in my pouch is titled *Hana Hou!*, a term translated on the masthead "one more time" or "encore." The magazine refers to Kaua'i, Maui, Moloka'i, Lana'i and Hawai'i as O'ahu's "Neighbor Islands," with a capital "N" and a capital "I." When I was here before, they were the "outer" islands, small "o," small "i." And no punctuation marks divided the vowels in "Hawai'i" or the other island names.

The plane takes off over the ocean, with Diamond Head on the left and the huge city stretching out beneath, then it banks right and heads northwest across the tip of the island. I see the billowy clouds, warm and bright white from above, cast cold black shadows on the planet's blue skin.

Soon after the plane gets up to full speed, it starts to slow down. I've just peeled open and begun to drink my fruit-flavored juice (self-fortified with alcohol) when the flight attendant announces the descent to Lihue Airport. An hour earlier I had downed a Vicodin from Sage's stash. I go riffing in my mind:

She pronounces it "Lay-*who*-way." I remember it sounding more like "Lee-*who*-we."

"Stink-eye." Classic.

I'll be on Kauai for the first time in thirty-one years. It feels like maybe ten. One of life's dirty tricks, Alt-O once reminded me: The older you get, the faster time moves.

Judging by the ads for beachfront hotels, prime real estate, and high-end residential communities, Kauai has done some maturing while I was gone. If that's what it is.

I saw the televised footage of Hurricane Iniki in 1992, followed the news as it beat the island into a state of arrested development. Homes were flattened, trees felled, power lines downed, people broken and demoralized. There was no electricity for months. Not enough carpenters, plumbers and electricians to repair the damage and rebuild the homes all at once. Not enough money, either.

But reportedly the island has bounced back. The hotels are rebuilt and repaired, the tourist industry is back on track.

Alternate-Oakley pops up and I ask him, "What about Hanalei and the road beyond? Did the bridges collapse? Did the north shore get hit hardest, as usual?"

He says, "Don't ask me."

"Three decades and a hurricane. Think I stand a chance of finding Taylor Camp?"

"Beats me."

## SURFING IS GOOD FOR YOU

Fresh from his four-month European sojourn, Oakley flew home to Los Angeles wearing a Beatle haircut and a trendy British double-breasted sportcoat he had purchased on Carnaby Street. His mother burst into tears and moaned loudly and deliriously, right there in the terminal.

"You look so strange! Frightening! You're turning into a degenerate! My only son has become a stranger to his mother."

"Helen," his father said.

"And you have even lost the common decency that compels a functioning member of society to dress and look at least a little like everyone else does."

"Not a priority, Mom."

"This all happened because those liberal professors poisoned your mind."

After a week at home, still suffering from culture shock and his parents' harassments, Oakley began looking for somewhere else to live. He and a fellow student and friend, Joe, found an apartment in the "dangerous" (according to the parents) neighborhood of Venice, California—dangerous because he would be living in close proximity to blacks and Chicanos.

His father scolded him about "sowing wild oats." Oakley had to look it up. It was weird: His father didn't seem to be criticizing him for anything specific. It sounded more like he was envious and spiteful about not being young in this new era of free love, when he could have gotten laid a lot, the scenario he imagined for his son.

But Oakley wasn't getting laid, not even a little. Not that he didn't want to. But the thought of the energy it would take to get close to someone new was discouraging. He missed Flora—Fleur—and wanted to be with her every day, but he didn't let that get in his way. He went on with his life. She was thousands of miles away, back in the arms of Ian.

He went on with his life. He was busy working for his MA.

The UCLA English department had a program with a name Oakley appreciated, the "Terminal Masters" program. If you were certain you didn't want a PhD, you could enroll in the Terminal Masters program and get your MA in one year. On the other hand, if you were to enroll in the PhD program and later decide to drop out, you would need two years of study to leave with an MA.

Oakley didn't want a PhD. He wasn't even sure he wanted a master's, but it would extend his student deferment, and it might come in handy someday. It was something that, as his mother liked to say, "You could always fall back on."

He passed his foreign language proficiency exam just in time, before his decent French had turned indecent prior to disappearing forever. He went to all his classes, did most of the reading and all of the writing assignments, and kept up his grades.

It wasn't long before Oakley felt the urge to get back into surfing. He bought himself a brand-new board, a longboard, despite the urging of the sales kid to purchase one of the new short boards that were, he said, "the future."

Oakley didn't bother to tell his mother about his renewed interest in surfing. He didn't want to set himself up for a new deluge of hysterical haranguing. What she didn't know she couldn't get all worked up about. But, of course, she eventually found out anyway.

To Oakley's surprise, she wasn't upset. Instead of digging up all the old objections she had once hammered him with, she said, "I'm so glad to hear you're surfing again."

He was too dumbfounded to reply. He let it go with a laugh of disbelief.

Thinking about it, Oakley could understand why his mother had made the turnaround. The nation's youth were getting involved in diversions far more threatening to their parents than surfing. Compared to hanging out in the Venice ghetto with blacks and Chicanos, shooting up heroin and robbing gas stations to finance your next fix, surfing was good for you—safe, healthy and wholesome.

The young people of Oakley's generation were gambling with their physical and mental health by "experimenting with" (a media cliché, but a good choice of words) marijuana, LSD, and sex. They were becoming politically active, placing themselves in jeopardy with the law. They were committing crimes and going to jail, or becoming fugitives and disappearing underground.

The world was changing too fast for Oakley's mother, and she was eager to believe that, at least in the most dangerous ways, her son wasn't changing with it. She was grateful that he had held onto an activity which, for her, had already become a nostalgic emblem of simpler, better times. And she was grateful that he wasn't taking LSD.

## FLEURRY

In mid-November, Fleur phoned him from Toronto.

"I miss you," she said.

"I miss you too. I love you."

"I want to come and stay with you if it's OK."

"It's more than OK." Oakley hoped Joe would agree.

"I'm leaving Ian. Forever."

"That's great—I mean, I'm sorry. Uh…I guess what I mean is both of the above."

"I need to get away."

Oakley persuaded Joe that having Fleur live with them would be OK, so eager and lovestruck that Joe really had no choice.

Oakley and Fleur spent their first twenty-four hours together in bed. The black hair, the strong body, the inner-directed smile, the weeping after orgasm—they all were back and Oakley was happy. They made love, slept, smoked pot, and ate in bed. Then they went to the ocean. Oakley drove her up and down the coast, showing her the surf spots.

After a week, he began to worry about cutting his classes. UCLA was on the quarter system and final exams were coming up soon. He told her he had to get back to school.

For a while she went with him, wandering the campus or Westwood Village while he attended classes. At night, she watched TV while he read his books and wrote his assignments.

On her own, Fleur wasn't motivated to explore — a strange alteration of her independent, self-contained behavior in Europe.

She wanted Oakley to take her places. But diligent Oakley was too busy. She soon grew bored. She stayed home, which wasn't always fun because she and Joe didn't get along.

After two weeks she had had enough. She told Oakley that Ian had been calling her. That they had made up, and he wanted her to come home. That she was flying back to Toronto as soon as possible.

Oakley had suspected it was coming, but that didn't stop it from hitting hard. He pleaded with her. He told her how much he loved her.

"If you really loved me you'd want to be with me all the time. Why do you always have to go to class? Nobody but you goes to class all the time. That's so…*square*."

Oakley was crushed. There was enough of the romantic in him to know that she had a point. If he really loved her, he would give up everything for her, including his fucking Terminal Masters degree. If he wanted to be in school more than he wanted to be with her, it meant that he didn't love her enough. She was right.

Acknowledging that she had revealed a serious flaw in him, all that was left for Oakley to do was let her go. Without protest.

—

## CHILLIN' WITH DYLAN

From the sky I watch our approach. Wind whips up whitecaps on the water beneath me, bright blue in the early afternoon sun. Near the shore the water turns viridescent, an emerald ring around the island. Beachfront hotels come into view, flanked by condominium complexes in rigid rows or bending with the shapes of seacliffs and coves. I'm pretty sure there were no vacation resorts on this part of the island before.

Waiting at the car rental counter, a half-dozen people in front of me, the sound system playing a Hawaiian-reggae version of "Country Roads" ("Almost heaven, West Makaha"), I put on my headphones and play a CD I burned especially for this trip, which I labeled "Taylor Camp Tunes." In the slow-moving line, oblivious to time, I listen to two renditions, back-to-back, of "Chimes of Freedom," Dylan's seven-minute version and the shorter Byrds version.

I remember the way Soundtrack sang the song at Taylor Camp. Hearing it now, in the hot, wet air of a Hawaiian afternoon, sends a shiver through me.

That's how I felt back then, that's how a lot of us felt, as if we were caught in a fantastic storm, thunder and lightning crashing all around us, and we were exhilarated, "starry-eyed and laughing," "spellbound and swallowed," we had hope, we had joy, we knew things were changing, we knew we were part of the change. The storm was cleansing everything, enlightening everyone, acknowledging every downtrodden soul on the planet, uplifting everyone to the same level.

"You know where I can rent a surfboard around here?" I ask, signing the rental agreement and handing it back to the young local woman behind the counter.

"Sure. Poipu Beach, Lihue, lots of places."

"What about Hanalei?"

"I think so. If not, then Kapaa. It's on the way."

"I know."

"You've been here before?"

"Thirty years ago."

"Wow. I wasn't born then."

"Do you know how many tourists come to Kauai every year?"

"I'm not sure. At least a million, I think."

"Do you have surfboard racks to rent? For the car?"

"You get 'em where you get your board." She hands me my copy of the contract and the keys. "Your car is a red Neon, parked in stall C-5."

"Thanks."

"If you're going surfing, try to park in places with other cars around. Don't carry any valuables, and lock all your stuff in the trunk."

"I'll remember to do that."

"See you next Tuesday."

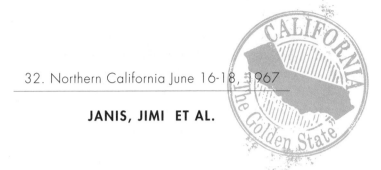

## JANIS, JIMI ET AL.

They took the scenic route, Highway 1, along the coast most of the way, three hundred miles through Ventura and Santa Barbara and Pismo Beach and Morro Bay and Big Sur. Five of the Seven Psychedelic Samurai crammed into Oakley's car for the trip.

No surfboards were strapped to the racks. This excursion was not for surfing. They were headed for the Monterey Pop Festival, the biggest rock show ever, with thirty-two bands scheduled to perform.

The samurai were three males and two couples. The males, also surfing companions, were Oakley, Norm (a curly-headed, scraggly-bearded, Jewish pot-dealer and Santa Monica apartment manager, an entrepreneurial soul housed in a stoned, psychedelic hippie body) and Oakley's apartment-mate Joe, who had earned his undergraduate degree and was now a conscientious objector serving alternate duty at the UCLA Neuropsychiatric Institute.

The couples were political activists Mark and Sage (Sage a knockout, literate and shapely and sexy, but she was with Mark, and that was that) and Dylan and Crystal (real names William and Jane), a heavy-set couple into organic food and lots of it. Dylan and Crystal couldn't join the group on this trip because they were on their annual pilgrimage to harvest peyote in Mexico.

Oakley and his friends left early on Friday morning to make sure they would reach Monterey for the opening night show: The Association, a Canadian group called The Paupers, Lou Rawls, Johnny Rivers, Eric Burdon and The Animals, and Simon and Garfunkel.

Oakley and company were well-stocked with food, drink, and drugs—strong hashish and pure, high-quality acid. They brought tents and sleeping bags and backpacks filled with cooking gear, intending to stay at a campground or maybe on a beach somewhere nearby.

It was evident that the residents of Monterey were not prepared to receive the throng that swarmed in for the festival. Roads were jammed, many of the road-jamming vehicles Volkswagen buses hand-painted with peace symbols and free love slogans. Scores of young people with backpacks were hitchhiking.

Oakley and his companions quickly learned through the grapevine that the hotels, motels and campgrounds were all full. Even restaurants were turning people away. Someone told them that the Perry's Boys' Smorgy ("All you can eat for $5.95!") had run out of food and temporarily closed. Gas stations, grocery stores, and drug stores were overwhelmed by the invasion. Shopkeepers were resentful and rude.

Faced with the situation, Oakley's carpool headed straight for the fairgrounds. Later, after the show, they'd find a beach where they could spend the night.

Inside the fairground a full-scale, freaky fantasy was unfolding—or, in the then-current vernacular, *happening*. Thousands of groovy, mellow hippies milled about, danced and pranced, sat at picnic tables, sprawled on the grass, or leaned against the stretched canvas walls of vendors' booths offering flowers, beads, crystals, god's-eyes, silver bracelets, books, bongs, and hash pipes. Food vendors sold corn on the cob and avocado sandwiches on whole grain bread. The air was thick with the aromas of stick incense, cigarettes, and marijuana.

Beautiful women wore lacy blouses and many-colored, raw-cotton dresses, long flowing skirts or miniskirts, and flowers in their hair. Cops had flowers in *their* hair. Long-haired, mustached, and bearded men wore animal-skin vests, embroidered jeans, headbands, beads, and feathers. Some dressed more garishly or comically, like a tall, skinny-legged man who sported a top hat, black cape, ruffled white shirt, vertically-striped bell-bottom trousers, and high-heeled boots.

Some wore American flags. Some had shaved and painted their heads. Almost everybody wore sunglasses.

There were straight people there, too, in blue jeans and solid-color shirts, with short hair. And Hell's Angels in black leather.

Hundreds of happy hippie kids ran around, many with painted faces. The very young were carried by their mothers, in their arms or strapped to their chests, or hung on their backs in slings, backpacks, or papooses.

Lots of people had cameras. Dogs ran free. Music was everywhere: guitars and flutes and conga drums and bongo drums. Huge balloons hung in the sky. Banners were slung from every booth, post, and pole.

Stretched across the middle of the stage, a long yellow banner proclaimed, "Music, Love, and Flowers—Monterey International Pop Festival." Sitting in metal folding chairs a hundred yards back, high on hashish, Oakley and his companions watched the show. They were close enough, and they had brought two pairs of binoculars to pass among themselves.

For Oakley, it was a lukewarm opening. Simon and Garfunkel, Lou Rawls, and Eric Burdon were OK. But Johnny Rivers? What was he doing in those hippie robes?

By the time the evening's musical entertainment was over, Norm the schmoozer had learned the whereabouts of a place where they could spend the night: a wooded spot next to the Denny's parking lot. It was within walking distance, so they retrieved their gear from the car, left the car in the fairground lot, and took the walk.

They were glad they had left the car behind. Denny's was closed, but its parking lot was full. People were sleeping in their cars. The little wood beside the restaurant was filled with tents—an instant migrant camp, minus grapes of wrath, plus tabs of acid.

They found a space that would accommodate their three tents: Mark and Sage in one, Oakley sharing his with Joe, and Norm in his one-man pup. As they pitched the tents and set up camp, neighbors came by, introduced themselves and offered food. All over the makeshift tent-town, people were offering to share whatever they had that others might need.

It was working out so much better than what they had intended to do. It was a bad idea to look in the dark for a place to spend the night on the beach. Now they were settled comfortably for the entire weekend. Norm had come through for them.

For breakfast they made oatmeal with raisins and honey, brewed coffee, and smoked a joint. After a long and relaxing morning, which included a couple of naps, the samurai walked back to the fairground for the Saturday afternoon show. A slender hippie woman offered to sell them some Owsley Monterey Purple, manufactured specifically for the festival.

Saturday afternoon. Canned Heat, "Rollin' and Tumblin.'" Paul Butterfield weeping into his reeds. Country Joe wearing a hard hat and painted cheeks, lead guitarist Barry Melton in an army surplus jacket. Steve Miller, Al Kooper, Quicksilver Messenger Service, The Electric Flag. And Big Brother & The Holding Company, fronted by Janis Joplin.

She screamed, stamped her feet, twitched her legs as if she were walking in place. She cried and pleaded and shouted her lungs out. There was a depth to her voice, a resonance. Her lungs were a vast cavern and her voice fortified by the depth of the source. She threw her soul into the microphone and out into the world, singing "Why does everything go wrong?"

They walked to their campsite and cooked dinner on the Coleman stove: brown rice with Italian sausage and zucchini, red wine, marijuana brownies for desert. Afterwards, they went back to the fairgrounds for the Saturday night show.

Hugh Masakela. The Byrds doing "Chimes of Freedom" and "Hey Joe." Jefferson Airplane, with Grace Slick singing, "Look at me here, you know I'm rooted like a tree here." Booker T. and the MGs backing Otis Redding: "I've been loving you too long," he cried, "to stop now."

In his tent on Sunday morning, Oakley swallowed a hit of acid. Just in time to be blown away by Ravi Shankar's four-hour-long performance. From slow and meditative to fast and furious, he never stopped playing, and the tabla drummer didn't either. The interaction was a conversation, at times reflective, at other times animated, like an argument.

The only problem was that the fairgrounds were too close to the local airport, and the planes flew low overhead, generating considerable noise prior to landing. With the other groups' electric instruments, massive drum sets and huge amplifiers, this was no big deal. But for the nuances of raga music, the planes were a distraction. At one point, Shankar stopped playing and told the audience, "Just pretend the planes aren't there."

Oakley pretended that the planes weren't there, and sure enough they disappeared, just as the entire audience had when he had gone to see Krishnamurti.

Oakley didn't go to the campsite for dinner, but bought food from the concession booths. He wanted to get good seats for the Sunday night finale. Big Brother and The Holding Company back for an encore. The Grateful Dead. Buffalo Springfield minus Neil Young, plus David Crosby. "Something's happening here," Stephen Stills sang. "What it is ain't exactly clear."

The Mamas and Papas fucked up on "Monday, Monday." At the end of the song, when the music stopped prior to starting up again, beginning with an intro from the bass player, the bass player started on the wrong note, and it threw off Mama Cass and Michelle, who sang the "Dah-dah, dah-dah-dah-dahs" in different keys. It took only a few seconds for them to get back on key, but the mistake had been made.

The Who took the stage, lead singer Roger Daltrey wearing a fringed cape and swinging his microphone by the cord. The lead guitarist, Pete Townshend, banged out rhythm chords with roundhouse swings of his arm. They did "A Quick One While He's Away," a five-minute rock opera, a story about infidelity that ends with the joyfully repeated chorus, "You are forgiven!"

Their finale was "My Generation." Daltrey stuttered out the lyrics, smoke pumped in from behind, and at the end Townshend smashed his guitar on the stage floor, bashed it repeatedly, then slammed it against his amplifier until it disintegrated. While everything else was crumbling into chaos before him, the drummer, Keith Moon, kept on playing until everyone else was gone—even the stage crew desperately trying to rescue the microphones. Then he kicked over his drums and walked off.

The Jimi Hendrix Experience, Hendrix and two Brits, a bass player and a drummer, Hendrix with his super-fast licks, playing the guitar behind his back, with his teeth, forcing feedback from the amps and using it. He finished the set with "Wild Thing," inserting a few bars of "Strangers in the Night" into one of his solo breaks, then going entirely into feedback, playing notes without strumming, no need to pick a note, it was all one continuous note, just move his other hand up the neck to change the pitch. He walked back to his amplifier and stood before it, humping it to distort the sustained note even more.

He went down on his knees and placed the guitar on the floor, the neck pointed toward the audience, emerging from between his spread legs like a phallus. He poured lighter fluid on it and set it on fire, coaxing the flames with upraised hands, feedback still screeching through the huge amps behind him.

At the end of the evening, everyone looked stunned, stoned, and strung out. They wrapped themselves in blankets, coats, and hooded sweatshirts against the cold night air. Oakley and his friends walked around the fairgrounds until everyone was gone, then crashed at the campsite.

The next morning they drove back to LA.

## SLOW YOU DOWN

I'm not sure where I'm going
    C              G
But I do know where I've been
    F                C
I have traveled this world over
    C                    G
With my patience wearing thin
    F                C
Waves float on the ocean
  Am              Em
In the soft warm evening breeze
      Am                  Em
Hawaii's bound to slow you down
  F    G        C      Am
But it won't set you free
    F  G       C

There's no method for forgetting

When it's underneath the skin

And there's nothing more unsettling

Than ashes in the wind

    [Chorus]

Some people will hurt you

Some people won't

Some people learn how to live

Some people don't

    [Chorus]

Currents cut the riverbank

Tides destroy the shore

What's the point of bothering

About it anymore?

    [Chorus]

## CULTIVATION/CONTEMPLATION

Oakley and Soundtrack were working together in the garden. Norm was on the way to Lihue, running errands with Fleur. It was midmorning but the air was still cool. From the two-acre clearing that contained the garden, the green volcanic mountains rose high and fast into a cloudless, bright blue sky.

Oakley hacked with a machete at the thick wall of jungle in an effort to enlarge the protective dead zone between it and the rows of planted vegetables. Pesticides were forbidden in the organic Taylor Camp garden, so this was the only way to keep grasshoppers from devouring their hard-grown food.

Soundtrack gathered Oakley's cuttings and tossed them into the brush, singing "Chimes of Freedom" a capella.

"I love that song," Oakley said. "In college I wrote a paper about it, for a poetry class."

Soundtrack dumped an armload of cuttings and motioned for Oakley to continue, swiveling his hands at the wrists in front of his face.

"I did it to challenge a professor. I analyzed it like a poem, using the jargon of literary criticism, playing the English-major game. I pointed out instances of synesthesia, one sense representing the impressions of another, in lines like 'bells of bolts' and 'bells of lightning.' I wrote about the ambiguity, the levels of meaning in addition to the literal one: Is Dylan describing just a storm, or are bombs actually exploding? Know what I mean?"

Soundtrack shrugged.

"The line about 'the city's melted furnace' makes it sound to me like a war zone. And there's the use of the first person plural: '*We* gazed,' '*we* watched,' 'when *we* were caught.' Who else is the poet with? A girlfriend? A group of companions? Or is he speaking for an entire generation, talking about a revolution and not just a thunderstorm?"

Soundtrack pointed a finger at Oakley, then gave a thumbs-up.

"The whole generation, right?"

Soundtrack nodded.

"The professor said that what I wrote was 'clever'."

Soundtrack smiled.

"Norm has a theory about you," Oakley said. "He believes you used to talk a lot, maybe too much, but you weren't aware of it until something happened. Who knows what? But something happened to you, and after that you got tired of listening to yourself. So you decided to shut up for a while. Is that right?"

Soundtrack shrugged his shoulders.

"Is it a religious thing, like a vow of silence?"

Soundtrack shook his head, then nodded.

"Yes and no," Oakley said. "Not religious like Roman Catholic, but spiritual maybe?"

Soundtrack nodded.

"Is it because you're sick of words? Because you never know whether people are telling you the truth or lying?"

Soundtrack nodded.

"William Burroughs says that language is the ultimate instrument of control. That abstracting words from the things they visually represent, the concrete images, is a way to disguise the truth and manipulate behavior. We're not killing our fellow human beings in Vietnam, we're fighting Communism."

Nod.

"You want to hear a story? You want to hear one really good reason I can relate to what you're doing?"

Nod.

## POLICE BRUTALITY/NEW REALITY

It was supposed to be a peaceful demonstration. In the mid-sixties, those who opposed the war in Vietnam were growing in numbers and no longer limited to the nation's radical fringe. The war was escalating and the death count was sixteen American soldiers per day.

On June 23rd, President Lyndon Johnson was coming to the Century Plaza Hotel in Century City, a new commercial/residential development in West LA, to attend a $1,000-a-plate Democratic Party fundraising dinner. Eighty antiwar groups had joined to organize a protest march.

Oakley had returned from the Monterey Pop Festival less than a week ago. It was the first time he had ever participated in a demonstration. He was opposed to the war but hadn't done anything about it because, until a month before, when he graduated from UCLA, he had avoided the draft with a student deferment. Now he was hoping to get another for the teaching job he had landed in a private high school in the San Fernando Valley. No way was he going to Vietnam. No way was he joining the Army. If he lost his deferment, he would immigrate to Canada. He would check in with Fleur in Toronto, maybe settle down there. She had written that she was no longer living with Ian, but that they were still lovers. Oakley still believed there was hope, while ridiculing himself for believing.

The demonstration was well-organized, with dozens of yellow-armbanded staff. It began with a rally in nearby Rancho Park. Thousands of people showed up, hundreds carrying picket signs. Not all of the participants were radicals. Most looked like average middle-class citizens. Oakley and his fellow long-haired college students were outnumbered by working adults, senior citizens, children, and parents. They were white, black, Hispanic, and Asian-American. They were Christians, Jews, and Buddhists.

The guest speakers were anti-establishment heroes Doctor Benjamin Spock and Muhammad Ali. Spock, whose theories about raising children had been widely applied to Oakley's generation, was now being criticized for his liberal leanings. Ali, for speaking out against the war, had officially lost his title as world champion heavyweight boxer.

The organizers had permits. The demonstrators' route had been laid out and carefully explained. From the park they would march up Pico Boulevard to the hotel on the Avenue of the Stars, take a few turns around a rotunda that fronted the hotel, then exit onto Santa Monica Boulevard, where the march would end.

Everything went well at the park. The crowd was enthusiastic but orderly and well-behaved. The air was charged with camaraderie and high hopes. The media were there. The march was going to be big news. It was going to help end the war.

When they reached the hotel, everything fell apart. Because he was in the front of the line, Oakley saw it all come down, all wrong.

Arriving to begin their circular course in front of the hotel, the demonstrators found that the rotunda had been barricaded by a line of sawhorses. Behind the sawhorses were black-and-white Harley Davidsons with members of the LAPD sitting on top. Behind the motorcycles was a phalanx of cops on foot, hundreds in all. The march came to a halt.

As soon as that happened, a policeman yelled through a megaphone that the assembly was unlawful because it wasn't moving. He cited the terms of the parade permit and a court order that restricted the marchers from stopping to demonstrate. He ordered them to disperse.

It was their fault they weren't moving, but that didn't matter. The problem was, there was nowhere to go but back, and that was impossible. Every minute hundreds of new arrivals came to a standstill. There was no escape to the field beside the rotunda, because the police had set up construction barriers. It was a well-built trap.

Confused and frustrated, the yellow arm-banded organizers didn't know what to do. Some yelled at the marchers to turn back. Some said to sit down. Some said to march forward. The police resolved the problem by removing the sawhorses, revving up their Harleys and edging them into the crowd, some of whom had obeyed instructions and sat down on the pavement. They had to get up fast because the Harleys weren't stopping. The other policemen followed on foot, poking and swinging their nightsticks, forcing the crowd back on itself.

Oakley watched the situation degenerate into chaos. He couldn't believe what was happening. He saw a cop hit a man on the head, hard. It made a sickening sound. The man, who had done nothing to provoke the attack, fell to his hands and knees in pain and disorientation. When Oakley stopped to help, the cop poked him in the ribs and told him to get moving. All around Oakley, police were pushing, poking, and beating people at random. One shoved an elderly woman out of her wheelchair. Others kicked and trampled fallen protestors. There was blood all over the place. Pretty soon the marchers dropped their picket signs and began to run. Oakley joined them.

Later that night, he attended a post-march gathering at the Los Feliz Theater. Onstage was political satirist Paul Krassner. What should have been a joyous celebration turned out to be a grim assembly of stunned, disillusioned people still reeling from the pandemonium of the demonstration. Krassner had already transformed the day's events into black humor, a sick stand-up routine that was impressive for its quick comic perspective on the day's events. But not many people were laughing.

Oakley felt that some good would result from the demonstration despite the police sabotage. The truth would be told by the reporters, illustrated by pictures of policemen pushing, clubbing, and kicking demonstrators. No one could ever again call the term "police brutality" an exaggeration.

Sure enough, in the next day's *Los Angeles Times* the demonstration-gone-bad was front page news. But to Oakley's astonishment, the whole story was a bundle of lies. And the single photograph that accompanied it showed the cop with his megaphone.

The article made no mention of the roadblock that created the standstill, no accusation of police misconduct or unprovoked and excessive force. All it acknowledged was that there had been a "confrontation between police and demonstrators," that people had been hospitalized, that fifty-one marchers had been arrested and that President Johnson had flown in on a helicopter an hour before the demonstrators arrived, landed on the hotel roof and quickly disappeared into the building.

A week later, another story appeared. It alluded to allegations of police misconduct, but the headline was "What DID Happen?" and the reporter still made no direct accusations.

A certainty, a reality that Oakley and thousands of others had eyewitnessed, had been converted first into a lie and then into an ambiguity. This was supposed to be America, not Russia, where, as everyone knew, the so-called news was propaganda created by the Communist Party and printed in *Pravda*. It wasn't supposed to happen in America.

Attending the demonstration, and then watching as the fictional version of it became reality for millions of people, permanently transformed Oakley. He did not become an outlaw, a radical, or even a political activist; the change was internal and fundamental. He became a permanent outsider, a resident exile. The process of alienation—not just from his country and his government, but from other people's reality—was complete.

It had begun in Europe the year before, when he had examined his life and his country from a removed perspective. After three months of foreign travel, he had returned to but never fully re-entered America. Now he had completed the final stage of the process: Oakley had seen behind the mask. He would never be the same again. He would always wonder what else he had been told to believe really wasn't true. He became skeptical, suspicious, cynical.

Even Oakley's parents chose to believe the newspaper over the testimony of their son. Why would the newspaper lie? Overnight, in their minds, Oakley had become a political radical, an unstable, deluded person. They asked him if he was taking drugs. It was the last question his parents asked him for quite a while, because he stopped visiting or even speaking with them for the next three years.

## 36. Kauai 1970

## ABSENT WITHOUT LEAVE

Dumping his non-biodegradable trash in the communal bin, Oakley spied a discarded envelope with the name "Dave" in the upper left hand corner but no return address. He couldn't resist checking it out. It was addressed to a Terri Sinclair in Des Moines, Iowa, but there was no stamp on the envelope and it wasn't sealed. Oakley couldn't resist. He took the letter with him back to his treehouse, sat on his oceanfront sofa and read it.

Dear Terri:

I bet you're wondering what happened to me. I'm sorry for disappearing but I had to do it. I want you to know that I love you and I miss you all the time. I miss our friends sometimes, and my parents never. But you I miss all the time. That's the way it is.

When you read this letter, you'll be the only person who knows I'm in Hawaii. I can't tell anyone else because I don't want to get caught. I shouldn't even be telling you, I shouldn't put this letter in the mail, but I can't stand the idea of you not knowing that I'm OK and not dead or something.

I'm hiding out in Hawaii, on Kauai island in a place called Taylor Camp, where you can stay as long as you want, for free. It's a pretty neat place, with lots of people living in tree houses right next to the ocean, in a kind of a jungle area between the road and the beach. I live in a tent.

My tent is nowhere near the tree houses. I set it up about a quarter mile away, across the big stream, where nobody can find it but me. I come and go from different directions so I won't make a trail that somebody could follow. You can walk right past my tent and not know it's there. Camouflage is one thing I learned in the Army.

Don't get me wrong, people know me. I'm not invisible. I probably *could* be, if I wanted to, but I happen to like to hang around. Everybody needs company, at least once in a while. I'm pretty sure that nobody here suspects I'm AWOL from the Army. But sooner or later somebody's going to come looking for me. So the less everybody knows, the better. Fortunately, people are pretty cool around here. They leave me alone when I want to be. They don't ask questions—or else they stop asking when I don't answer.

Except for Fred. Also known as "Fred the Zen," because some people around here think he's some kind of guru. Not me.

Everything would be OK if it weren't for Fred. He's always on my case, and it's irritating. I'm not the only one. He taunts this guy Patrick about the hippie thing, his long hair and the beads and the tie-dye T-shirts, saying if he's supposed to be so different from straight people, how come he's wearing a uniform? He ridicules this other guy Oakley about his education, of all things, telling him his book learning is useless, "real knowledge comes from inside" or some shit like that.

I don't care what Fred says to anybody else, but if he keeps bugging me in front of other people he could blow my cover.

If you ask me, he's a phony. What kind of so-called "guru" drinks, smokes dope, and spends most of the day causing trouble? He's always clowning around, farting and swearing and talking about sex. He's about as spiritual as a truck driver. He pisses people off, gets too personal, noses into their private business, makes them uncomfortable.

And what kind of guru tries to seduce every woman around? Even that old biddy, Margaret, five feet tall, three feet wide, and at least fifty years old. If I woke up in bed with her I'd run off screaming.

Fred's got two girls living with him in his tree house, Marsha and Sandy, and he's fucking both of them. Marsha's a short, chubby girl with freckles who says she's nineteen, but she looks about sixteen. Kinda pudgy. Sandy's a black woman in her twenties, real slender, real shy, moves like some kind of cat. Her eyes are green.

Fred must be sixty. What does he need Margaret for, anyway, when he's got two young babes like Marsha and Sandy hanging all over him? Whenever he comes on to her, which is just about every day, she laughs at him and tells him to fuck off. But she's blushing a little, and I can tell she's flattered in a way.

Fred never calls himself a "Zen Master," but everybody else does, and he never goes out of his way to deny it. I have no problem with other people thinking he's a guru. The problem is, he's no guru to me.

But just because I don't fall for his bullshit doesn't mean he leaves me alone. I try not to let him bug me, but the bastard never gives up. He's getting on my nerves.

The first time we met, I introduced myself. "I'm Danny," I said (I'm using a fake name). "Nice to meet you." I held out my hand.

Fred the Zen shook it up and down, pretending to be amazed at the ritual of shaking hands, like it was new to him, and saying "Nice" twice or three times, like it was a foreign word. Then he just looked at me, eye to eye, not letting go of my hand.

Finally he said, "Clean-up time, Danny."

I said, "Huh?"

He said, "You can't get to the business in front of you without cleaning up the mess you left behind."

I said, "I don't know what the fuck you're talking about."

He stared at me some more, all the while smiling this big phony smile, then said, "Have it your way, Danny. Keep it to yourself, private."

That was weird, because the way he said it sounded kinda like he wasn't saying "keep it private," but calling me private, which was my rank when I split. There's no way he could know about that, unless he's some kind of mind reader.

I didn't last long in the Army. Couldn't get used to taking orders from assholes who were always screaming at me, calling me a "shitty puke," making me dig holes and fill them up again. And then they send you to Vietnam to kill people, or die. Or both.

I got the hell out of Fort Lewis, bought a plane ticket under a fake name to Hawaii, the farthest away I could get without a passport. I wanted to call you and tell you where I was going, but I didn't want to leave a trail. I hope you understand and will forgive me for not letting you know what I was doing.

On my second night in Waikiki, I heard the scuttlebutt about Taylor Camp. It sounded like a good place to disappear. And, because I was a tourist, I could fly to Kauai for seven bucks. I had about three hundred, money I saved in case I ever needed it, like I do now.

So here I am in paradise, safe and secure, at least for the time being. It's a pretty good life. I mean, the ocean is great, the hiking trails are incredible, I'm learning how to surf, I'm cooking my own food, and I quit smoking—except for joints, of course.

The only problem is, I'm getting paranoid about Fred. I'm thinking he's on to me. There was that "private" thing, and there's the way he always says "Danny," like he thinks it's not my real name. At least he's wrong about that.

Maybe he sees some mannerisms I picked up in the Army that I'm not aware of. Maybe he was in the military himself, a long time ago. It's hard to tell because the guy has got to be schizo. He's always imitating other people. He can imitate your voice. He takes what you say and turns it back on you, saying it in just the way you said it, but making it sound silly. He makes people laugh at themselves. And it's not just his voice. He picks up on mannerisms. He imitates what you do with your eyes when you talk, with your hands, with your head.

He does impersonations, too—Nixon, Kissinger, Bob Dylan, Phyllis Diller. He can sound Jewish, Irish, French or Chinese. I have to admit, sometimes he's pretty funny.

And he's pretty limber, for an old man. He can jump like a monkey if he wants to, or march around like the Gestapo. But then, the next minute, he's shuffling like an eighty-year-old, all bent over and slow. He's lean and muscular, looks pretty healthy. But he can also look like he's about to kick the bucket. It has something to do with the way he can change his posture.

Yesterday he scared the shit out of me. It was super humid, no wind, the kind of day when your skin is sweaty and shiny all the time, and everything you're wearing is soaked. You're never not wet. At Taylor Camp there are three good ways to cool off: jump in the ocean, lay down in the stream, or go for a swim in the wet cave pool. I was so uncomfortable, I decided to do all three.

I was in the ocean, swimming around in the calm water inside the reef, when I bumped into something. It was Fred.

"Hot enough for you?" he asked.

He was dog-paddling, just his head showing above the water, grinning at me, like the two of us were in on some kind of secret nobody else knew about.

"Before you get cooler, you need to get hotter," he said.

"What's that supposed to mean?"

"Out of the frying pan, into the fire. Then get out of the fire, and you're home free."

I didn't know how to deal with that kind of gibberish, so

I just swam back to shore, fast, to get away from Fred and his weirdness. I left him floating there, a head bobbing on the water, grinning like the butcher's dog.

When you get out of the ocean you're all salty, so I like to wash off in the stream. Where it flows out of the jungle onto the beach it gets wide and shallow, and the bottom is sandy. You can lie down horizontal and let the water rush over you, fresh from the mountains, cold and clean. It feels great.

The problem was, when I got to the spot, Fred was already there. I don't know how the fuck he got out of the ocean and into the stream without me seeing him pass me. But there he was, on his back, his eyes closed, his arms stretched out like Jesus on the cross. It was creepy. As I looked at him, his eyes opened and he was staring me down again.

Before he could say anything, I split.

The wet cave is about a ten-minute walk from the stream, through the camp and across the road. I ran the entire way, just to make sure he wouldn't follow me, even on the little dirt trail that winds up the side of the mountain to the cave. I stopped at the top to catch my breath.

From the cave mouth you walk down a short, steep slope to a small beach of packed soil and the pool. The whole place was deserted, quiet and eerie.

The air smelled moldy, but the water was cool and clear. I floated there, looking out the cave mouth, an oval-shaped picture of sky and clouds, feeling like Jonah, swimming in stomach fluids, looking out the mouth of the whale. It was great to be alone. Peaceful.

Not everybody knows this, but there's a second pool in the wet cave, hidden from view. To get to it, you dive under a wall of rock at the back of the cave, and you come up into this completely enclosed grotto. The only light comes from the cave mouth via the water, so it's dark except for the green glow you're floating in.

When a couple of tourists appeared at the cave mouth and spoiled my privacy, I dove under the wall and swam into the grotto.

The instant I came up for air, I saw him—Fred the grinning head, lit up all green and grotesque, like a Halloween mask. I almost had a heart attack. I didn't scream; it was more of a yell. Fred laughed. I was pissed.

"Jesus *Christ!*" I shouted, my heart pounding. "What are you trying to do, freak me out?"

"It's like a three-course meal, isn't it?" he asked. "The ocean is the main course, the stream is the salad, and the wet cave is dessert. What's your favorite, Danny? Wait, don't tell me. I think I know. Dessert. Am I right? *Dessert?*"

I didn't stick around to answer that idiotic question. I dove under the wall back to the main pool, surprising the tourists who were just wading into it, scrambled out of the water and got the fuck out of there, wondering how in hell Fred could have reached the wet cave before me when I ran all the way there.

I went back to my tent, the one place Fred could never find me. I went off the main camp trail and made a wide arc through the jungle, passing the tent and coming back around, approaching from the east, the way I always do to shake off anybody who might be following.

I sat on my wooden box under the tarp, trying to calm down. It was too hot to go inside the tent. Besides, during the day I keep it zipped up and try not to go in and out too much, to keep the mosquitoes from getting in.

I sat there trying to convince myself that what Fred had done was physically possible. Because if it wasn't, he was some kind of evil spirit trying to drive me out of my skull. Even if what he did *was* possible, how did he know where I was going next?

I got so worked up and paranoid I needed a drink. I keep a bottle of Jack Daniels in my backpack, in the tent. I went to fetch it, pulling down the zipper on the nylon door. And got another jolt of pure fear.

Fred was inside, sitting cross-legged, staring out at me as I opened the tent. He squinted in the light like a mole leaving his hole.

My fear turned into rage. "Get the fuck out of my tent!"

"I was hoping you'd say that," he said, stepping out, gasping for breath— faking it, of course. "There's no circulation in there."

I called him at his game. "Why are you doing this to me? What do you want?"

"The longer you wait, the more time you waste, the worse it's going to get."

"The worse what's going to get?"

"Do it now. Face the music. Get it over with, and get on with your life."

"What are you talking about?"

"Getting rid of your hang-ups. Whatever's hanging you up."

At that point, I didn't know if he was talking about psychological hang-ups or my personal big hang-up, the AWOL thing he couldn't possibly know about. I couldn't tell anymore what he knew or didn't know. Was he just a close observer making good guesses, or some kind of psychic? Either way, he was freaking me out again.

"Just get out of here," I said. "Leave me alone."

"'Only when you have no thing in your mind, and no mind in things, are you vacant and spiritual, empty and marvelous.'"

"And please spare me the Zen crap."

Fred went down on all fours, howling and whimpering like a beaten dog, and scurried off into the jungle. If he'd had a tail, it would have been between his legs.

This morning I woke up in the dark knowing I didn't want to deal with Fred, or anybody. So I packed an avocado, some beef jerky and a Hostess Twinkie and left at dawn to hike the cliff trail into Hanakapiai.

For the first hour on that skinny winding trail, every time I turned a corner I half expected Fred to be there, waiting in ambush. The trail cuts back and forth, inland for a few hundred yards, tucked against grooves in the cliff, then back out to these overlooks where you can see the ocean and the coastline. At any turn it would have been easy for him, without pushing or even touching me, to spook me off the edge of the trail and watch me fall five hundred feet to my death.

After a while I stopped thinking about Fred and started thinking about getting out of here. Going home. Turning myself in.

The deal is, I realized, if I go back voluntarily, I'm just AWOL. If I don't, and they come and get me, then I'm a deserter. What they do to AWOL soldiers is nothing compared to what they do to deserters.

A while later I stopped thinking about everything and began to enjoy the scenery, the vertical cliffs rising out of the sea, the huge expanse of ocean and sky, the ferns growing out of the rock walls. The morning was cool, the trade winds had picked up again and blown the clouds away, and the sky was clear blue. I was alone; nobody else passed me on the trail, going either way. By the time I reached the Hanakapiai overlook, I was feeling good.

That's when I found the envelope. I turned a corner and there it was, stuck onto a twig of a tree branch hanging out over the trail. Addressed to me, "Danny," the name in quotation marks.

Fred again, obviously, I knew. But how could he possibly have been there before me? How did he know I would be on that trail? Was he watching me at that moment?

I opened the envelope and pulled out a piece of paper. Written in pencil, in imitation of a child's awkward attempt at hand-printing, were the definitions of two words:

Dessert: cake, pie, ice cream, etc.; the final course of a meal.
Desert: to leave without intending to return.

I yelled out loud, "No shit, Sherlock! I already figured that out!"

I heard a rustling on the trail behind me. I looked around but no one was there. My heart was pounding again. For a while I sat on a rock at the lookout, then headed back. I wasn't in the mood to go any farther.

Now here I am, back at the camp, sitting alone on the beach, watching the sunset. Fred's nowhere around, although he'll probably show up any second now—drop out of the sky in a parachute or pop up from the sand where he has buried himself, right where he mystically knew I would choose to sit.

Why is he hounding me? What am I, his pet project or something? If he'd just get off my back, I could get my shit together.

I don't know when I'll see you again. I'm not sure how long I'll be able to stay here without someone finding out. If I get caught, I'm in trouble. I don't know what to do. I sure hope you won't forget about me, or find someone else. I'll be back someday, I promise.

I love you (whatever that means),
Dave

Oakley folded the letter and put it back into the envelope. He thought about it for a while, looking at the waves in the water and the clouds scudding across the sky. He thought about Fred the Zen, a different person to everyone, possibly a man from another planet, or at least a higher level of consciousness. And he thought about Danny—Dave—and the girlfriend back home. Danny was too paranoid to throw out a letter like that so carelessly. He would have torched it.

So: Did Danny plant it for him to find? Had Danny been shadowing him, waiting for the opportunity? If so, why?

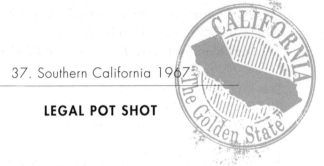

## LEGAL POT SHOT

After Fleur flew back to Toronto, Oakley burrowed back into his studies. Joe was taking care of residents at the children's wing of the UCLA Neuropsychiatric Institute, who had various mental problems such as retardation and autism.

Joe loved every minute of it. He invited Oakley to play guitar with him while he sang songs for the kids, and Oakley was amazed at the way Joe was connected to them, opened them up, made them happy. They sang a Woody Guthrie song: "Take me for a ride in your car."

Joe had refused to serve in the military on the grounds that he didn't want to kill anyone. To receive his 1-0 classification approving him for alternative civilian service, he had to pass interrogations conducted by Selective Service Agency officials. He had described one to Oakley.

"I'm sitting at a table with this guy in a suit. He asks me to tell him what I would do if I were to find myself in this situation: I'm in a car, driving down a mountain on a narrow two-lane road. On the left, there's a wall of rock; on the right, a thousand-foot plunge off a cliff.

"I turn a corner, and standing there on the road in front of me is a little girl. In the oncoming lane is a truck. I have three choices: Run over the girl and kill her; pull into the other lane and hit the truck, killing myself and the truck driver; or drive over the cliff and kill myself. Which alternative would I choose?

"I look at the guy in the suit. I think about the question for a minute. Then I tell him I would press the 'fly' button on my dashboard, and wings would sprout from the sides of the car. I would scoop the little girl up off the road, then my car would take off in time to clear the oncoming truck. No one would be harmed.

"The guy in the suit says, 'That's not a real answer.'

"I say, 'That's not a real question.'

"He says, 'It's a hypothetical question.'

"I say, 'It's a hypothetical answer.'

"Two weeks later, my status is approved."

Joe told Oakley about the marijuana experiments at UCLA conducted—"Jointly," he put it—by the Neuropsychiatric Institute and the Psychology Department. They were looking for volunteers. Oakley signed up.

He was paid twelve dollars an hour to smoke weed and take tests afterwards. The experiment required four ninety-minute sessions over two weeks. He earned seventy-two dollars. It was well over minimum wage, and he got free highs.

The joints were pre-rolled, with black numbers on one end. He was told that the marijuana came from different sources and that, as a control, some joints were placebos containing alfalfa. The control group was given alfalfa and the experimental group smoked real pot.

In an examination room, a graduate student would sit beside Oakley, insert a joint into a glass pipe, hold it for him and light the joint. After he inhaled a measured amount of smoke, the student would signal him to stop and remove the pipe from his lips. Oakley would wait for the next signal, fifteen seconds on the student's stopwatch, to exhale. This process was repeated three times.

The grad student, a young woman in a white lab coat, would then leave Oakley alone in the exam room for ten minutes, to allow the weed to take full effect. When she returned, she conducted tests: eye exam, motor skills, coordination, mental stuff. She asked him how he felt: Nervous? Anxious? Clammy? Cold? Hot? Happy? Sad?

The problem for Oakley was that his examiner was behaving toward him with unconcealed hostility. Obviously she didn't approve of marijuana. It influenced his mood and therefore his answers to her questions.

It was a problem of set and setting, "set" being the attitudes, preconceptions and intentions that Oakley brought to the table, and "setting" the milieu or environment where the experience took place, including any other people who were there. Oakley had read that early LSD experiments produced contradictory results because of glitches in set and setting. One problem was that, during the LSD studies, people who took the drug were surrounded by white-coated lab technicians who were predisposed to look for schizophrenic behavior.

He asked the grad student if she knew about set and setting. She was insulted by the question. He told her that, whatever the effect of the pot, her contributions to this setting were detrimental to his emotional comfort. He told her that she was impersonal, intolerant and rigid.

## 38. Kauai 2001

## ANOTHER FLOWER

It's a short drive past two mini-industrial parks to Lihue town. The streets are torn up, new drainpipes being installed, traffic bottlenecked. On the car radio, a strange assortment of oldies: "Wild Thing," "Baby Elephant Walk," "Spirit in the Sky." Quicksilver Messenger Service: "Take another hit...of fresh air." Neil Young: "Look at Mother Nature on the run in the nineteen-seventies." Spirit: "It's nature's way of telling you...something's wrong."

Must be Alternate-Oakley at work again, selecting songs for me. Musical messages on the air waves. What *is* wrong?

Ahead on the main drag is a landmark I recognize, the Lihue Theatre. Its old-style marquee leans into the street. I saw a movie there, one movie in the four months I was on Kauai. *The Wild Bunch*.

But it's not a theater anymore. The red letters on the marquee proclaim its new identity: *Lihue Theatre Senior Apartments*. The glass-enclosed box office is now the security guard's booth.

I look for a place to get a late lunch—a local diner—but I can't find one. My choices are Kentucky Fried Chicken, Burger King, McDonalds, and Jack in the Box. They weren't there before.

I pull into a gas station to use the phone booth. I have a number but no name, only the email address, Kalana. First name, last name, man, woman? I dial the number.

"Hello?" A male voice.

"May I please speak to Kalana?"

"Who?" He sounds put off.

"Uh, Kalana?"

"Nobody here name Kalana."

"That was the email address they used. I don't know the name, but I was given this phone number."

"Oh, wait, you da kine? From da Mainland?"

"Yeah, that's me."

"Hole on." Away from the phone, the man yells, "Pua!" I hear a voice answer, hear the man say "Yoah coas' haole."

"Hello, is this Oakley?"

"Yes, hello."

"Where are you?"

"In a phone booth at the Aloha gas station in Lihue."

"Can you meet me in a half hour?"

"Sure. Where?"

"Okamura's Okazu-Ya, on Rice Street. You know where Rice Street is?"

"I remember."

"See you in a half hour."

"How will I recognize you?"

"I'll find you. It's easier."

"Your name is Pua, right?"

"Pualani."

"Beautiful flower."

"Haole boy knows some Hawaiian."

"Haole no mo' boy."

"Pidgin too. If you're hungry, don't wait for me."

"One more question? What's a '*coze* haole'?"

"*Coast*. West Coast. California specifically. We know who you are."

Okamura's doesn't serve alcohol. I'm working on a bowl of noodles when Pualani joins me in the booth. She's slender, very little body fat, in good shape for her age, which must be somewhere in her mid-forties. She's wearing jeans, a T-shirt, and a purple daypack. Her skin is finely lined, firm and healthy. Her straight black hair is streaked with gray. Her mouth is wide when she smiles at me. I like her smile.

"Thanks for coming."

"Thanks for the ride. Want something? Food? Beverage?"

"I'm fine."

"I never knew until today that you were a woman."

"What difference does it make?"

"None at all. Just an observation."

"How long will you be here?"

"Six nights, seven days. I got a weekly rate on the car."

"Where are you staying?"

"Two nights in Poipu at the Sheraton. Four nights in Hanalei at a B&B."

"What are you going to do?"

"Surf if there's waves. Look for Taylor Camp."

"Taylor Camp? It's long gone."

"I know. I just want to find the place where I lived, where I built my treehouse."

"I never spent much time on the north shore, but I remember that the State couldn't wait to get rid of everybody and tear everything down. They said it was bad for tourism. They called it an eyesore."

I shake my head and take a drink of water. "For me, it was a sight for sore eyes. It was a civilized little settlement in the jungle. The treehouses were beautiful. The people were friendly and unselfish. Everybody shared what they had with everyone else."

She smiles. "Sounds like a fairy tale. Maybe your memory is smoothing things over."

I smile back. "Maybe a little bit." I eat my noodles, think about it. "No, I take that back. I don't know what everybody else felt about it, but for me Taylor Camp was the last good thing that happened before this country started going bad."

"I'm not sure what you're talking about."

"I'm talking about the way young people were beginning to change the world. It was a threat to the power structure. It undermined consumerism and capitalism. Something had to be done about it, and something was."

"Like what?"

"Like steering Americans away from everything we had been learning. Making sure that the next generation would not learn to think. Dumbing them down and demoralizing them. Breeding a herd of mindless consumers. Making 'liberal' a dirty word."

"Who did all this?"

"People in power. The people behind the politicians. The owners of corporations. The captains of industry."

"Sounds paranoid."

"It's not. History was rewritten. The dreams and accomplishments of a generation were maligned and trivialized. We were dismissed as 'hippies' and 'flower children.' We were condemned as sexual libertines, anarchists, and drug-addled freaks."

"You can't deny the drugs, though."

"The drugs were there, but only some of us were addled. I think most of us learned what we could from drugs; maybe they accelerated our acquisition of some new perspectives on reality. Maybe not. Whatever the drugs did or didn't do, I have no regrets about using them."

"Using which drugs specifically?"

"Marijuana. Hashish. Mescaline. Peyote. LSD."

"But here you are, alive and healthy. And not insane, I hope. What do you do back in California?"

"I teach literature and writing at a college in Northern California."

"That explains your vocabulary."

"What explains yours?"

"Kauai Community College."

I finish my noodles and look around for the waitress. "Sorry for blabbing so much," I say.

"Don't apologize. I'm enjoying it."

"I think I'm still working it out in my head. I guess Taylor Camp has become a symbol of something for me. It was a place suspended in time, an island on an island, a little cluster of foreigners. It was 1970. We were refugees from the sixties."

"I was eighteen then. How old were you?"

"Twenty-five." I catch the waitress's attention. "I'm going to have a cup of coffee," I say to Pualani. "You want one?"

"I'll have an iced tea. Thanks."

I order as the waitress clears the table.

"Nineteen-seventy was a year of disillusionment. When we idealistic young Americans finally woke up from our naïve dream of instant mass enlightenment and peace on earth."

"Why that year in particular?"

"I don't know, it was just that a lot of things happened. Nixon lied to us about ending the war. The National Guard killed four student protesters at Kent State. Ronald Reagan was governor of California, saying stuff like 'You've seen one redwood tree, you've seen 'em all' and 'If the protestors want a bloodbath, we'll give them a bloodbath.' Rock stars were dying of drug overdoses. The Beatles split up. Cesar Chávez went to jail."

"Cesar Chávez?"

"The man who organized the immigrant farm workers in California. Remember Angela Davis?"

"No."

"A radical philosophy professor at UCLA. A member of the Communist party and the Black Panthers. In 1970, she lost her job. But that wasn't enough. The FBI claimed that guns used in a shootout were registered in her name and issued a warrant for her arrest. She went into hiding, got caught, charged with murder and kidnapping, and spent a year and a half in prison. Later all the charges were dropped and they let her out."

The waitress brings my coffee, Pualani's iced tea, and the check.

"Remember Timothy Leary?"

"Him I *do* remember."

"In 1970 the FBI was after him, too. A judge called him 'the most dangerous man in the world.' That's how afraid they were."

"Of what?"

"He was responsible for young people becoming aware that there was another reality, different from the one that was being beaten into our heads by our elders. In that sense, he *was* dangerous. To the status quo."

"Remind me, Oakley. What does all this have to do with Taylor Camp?"

"I don't know, it's just seems to me that—well, after I left and went back to California, it seemed like everything started going downhill. Taylor Camp was the last place where everything seemed to be heading in the right direction."

"Why did you leave?"

"Thought I should be doing something to turn the tide. Everyone was drifting and floating, 'going with the flow' we used to say. The dream was dead, but nothing was there to replace it. We hadn't changed the world as fast as we wanted to. We were still unwilling to make a realistic commitment or strike a compromise. It would have been too mundane. At Taylor Camp life was a game, a cosmic joke. After a while, for me it wasn't funny anymore."

I finish my coffee and take out some cash to pay the check.

"You're a deep dude."

I laugh. "Sorry for rambling on. Being here again is stirring up memories."

"Is your room at the Sheraton a garden view?"

I nod. "Best rate."

"My cousin's in marketing there. He can upgrade you to oceanfront."

"You don't have to do that."

"Maybe I want to."

We smile at each other.

"I'm sorry if this camera business is weird for you," she says. "It's just something I need to do."

"Being here is weird for me, but in ways that have nothing to do with the camera. You stole it the day I set foot on this island. I got over it. Don't feel bad about it."

"Still, I apologize. I was a kid, hanging out with the wrong crowd."

"I accept your apology."

"Thank you." Again, the smile. Kind of sexy.

"I'm curious about your church, the one that wants you to right all the wrongs you've ever done. What religion is it?"

"It's just a church group, really. Not an entire religion. A little group called The New Disciples of Jesus. Just some people making suggestions."

"You're not headed for outer space anytime soon?"

"Come on, it's not a cult."

"I'll take your word for it."

"Why would you do that?"

I haven't had this kind of conversation for a long time. We're having fun, making connections.

"Because I trust you, I guess. After all, you're returning my camera. If this group works for you, that's great. I'm just not much for organized religion, I guess."

"You know, I'm beginning to think I'm not either. There are some good people in the group, but some are—well, kind of pushy."

"In what way?"

"I don't know, they just think they have some kind of unique access to God. Why would a dinky little church group in Hawaii have privileged information that Catholics or Protestants or Jews or Muslims don't? What makes them so special?"

"Everybody has a different version of God. That's one reason for discrimination. For war."

Pualani looks at me for a moment, then digs in her pack for the camera. "Anyway, here it is."

She hands me the Mamiya Sekor. It looks clean, taken care of.

"Does it still work?"

"I think so. I hadn't used it for years, so I sent it away for maintenance and servicing, and they said there was nothing wrong with it." She looks in her purse again, comes up with a box of film. "Take this, too in case you want to try it out. It should work. If it doesn't, call me and I'll get it fixed. Or replace it, whatever."

I put the film and the camera on the seat beside me.

"What does your husband think about all this? Does he belong to the same church group?"

"Husband?"

"The guy who answered the phone when I called."

"That's my brother. My husband, my ex, is on the Mainland. Haven't seen him for years."

The waitress brings the check.

"The north shore isn't happening," Pualani says, "but there's a south swell. First Break should be good."

"You surf?"

"A little."

"I don't know the south side. I only surfed the north shore."

"First Break and a couple of other good spots are at Poipu, down the beach from your hotel. You have a board?"

"Thought I'd rent one."

"Miles will loan you one. My cousin. Miles Kashiwada. He surfs. When you check in, ask for him first thing, OK?"

"I'm not sure I'd be comfortable doing that."

"Look. Maybe he can't upgrade your room, maybe he can't get you a board. But you should meet him anyway. Just introduce yourself, let him show you around the hotel, give you the PR tour."

I go to pay the cashier and come back to the booth.

"Guess I'd better head out."

"Yeah, you might catch some evening surf."

"You want to come up to the Sheraton tonight, and I'll take you out to dinner?"

Pualani tilts her head, as if my question has slightly altered the axis of her perceptions.

"Not tonight."

"Tomorrow night?"

She zips up her pack and slides out of the booth.

"I'll tell you what. When you come back through town on your way up to Hanalei, call me and I'll meet you for lunch."

"Great. See you Friday, then."

We walk out together from the cool, shady restaurant into the glaring sunshine and motionless, moisture-saturated air. Pualani has a bicycle. Before she rides off, I say, "One more thing. If your email address is 'kalana,' is your name Pualani Kalana?"

"No. Kalana means forgiveness."

## 39. Southern California 1967

## ACID REIGN

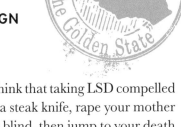

To read the newspapers you would think that taking LSD compelled you to cut your father's heart out with a steak knife, rape your mother or sister, stare at the sun until you went blind, then jump to your death from a third-story window.

While this hysteria was being shot through the veins of the media, Oakley was dropping acid once a week and having a fine time during his year of graduate school at UCLA, getting straight A's and feeling a certain disconnect from the conventional wisdom, a cognitive dissonance. Reading one thing about the drug and experiencing something completely different. Dropping acid was an eye-opener that went beyond the eyes to open every sensory organ, cell, and molecule in his body. It removed him, however temporarily, from his context and conditioning. It could be profound, enlightening, fun, or frightening, but always intense.

Oakley met once a week with a group of six friends, who would embark together on a series of LSD-laced adventures at predetermined locations: sunrise on the beach followed by a psychedelic surf session; literary readings (*Mount Analogue, Steppenwolf, Stranger in a Strange Land, The Tibetan Book of the Dead*) and music appreciation (The Beatles, The Doors, The Incredible String Band, Ravi Shankar) in Oakley and Joe's apartment; a visit to the Museum of Science and Industry via freeway in which Oakley (the driver) became a blood cell coursing through an artery in the heart of the city; field trips to shopping centers to observe the habits of straight people in the consumer society; an excursion to a movie theater for a viewing of *The Seven Samurai*. That was when they had begun calling themselves the Seven Psychedelic Samurai.

On a samurai acid field trip to the beach at Point Dume, north of Malibu, a windy afternoon, wind blowing sand across the broad, deserted beach, whitecaps on the water, Oakley strolled up to Crystal who was staring intently at a large rock.

"Check this out," she said, beckoning Oakley to her side. "On this rock is the history of mankind, the explanation for everything."

The rock was covered about equally with lichen in two colors, red and green.

"Wow," Oakley said, trying to hook into Crystal's enthusiasm. "Lichen is beautiful. But, I don't know…the history of man?"

"Don't you see?" She was fervent. "One rock, two different races. They both want the whole rock, they don't want to co-exist peacefully. So they're at war."

Oakley leaned in for a closer look at the lichen. "How do you know they're at war?"

"It's obvious! You can see the front lines. The red and the green are fighting, gaining and losing territory. The occupied territories keep exchanging hands." She fell silent, laughed softly, and rubbed her neck. After what might have been five seconds or five minutes, she said, "You can see the traces of both colors."

Crystal was right. Oakley could see it.

"But surely this is not the story of mankind. I mean, don't we have a little higher consciousness than rock lichen?"

"If we do, they why do we keep fighting for territory, all over the world, pushing the borders back and forth, killing people colored different than we are, or who speak different languages, or believe in a different god?"

"I guess you're right." Oakley didn't want to argue. An acid trip was not the time to engage in formal debate.

A week later, Oakley sent Crystal a letter. He wrote "Acid Reign" on the envelope. He wrote, "Here's a counter-argument in our rock lichen discussion," followed by a quotation:

Man is, before all else, something which propels itself towards a future and is aware that it is doing so. Man is, indeed, a project which possesses a subjective life, instead of being a kind of moss, or a fungus or a cauliflower.

— Jean Paul Sartre

One winter morning Oakley, Joe, and Norm dropped some Window Pane and drove up the coast to the surf spot called County Line, where Los Angeles ended and Ventura began. They sat in the car, engine and heater on, smoking a joint and checking out the waves. The surf was up, but a stiff wind was blowing. They left the cozy cocoon of the car, got into their wetsuits, and paddled out.

In the water, Oakley began shivering uncontrollably. While Joe and Norm caught their first waves, he sat on his board beyond the lineup, hunched over, hugging himself, trying to stop shaking. His head ached. He was miserable.

Then something snapped. Into his consciousness came a question—*Who is responsible for this situation?*—and, at the same time, the answer. He sat up straight and turned his attention outward, defying the cold, fighting back, summoning strength, taking action. His shivering stopped. His headache dissolved. He caught wave after wave, confident and surefooted. The wind blew, the air and water were cold, but Oakley didn't feel it anymore. Sometimes, reality is what you make it.

## FIRST DAY, FIRST BREAK

To Miles Kashiwada, I'm just another haole tourist. He hardly
says a word as he drives me around the twenty-acre resort on a golf
cart, except for what must be his standard patter, pointing out the
restaurants, facilities, club house, pool and spa.

"How's the surf?" I ask.

He gives me a skeptical look. "You surf?"

"Not as much as I used to. The ocean's pretty cold where I live."

"There's some juice out there. Two spots you can walk to from
here. First Break is a right peak off the reef about a quarter of a
mile out. Steep take-off and drop, fun wave. It needs a five-foot swell,
which we've had for the last couple of days, so it's been going off. It's
worth the paddle out. Farther down the beach is Waiohai, a thick
left slide that breaks off a point. The inside wave turns hollow. But it
breaks on the reef, so it's better at high tide."

"When's that?"

"Check it out at about ten in the morning." Miles looks at his
watch. "I'm pau at five this afternoon. I was gonna check out First
Break. Want to join me?" He says it like a challenge.

"I didn't bring a board."

"I can get you one. Short or long?"

"Either one, but short is better."

"Meet me at the beach concession at five-fifteen."

My luggage has been sent to my room. My upgraded room, on the
second floor of the Ocean Wing. Below the lanai is a paved walkway
and a wide green band of lawn which gives way to the rugged black

rocks of a lava peninsula. Beyond that, blue sea all the way to infinity. My room is on the edge of the island, all sea and sky outside the floor-to-ceiling sliding glass door.

On a table beside a dresser are a bottle of champagne in a silver ice bucket and a large basket of fruit wrapped in cellophane and tied with a green bow, containing a pineapple, four bananas, two papayas, and two oranges. Beside the basket are a knife, a fork, and a linen napkin on a plate, with a card that reads: "Enjoy a taste of the Garden Island. With best wishes from Pualani and the management and staff of the Sheraton Kauai Resort."

I help myself to a banana, pour myself a glass of champagne, unpack. I change into shorts and a T-shirt, stretch out on the queen-size bed and close my eyes.

Disconnected. Sealed off. Air conditioned. No bugs. No mildew. No jungly smells. What the fuck am I doing here?

If we really have alternate selves living an infinite number of different lives, I want to be able to jump back and forth across those parallel worlds. See what happened when I took those different paths. *Be* what happened.

I can't help it. What if I hadn't been with Sandy? Or what if she had made it through her depression and we had stayed together? What if I had never gone to Taylor Camp in the first place? What if I had gone to Canada, or back to France and stayed there, really learned the language, lived there permanently? Never met Sage. Where did I make the wrong turn? Sometime after Taylor Camp. Where did the world make the wrong turn? And why?

The afternoon breeze is stilling. Miles, in great shape, paddles out ahead of me to the lineup on the left side of the reef. The sun is low over the horizon to our right, behind the approaching waves. The wave faces are in shadow, but as their tops rise, curl and stretch thin, they turn to glittering gold, backlit by the sun.

The surf isn't big, maybe head-high, but to me it looks menacing enough. A half-dozen others are out, catching the waves deep and late, just before they pitch. Making quick drops and turns, pivoting off the curling crests, illuminated by the golden glow.

Miles catches one, but I take my time. It's been a while—at least a year—since I've been out, and that was in far less powerful waves. I get into position, but let a good wave pass.

I remember my red badge of courage—the wave I caught thirty years ago at Impossibles, and the next one that I didn't make, sliced up my back on the coral and chalked up another Zen lesson. Those were hairier waves than these by far. I paddle before an oncoming swell, get swept up into the rising surge as it tilts my board downward. I stand to take the drop, watch the wave take shape, form into a tapered path, and show me that if I don't screw it up I'm in for a fine ride.

The board feels stable and responsive as I swing it around at the bottom of the drop. I don't even try to carve my way back up to turn off the lip; instead I find a slot and lock into it, ducking under the curl like I used to in my longboard days, still and calm in the midst of the churning energy.

We ride wave after wave, both of us getting our share. On one wave Miles, paddling out as I slide along, raises his arms and shapes his thumbs and forefingers into a rectangular frame, and presses an imaginary shutter with his pinkie.

We're still in the water, we're the last ones out there, long after the red clouds of sunset fade to black. The rising moon, just past full, adds a new quality of light. The lights come on in the beachfront hotels and condos; luau music drifts out over the water. By the time we're walking up the beach, the moon is halfway to high.

Miles has become a bit more receptive. Not exactly friendly, but getting there. So I invite him to hang out, share some champagne and fruit. Surprisingly, he accepts and goes to his car to change.

We sit outside on the lanai. Miles produces a joint and we smoke it while, a few yards away, night-strolling hotel guests illuminated in white moonlight parade past us on the walkway.

When we're driven inside by mosquitoes, Miles calls up and comps two room service meals and a pricey bottle of wine. After dinner, he turns on my bedside clock radio.

"Find this station on your car and leave it there," he says. "FM 91.0."

"Thanks for all this," I say.

"It was Pualani, you know."

"I know. But it's a small matter between us. It doesn't require this kind of treatment. You know, she already paid for my airfare."

"I didn't know. She doesn't tell me these things."

"You do know about the camera?"

"Yeah." Miles chooses his words. "Long time ago, she was not so nice."

"And now?"

"Now she's cool."

"In what way?"

"Every way. She turn' her life around. I do what she asks because I welcome the times she asks me to do her a favor. She's the one always doing the favors. I pay her back gladly."

Basement tape, Dylan and The Band, "Nothing Was Delivered."

"Know what she does for a living?"

"I never ask." I'm starting to adopt Miles's mild pidgin.

"Nothing she gets paid for. Volunteer work. Wherever she can find it. For the elderly, abused wives, orphan kids, the hospital, and the library."

"Where does she get money to live on?"

"From her ex. When he sends it."

"She lives with her brother?"

"And his wife and kid. Pualani has a cottage out back. More like a room with a lua. And a lanai. She cooks for the family, gets free room and food."

"Is she OK with that?"

"What do you think?"

"That she deserves better."

"Family is good. What's better?"

"A little privacy and independence."

Tom Petty's "Freefallin'" comes on the radio.

"You remember anything about Taylor Camp?"

"I was born in '75. When they shut it down I was two years old. All I know is what I hear people say."

"What do they say?"

"Just the conventional bullshit, you know? It's in all the guidebooks, pretty much the same story. Howard Taylor pissed off at the state over the zoning. Hippies turned squatters. Taking drugs. Sunbathing nude on the beach. Practicing free love. The usual."

"Taylor Camp is mentioned in the guidebooks?"

"Drop by the Business Telecommunications Center tomorrow after lunch. There's something you might want to see."

### THE KEY OF JESUS

      G
Used to sing my songs alone

        G
They sounded fine to me

     C
But that was long before

      G
I heard life's melody

    G
It filled my eyes with tears

    C
It touched a chord in me

    C    D  G
The perfect harmony

                D
    Though I've never met the Man

          G
    And I can't endure the freaks

        C
    I can feel the harmony

     G
    In every word He speaks

         G
    Now my music's in the air

         C
    And my song is everywhere

    G          D G
    My life's in the Key of Jesus

I finally read the score

The four-part harmony

And while the music played

A question bothered me

When people take His words

And use them as they please

Who gets the royalties?

    [Chorus]

## 42. Kauai 1970

### SURFIN' SATORI

At the end of a sunny day, Taylor Camp residents emerged from the jungle onto the sand, set out their beach towels and blankets, turned their faces to the west, and observed the ritual of the setting sun, which seemed tonight like a ball of butterscotch taffy melting in the water.

Oakley joined Fred, Marsha, Danny, Sandy, Soundtrack, and Patrick on the beach. They were munching on an assortment of packaged snacks, passing a gallon jug of red wine and sharing a joint. Fred was dressed in long pants and a long-sleeved shirt; the others were wearing shorts or bathing suits. Danny had a surfboard. Oakley watched for an indication from Danny, a signal that Danny knew he had read the letter. Nothing.

"Join the pilgrimage, Oakley," Fred said. "Good friends, good wine, sun worship, moon worship, everything you need to find a companion for the night."

"I wouldn't call this good wine," Marsha said. She wore her trademark cutoff jeans and a beach towel around her shoulders to shield her freckles from the sun.

"I wouldn't even call it wine," Patrick said. "In fact, it's illegal to call this stuff wine. It's about two percent grapes and ninety-eight percent chemicals. Look at the label. It doesn't say 'wine' on it anywhere."

"It's written right here," Danny said, "'Burgundy'."

"But it doesn't say *wine*."

"Who gives a fuck, you get a buzz from it. Pass it over."

"Hey, Danny," Marsha said. "The surf looks good. Why aren't you out there?"

Just beyond the protected calm waters beside the shore, not more than fifty yards out to sea, the swells rose up and crashed against the shallow coral reef.

"No way," Danny said. "Not those waves."

"They look rideable," Oakley said. "Does anybody ever surf out there?"

"I've seen some locals riding it. They call it 'Impossibles'."

"Hmmm."

"The wave is makeable," Danny said, "but only at high tide. Otherwise it sucks out over the reef, and suddenly there's nothing below you but coral."

"The tide looks high right now."

"The high was two hours ago. It's going down. It's too late."

"Come on, Danny, let's give it a try."

"Hey, Soundtrack," Patrick said. "How about some surf music?"

"Anything but that Jesus freak stuff," Marsha said.

"That song is just the opposite," Oakley said.

Soundtrack played the surf-rock instrumental "Pipeline."

"Say, Patrick, maybe you can answer a question that's been bothering me lately," Fred said. He made the peace sign with one hand. "If this means peace for all mankind, then why does this," he said, making a second peace sign with the other hand, then extending both arms over his head, "mean victory for Richard Nixon?"

"Why don't you ask Nixon?" Patrick asked. "And stop assuming I'm a spokesman for the entire counterculture."

"You define yourself by your appearance," Fred said. "You look like a hippie, why can't you speak for them?"

"Because there's no such thing as a hippie," Patrick said. "It's a media myth."

"You're myth-ing the point, Patrick. You're making the myth a reality. You look like a million other young people. Same clothes, same hair, same accessories. You're making the cliché come true."

"Come on, Danny," Oakley said. "Let's ride that wave."

"It's almost sunset," Danny said.

"But it won't be dark for another hour."

"Where's the old courage, Danny?" Marsha asked. "Can't get it up?"

"There's a difference between courage and stupidity."

"There was a famous wrestler named O-nami," Fred said, "which means 'Great Waves.' He was strong and he knew all the techniques, but he had a problem. In private he could defeat his teacher, but in public he was so self-conscious that even his students beat him."

"Is this another idiotic Zen story?" Danny asked.

Fred smiled pleasantly at Danny. "O-nami went to a Zen master for advice. The Zen master told him to spend the night in the temple meditating on his name. He told him to think of himself not as a wrestler who was afraid, but as huge waves crashing on everything in their path. O-nami did as he was told. As he felt the waves in his meditation, they swept away everything in the temple. Before dawn all that was left was O-nami in the middle of a vast ocean. In the morning the teacher found O-nami with a smile on his face. He told O-Nami that nothing could bother him anymore, that he had become the waves, that he would sweep away his opponents. The next day O-nami won his match. And after that, no one was able to defeat him."

"What's that supposed to mean?" Danny asked. "We're not people, but waves? We're supposed to merge with nature or something?"

"Whatever it means to you, Danny," Sandy said, "is what it is." She was wearing a white one-piece swim suit that looked made for competition rather than fashion.

"Right on," Fred said.

"Well, my name's not O-nami. So I'm not big waves, I guess."

"Your name is Detour, and what does that suggest?"

"Gee, Fred, I've never heard this one before."

"You're off the main road for some reason. I wonder what it is?"

"By the way, it's pronounced de-*tour*, not *dee*-tour."

"The question remains," Fred said, "why did De*tour* de*cide* to de*sert*? Is it the way he tells it, like a good flower child, that he didn't want to kill anybody? Or is it really just the opposite? Is it really because he didn't want anybody to kill him? And either way, why doesn't he just take care of it? Why doesn't he turn himself in and get it over with? So he can get on with his life."

"Hey, Soundtrack," Oakley said. "You heard of Ramblin' Jack Elliott?"

Soundtrack nodded.

"Do you know the song I'm thinking about?"

Soundtrack smiled and began to strum and sing, imitating the adenoidal voice and flatpicking guitar style of the cowboy from Brooklyn.

"Dee-*tour*, there's a muddy road ahead / Dee-*tour*, paid no mind to what it said / Dee-*tour*, oh these bitter things I find / I should have read that detour sign."

Soundtrack got a round of applause, except from Danny.

"You assholes don't know shit!"

"Who knows shit," Fred said, "better than assholes?"

Oakley left to fetch his board. When he got back, Danny was still sitting there.

"Come on, let's go."

"Onward, Danny," Fred said. "Into the sea of death! Remember the buddy system. Don't let Oakley perish alone!"

"You're on your own, Oakley. You probably won't even make it outside."

"No pouting, Danny," Marsha said.

"If it weren't for these assholes," Danny said, "I'd hang around just to watch you die."

He walked off into the jungle.

As soon as Oakley hit the water, he was sorry he did. The waves looked much bigger than they had from the shore, and encroaching darkness added to the sense of danger. He paddled through a small cut in the reef and immediately was hammered by one breaking wave after another. Finally there was a lull and he made it out past the impact zone into the deep water.

Oakley had come to understand that the waves in Hawaii were different from the waves in California where, from the open ocean, the swells approached a gradually-shallowing sandy bottom and presented no real surprises. Here, when the swells hit the reefs they underwent a frightening transformation. They suddenly leapt up to double their size and shape-shifted from benign floating humps to dangerous, rising walls of hurling water that hollowed out and crashed heavily onto razor-sharp coral.

Oakley wished he hadn't paddled out, but it was too late to turn back. He would have looked ridiculous paddling back in without catching a wave. Besides, even if he were to attempt paddling in, he would have been hit by waves and possibly smashed against the reef. The only way in now was to ride a wave.

One leapt up in front of him, but he let it pass because the shape didn't look right. Sure enough, he watched from behind as it closed out, crashing across its length rather than curling to create a pocket where a surfer could ride.

Oakley tried to calm his rising panic. He went through the litany: The real danger was himself, he needed to conquer his fear, assert his mind over the watery matter.

The next wave had the shape, but it was considerably larger. As it approached the reef it rose and began to turn concave. His heart pounding in his ears, Oakley paddled toward shore, until he felt his board joining the wave's motion. He stood, slid down an eight-foot face to the bottom, leaned hard to turn and squatted low as the wave began to break over his head. He found a track and stayed on it, hoping to make it out the other end of this rotating barrel, one hand on the rail of his board for stability, the other outstretched for balance, his puny platform sliding sideways, his body enclosed by moving water.

For an instant, he was surrounded by silence, shut off from light and all sensation of motion. Time slowed down and stretched out in front of him. Images flashed through his head, a mental slide show that seemed to last for many minutes: a child wading in nearshore waters, a deserted stretch of coastline in southwestern Spain, the naked body of a woman in a blue nylon tent, a cold morning sitting in a warm car in

Ventura county, a cool dip in a desert stream, a closeup of nails being hammered into bamboo, the grinning face of Fred the Zen.

Then a fine spray of water hit his back and, suddenly, he popped out of the wave into the world again. Back in control, he kicked his board upward through the white water, escaping the wave before it threw him onto the reef.

Grinning in triumph, thrilled by the feeling of a perfect ride, Oakley started to paddle to shore. But when he saw the group cheering him, up on their feet, stamping and hooting and gesturing, he decided to stay.

He paddled for a larger wave in the next set. As soon as he was standing, he knew he was in trouble. The wave was pitching more severely over the reef. He couldn't drop to the bottom because there was no bottom, no water to bank against, because the reef was exposed. So he made his turn halfway down the face, hoping to accelerate and get the hell out of there. But the water wall bent on him and the fin of his board popped out of it, sending him into freefall with the board, the lip of the wave coming down from above, the coral floor rising from beneath.

He buried his head in his arms and waited for the impact. The wave swung him up, over and down. It felt like a bounce as he landed on his back with a thud and was then immediately lifted up by the galloping white water and dragged the rest of the way across the reef. He ended up in the protected pool, his board a few feet away. He hopped back on and paddled to shore, feeling lucky to be uninjured.

"Hey, man," a long-haired teenager wading in the shallows said. "You OK?"

"Yeah, I think so." Oakley's back hurt a little, but nothing felt broken.

"Your whole back is bleeding."

When Oakley reached the shore, Sandy was there.

"You're cut up pretty bad. Might need some stitches. I can't tell, there's too much blood."

But Oakley's pain was minor compared to his state of mind, which was bordering on the ecstatic.

"Did you see that first wave?"

"It spit you out!"

"I felt the spray!"

"The next one, we thought you were a goner."

"I bounced off the fucking reef!"

Back with the group, Oakley was the center of attention.

"You shouldn't have been out there," Marsha said.

"It was all in my head! Mind over matter."

"You almost killed yourself."

"But I didn't!"

"Mind over sanity, Mister O-nami. Another convert for Fred the Zen."

"How about it, Fred?" Patrick asked. "Is this Oakley's big one? The moment of satori?"

"Who says there's only one?"

Soundtrack played the Beach Boys "Surfin' Safari" but changed the words: "Come on, babe, surfin' satori, come on, babe, surfin' satori…"

Sandy said, "I've got some hydrogen peroxide."

"For what?"

"To kill the coral, so it doesn't grow in you."

"Hey, Patrick," Fred said. "Where's Heather?"

"None of your business."

"How come we never see her?" Fred asked, one hand idly caressing his crotch. "Is she shy, or acting under orders? I'm curious. I've only caught a glimpse or two of the mystery woman, but it was enough to see that she's not fulfilled! Which makes me more than just curious."

"Shut up, Fred! I don't need any of your bullshit."

Patrick jumped to his feet and left the group.

"You're such a fun guy, Fred," Marsha said.

"The truth hurts, but it feels so good," Fred said.

Soundtrack picked out the theme from "Looney Tunes and Merrie Melodies." First he did it note by note, then he worked in some chords.

The sun went down, flashing a green light to all those gathered on the sand, the receptive, susceptible acolytes of Ra.

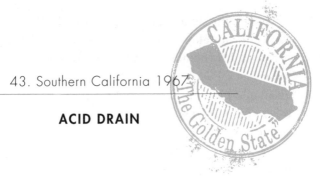

## ACID DRAIN

One Friday morning the Seven Psychedelic Samurai, crammed into Oakley's Chevy, went to Tahquitz Canyon, a reportedly sacred site not far from the profanity of Palm Springs.

The first night they camped out at the canyon bottom, pitching their tents in a hidden clearing surrounded by tall brush. The next morning they rose at dawn, dropped some Window Pane, left camp and hit the trail up the mountain. Oakley had his Kodak snapshot camera to record the adventure.

The trail went up the left side of a stream that came down from the mountaintop a couple of thousand feet above them. Its water was cool and clear. They were climbing in the high desert, cool in the morning but hot in the afternoon. The rocks were gray, smooth granite; the sky was clear blue, and the group was high and lucid.

They climbed quickly, enjoying the motion of their bodies working, the sweat popping out of their foreheads, the undulations of not only the flowing water but the very ground beneath their feet. LSD can do that to you. They hiked on and up, past rapids and waterfalls, on the trail that held close to the water.

Oakley was falling in love again. That dark, straight hair. That oval face with those full lips. The smile. The easy laugh. Her quick wit and engaging intelligence. Her short shorts and a tank top with no bra. Her perfectly round breasts. Oakley couldn't stop staring at Sage.

He knew he would do no more than look. It was uncool to hit on a friend's girl. Besides, Sage was happy where she was. Sage was warm and friendly toward Oakley, but not romantically or sexually interested.

By noon the stoned hikers had reached a horizontal plain near the top of the mountain, where they stopped beside a large pool of water surrounded by boulders. They smoked some weed, ate lunch, swam in the water, hallucinated on the sky and terrain, talked and napped. Dylan and Crystal disappeared temporarily, reappearing with corny smiles and flushed faces.

The spot was so peaceful and inviting that is was late afternoon before they realized that they had better start back or they wouldn't make it to their camp before dark.

At Mark's suggestion, they started down the stream on the opposite side they'd hiked up. After two hours, it proved to be a mistake. They came to a spot where the trail ended, and the water plunged downward in a fifty-foot waterfall. For some reason, this had been no obstacle when they hiked up the trail on the other side.

The sun was sinking, the air was cooling, and the hikers realized they were in trouble. Mark wanted to climb back up to the pool and connect to the other trail, but Oakley said there was no time for that, it was too late in the day. He suggested climbing up the side of the mountain, where there was no trail, but where they could skirt the dropoff and then return to the trail beside the stream.

Oakley's plan won out.

Climbing around the drop took at least an hour. Up the side of the valley, across the ridge, and back down far below the waterfall. The sun was gone and the temperature was dropping fast. It was summertime, but in the high desert it would be a long, cold night in their skimpy clothes. They had little water, no food, no gear.

Oakley wanted to scout ahead to make sure they could find their campsite, but he stayed back to make sure the group stuck together. Dylan and Crystal were lagging behind, breathing heavily, slowing everyone down. But they weren't complaining, and no one criticized them. No one said much of anything. The rush of the LSD had been replaced by the damper of fear.

It was twilight when they finally returned to the stream at a point where they could ford it and connect with the original trail. As they crossed, Oakley dropped his camera into the water. He pulled it out and dried it off, hoping it wasn't ruined.

They found their tent camp in the dark. They straggled in, exhausted but relieved. They made a fire, cooked dinner, passed around a jug of red wine and a couple of joints, and disappeared into their tents.

In the middle of the night Sage climbed into Oakley's sleeping bag, informed him that this was a one-time event, that Mark approved, that it would in no way alter their relationships. They kissed and fondled. Oakley didn't know what to say, but he wasn't about to refuse the offering of such a gift. They made love, Oakley touching the body he loved to look at, being intimate with the woman he appreciated in so many ways, hoping Mark would really be okay with it.

The next morning before they broke camp, Oakley rewound the roll of film in his camera, removed it, and left the camera open to dry out.

Later that week, he had the film developed. The slides came back streaked with ink that had flowed down the images like a curtain of water. Accidental surrealism. Acid stain. Acid refrain.

## GREEK TRAGEDY

It was twilight on the beach, but almost dark in Oakley's treehouse. He fired up his Coleman lanterns and a mosquito coil outside. His back was sore and tender from the coral-reef pounding. Sandy showed up with a clean cloth, a brown plastic bottle of hydrogen peroxide, and a bucket of fresh water from the stream. She was still in her white swimsuit.

"Don't you get eaten alive like that?"

"Maybe they don't like black people."

Sitting him on a wooden crate, she poured peroxide into the pattern of cuts and gouges that covered his back. It sizzled and stung.

She coated the cuts with antibacterial cream, then criss-crossed them with adhesive strips, depleting a half tinful, covering his back with band-aids.

"Wish I had some gauze tape," she said.

"You're doing great," Oakley said. "It's weird that humans can't take care of our own backs. We can't even touch some places."

"Right now, you don't want to. And you better stay out of the water. Keep it dry."

"I will. Thanks."

Oakley pulled on a T-shirt. His back hurt a lot more than it did before. The high price of enlightenment. And now Sandy was here dressing his wounds, standing so close he could see the fine hair on her skin, smell its sweetness, performing an act as intimate as making love. She was actually speaking to him, and looking beautiful against the fading twilight backdrop of sea and sky beyond the jungle.

"I have a roach," he said. "Want a hit or two?"

"No thanks."

"Me, neither, actually. Just Taylor Camp protocol."

To Oakley, Sandy's faint snort was the equivalent of a belly laugh.

"You want some pretzels? They're not stale yet."

"No, thanks. Gotta get back for dinner."

"You cooking?"

"Not tonight. I have some time."

They sat silently for a moment.

"You haven't really seen my place," he said. "Can I show you around?"

"Sure."

"Well, you're in the kitchen and dining room. Here's the fireplace. Up the steps are my den and bedroom. Come on up."

Oakley brought one of the lamps inside. The triangular opening was covered with a double-layered door, one layer plastic sheeting and the other green, fine-mesh mosquito netting. Oakley peeled back and tied open the plastic, then carefully tied down the netting, sealing the room off from mosquitoes, termites, moths and other winged invaders.

They sat on wooden folding chairs at the front edge of the platform, facing one another. Through the netting, they could see down the tapering canopy, illuminated by the lantern outside. It was like looking into an angular tunnel.

Still feeling the rush, Oakley decided to take a chance with Sandy. "So, you're pretty much together with Fred, right?"

Sandy stood up. "What?"

"Nothing! I'm sorry. Sit down. Please."

She remained standing. "You want to know about me and Fred?"

"It's none of my business."

She sat back down. "No, it's all right. He's been good to me. He's helping me. I owe him a lot."

"And?"

She stood again. "And what?" Almost in tears: "What do you want me to say?"

"Nothing! It's OK! I'm sorry. Please sit down."

She turned to leave, then turned back. He stood, thought about putting his hands on her shoulders, but decided against it.

"Listen, I'm really sorry. It's just that I like you, but if you're exclusively with Fred and you don't want me to bother you, then I won't."

She sat. "You like me?"

Oakley sat. "Sure."

"Why?"

"What do you mean, why? You're beautiful. You're intelligent. You're nice."

"No I'm not."

"Not what?"

"Not any of those things."

"I disagree."

"You don't know what I can do."

"What does that mean?"

"Nothing."

"What can you do that I don't know about?"

"I can make bad things happen."

"How?"

"I don't know. Maybe I'm a witch. I cast bad spells. But I don't know when I'm doing it."

"Come on, you're not a witch."

"You don't know me. You don't even know my name."

"Sure I do."

"It's a nickname. You don't know my real name."

"Sandra?"

"Guess again."

"Uh, Alexandra?"

"Nope."

"I give up."

"Cassandra."

"Really?"

"Yep."

"Well, it's a pretty name."

"But…"

"I didn't say 'but.' It's a pretty name."

"You do know who Cassandra was."

"Yeah."

"Yeah. Well."

"You have the power of prophesy?"

"Maybe."

"How do you know?"

"I told you. I think bad things, and then they happen."

"I don't believe that."

"Nobody believed Cassandra. Apollo made sure of that."

"You're no different from other people. We can all make things happen."

"Like polluting the earth."

"We can make good things happen, too. We can clean it up."

"Not enough people are doing that."

"Not yet, but more and more people are starting to."

"Then why does it *rain* all the time?" Sandy asked with a despairing moan. Tears made her emerald eyes gleam in the lamplight.

"It doesn't!"

"Yeah. Only when I'm feeling bad!"

"Give me a break! If you can make it rain, you can make the sun shine too. You make it shine for me."

Sandy stood up. "Bullshit. You fucking men!" She untied a section of the net, ducked under it, and ran off into the night.

"Great," Oakley said to himself. He picked up Fred's little Zen book, opened it at random and read aloud.

"'The wild geese do not intend to cast their reflection. The water has no mind to receive their image.'"

He closed the book.

He sighed and said, "Words to live by."

## 45. Kauai 2001

# A REGIME OF PLANTING AND FISHING

I'm up at dawn, the wakening day in Hawaii too good to miss, something I still remember from my time at Taylor Camp. The air is cool and clear, the brilliant blues of sea and sky unbleached by the haze that will appear as the morning progresses.

I sit outside in a metal chair at a metal table, dressed in swim trunks and a tank top, drinking room-made coffee, eating banana, papaya, and sweet, juicy slices of pineapple, watching the ocean. Although the morning air is still, the ocean is alive, jumpy, as if responding simultaneously to several contradictory currents or the agitating rhythm of a thousand tiny fish swimming just beneath the surface.

At 7:30, coated with waterproof sunscreen, borrowed surfboard under my arm, I head up the beach past elderly tourists strolling, young athletes running and swimming, surfers checking out the waves. First Break looks crowded, so I keep walking to Waiohai, the left Miles told me about. It looks like a good wave, about chest high this morning, with less than a dozen surfers out.

The ocean's surface is still bristling, the sun is already hot and bright, and a heavy salt scent permeates the moist air. I paddle out, savoring the sensations of fluidity, the harmless impact of the oncoming white water, the energy surging above me as I duck-dive under the waves. After yesterday evening's session I'm more at ease, confident that I still possess the skills I acquired over many years of surfing. The waves are friendly and accommodating, the surfers mellow and courteous in the early morning. I feel balanced and coordinated. I stay in the water for three hours.

After a turkey sandwich, a Caesar salad and a Big Island wheat beer poolside at the Oasis Bar & Grill, I head for the business center. Miles gets onto the Internet and connects to a website featuring a map of the Pacific Islands. He moves the arrow to the little fingernail-cutting-shaped cluster of Hawaiian Islands in the center of the North Pacific, touches the tip to the island of Kauai, and a title pops up: "Ha'ena, Kaua'i, Hawai'i."

A couple of more clicks and a page appears with the title "Taylor Camp."

I laugh. "This is great! What is it?"

"Take a look. It's sort of a scientific paper. What happened was, an archaeology class from the University of the Pacific did a dig there, looking at Taylor Camp like some ancient city in Egypt. They theorized what the society was like from their findings."

"Sounds like *A Canticle for Leibowitz*."

"What's that?"

"Book I read, science-fiction. About people in the future trying to figure out what happened in the past. They get it all wrong."

Miles stands and gestures for me to sit.

"How'd you find this?"

"Pualani. She thought you might be interested."

"I am."

"Enjoy. Print it out if you want, it's all comped."

Sure enough, it's a paper from the *Field Museum of Natural History Bulletin*, published in 1979—two years after Taylor Camp was shut down and destroyed. Authors: Thomas J. Riley and Karma Ibsen-Riley. Title: "Taylor Camp, Hawai'i: The life and death of a hippie community." Karma. Ibsen. Hmmm.

I save the file, log off, and open the text editor. I read:

> *"By 1972 there were 21 permanent houses at Taylor Camp...Some were quite elaborate indeed, with large bamboo pole foundations, clapboard siding, and windows facing the sea...there was a communal shower, an open air toilet, a small church, and even a cooperative store."*

I remember the "communal shower" and "open air toilet," but not the church or store. Norm designed the shower and toilet. I helped build them.

*"Near what must have been the center of the camp was the communal toilet, an open air 'throne' mounted next to a concrete septic tank (a requirement of the local Department of Health) as well as the shower, a contraption ingeniously rigged from 55 gallon oil drums."*

The toilet was not at the center of the camp. It had to be several hundred yards away from the nearest place where people prepared and ate food, somewhere beyond the maximum cruising range of a housefly. We built it to Health Department standards and regulations because, if we hadn't, they would have closed us down.

*"On the west side of the camp were the gardens, about two acres in extent, which are still producing a few vegetables today."*

"Today" meaning 1979. Surely by now there can't be anything left, not even a trace.

*"The small size of the garden area—a little less than two acres—demonstrates that planting played a secondary role in the subsistence of Taylor Camp residents."*

For some of us it played a primary role, for others a nonexistent one. We didn't all behave identically. Some of us ate Twinkies, others collard greens.

I lived without electricity, plumbing, climate control, radio, or television. I learned the names of trees and plants and how to use them for food and medicine and construction materials. I learned the meanings of Hawaii's place names and read stories of the Islands. I took long walks. I meditated.

*"Many local Ha'ena residents claimed that the economy of the camp was based on welfare support from the county and state and on the production and sale of Cannabis sativa, which Hawaiians call pakalolo ('crazy weed') and we often call marijuana."*

No one was growing and selling, at least when I was there. We weren't that stupid. We would have been busted in a minute.

I didn't know anybody on welfare. A woman with a five-year-old son was receiving child support checks in the mail, and one guy I knew was collecting unemployment.

*"The archaeological remains that we mapped and uncovered…
suggest to us that [the residents'] perceptions of being close to the
land included isolation from the main centers of trade and commerce
on Kaua'i rather than dependence on the land for subsistence."*

True. Nobody ever claimed to be living off the land. I supplemented
my food expenditures with stuff from the garden. For the first time in my
life, I actually *gardened*. Not being all the way there (completely dependent
on nature, totally living off the land, no cash expenditures) wasn't the
point. I had some money in the bank, a $600 account I opened up in
Hanalei and drew from when necessary. But I was a lot closer to nature
that I had ever been, and a lot closer than most people get to living even
a short stretch of their lives without electricity, plumbing, heating, air
conditioning, and sophisticated sanitary fixtures. No television, either.

*"The lack of participation of camp members in community affairs
and structures, the nudity, and of course the presence of 'drugs' all
contributed to the suspicion with which the older, more fixed residents
of Ha'ena viewed Taylor Camp."*

True, but why is "drugs" in quotation marks?

*"A tremendous value seems to have been placed upon mobility in the
form of the automobile. The subsistence of the camp was based on
a cash economy that required considerable monetary inputs rather
than on a regime of planting and fishing."*

This irritates me. No one followed any "regime." Personally, I lived
on a combination of vegetables from the garden, fruit and nuts from the
trees, fish from the sea, and packaged food from the Ching Young Store.

We planted and we fished, it was all part of the mix, but we never
intended that it would be everything. There was no single source for what
we ate; we were not purists about food or anything else. We drove nails into
bamboo and lashed it with nylon cord. We used plastic sheeting for walls.
We were not Luddites. Technology, whenever available, was our friend.

Another point: We were ultra-conscious (as most people with little
or no money must be) of the value of everything. Someone's discarded
chair was quickly retrieved from the trash, repaired, and adopted by
someone else.

Taylor Camp was not an organized or structured community. It was a bunch of people living independently in an unfamiliar place, getting to know it and figuring out their own ways of dealing with it. Using whatever resources they had, including cash. And cars.

Not everybody had a car, including me. Maybe ten percent of us. The rest had to hitchhike or accommodate our needs to the convenience of those who did have cars—whether we enjoyed their company or not. Fortunately Norm had one, he even let me borrow it, so I didn't need to solicit transportation. Thanks to Norm I could ride two miles to surf at Tunnels, seven miles to Hanalei, or thirty miles to Lihue. We went to Lihue at the most once a week. Not a lot of driving.

*"Taylor Camp was an experiment in living in the late twentieth century that was spawned by an attempt at rejection of many of contemporary America's superficial values. But it was an experiment in alternative leisure styles rather than a Utopian settlement designed to explore the economic and organizational frontiers of human settlement."*

These people are academia nuts. "Alternative leisure styles" sounds like a fashion show. We were definitely no "utopia," but we were on a "frontier" of sorts.

The archaeologists find wine bottles, tin cans, candy bar wrappers, pop tops, cigarette butts. They conclude that the inhabitants of Taylor Camp were not as disciplined, as spiritual, as health-food conscious in their lifestyles as hippies were presumed to have been. They label and group and classify us according to the contents of a collective pile of non-biodegradable trash.

But that's what happens when you become a thing of the past. You become what anybody decides you were. Archaeology deals with limited evidence because it can't get inside people's heads. But at Taylor Camp, that's where everything was happening—in our heads. That was even what some people called us: "heads."

At dinner I'm a loner at the steak and seafood restaurant, surrounded by couples and families, uncomfortable alone. I should have brought a book.

My after-dinner walk on the beach is another bad decision. The moon, a slice thinner tonight but still round and radiant, shines on couples strolling the sandy promenade in an assortment of affectionate connections: hand in hand, arm in arm, head on shoulder. I detour for the parking lot and drive two miles into Koloa town, looking for the liquor store Miles told me about.

Back in the room with my booty: a bag of pretzels, several bottles of a locally-made, "healthy and natural" fruit juice blend of mango, papaya, guava, and lilikoi, and a fifth of Ketel One. There's no room in the mini-fridge, so I leave it all on the counter and fetch a bucket of ice cubes.

Hawaiian-style highball in hand, I surf the boob tube until I can't take it anymore. Twenty minutes.

I inspect my camera, try out the shutter and the film advance lever. I pop open the back and put Pualani's film in. It's not like retrieving an old friend; I only had the camera for about a week. But I remember what I bought it for: all the traveling I would do in my exciting, peripatetic lifetime. I didn't need a camera after all. I practically stopped traveling after Taylor Camp. At least traveling in the sense of staying in places for longer that a week or two.

I put away the camera and pick up my current read, Annie Proulx's *The Shipping News*, about a loser who transforms into a winner. It happens partly by circumstance, but mostly because he has a good heart. At this time in my life, I feel the opposite, once a winner who has slowly become a loser. Fred the Zen was right after all.

What to make of a diminished thing.

I read, drink, munch, turn the TV on again, off again, think about masturbating to ease my yearnings, don't feel the urge. My head is spinning. I step out of the room into the night, moon still shining, nobody out at this hour, sea washing against lava rock, sending molecules of ocean into my nostrils.

I go to sleep thinking about Sage, then and now.

Too drunk to dream.

## FIVE-FINGER DISCOUNT

Fred and Oakley were back from Lihue, carrying bags of groceries and supplies to the banyan treehouse, dumping them on the table in Fred's kitchen. Oakley was wearing cut-off jeans and a T-shirt. Fred was a grotesque parody of a tourist, dressed in black shoes and socks, striped Bermuda shorts, a pink T-shirt that read "*Poipu Beach, Hawaii,*" and a straw hat. Marsha climbed down her ladder. Sandy was nowhere in sight.

"What a trip!" Oakley said. "Fred drives slower than the locals."

Marsha said, "Tell me about it."

Oakley separated out the few items belonging to him: a five-pound bag of brown rice, smaller bags of flour and sugar, jars of soy sauce and instant coffee, and an orange box of powdered milk. Marsha helped Fred stash their goods in the makeshift cabinets and drawers. Out of one bag she pulled a garish aloha shirt with the price tag still attached.

"You bought this, Oakley?"

"Uh, no. It's Fred's."

"Nice, eh?" Fred asked. "Shall I model it for you?"

"Fifteen ninety-five? You only had forty dollars. How could you buy this?"

"It was on sale," Fred said.

"Five-finger discount," Oakley said.

"You *stole* it?"

"Not me. Although I was sort of an accomplice."

"*You* stole it?" Marsha asked, glaring at Fred.

"Like you said, we couldn't afford to buy it."

"Take it back."

"Why? There's nothing wrong with it."

"There's something wrong with *you!*"

"Actually, he did it for my benefit," Oakley said. "He was demonstrating the connection between freedom and external appearances. I look like this, and Fred is dressed like a tourist from Nebraska, and we go into this variety store—you know the one near the movie theater, Imura's I think it is? And the sales clerks follow *me* all around the store, watching my every move. Meanwhile, Fred is strolling around like the Invisible Man. I saw him take the shirt, but nobody else did."

"There's no excuse for stealing."

"That store won't even miss it."

"You didn't rip off a store, you ripped off *people*." She ran a hand through her spiky red hair.

"The *people* will never know it's gone."

"That's not for you to say."

"Charging sixteen dollars for that shirt is stealing."

"You're not responsible for their actions. You're responsible for *yours*." She walked up to him, looked up, her face level with his chest, and gave him a shove. He didn't budge. "Give it back!"

"You know something, Oakley?" Fred asked. "Marsha's right. I fucked up. In my desire to teach you a lesson, I upset the balance of the universe. I'll take it back right now."

"You're kidding," Marsha said.

"By the time you get there," Oakley said, "the store will be closed."

"Can it wait 'til tomorrow?" Fred asked Marsha.

"Are you serious?"

"What do you think?"

"I think you're serious," Marsha said.

"Is tomorrow all right with you, Oakley?"

"You want me to go with you?"

"I'll need my decoy again. I'm going to sneak this shirt back into the store. Replace it without leaving a ripple in the cosmic pond. Unsteal it."

"Thank you," Marsha said. "I appreciate that."

"We'll leave at nine. Gonna be here, Oakley?"

"Why not? Should be fun to watch."

Oakley watched Fred and Marsha put away their purchases. Marsha seemed moody, but Fred was lighthearted and happy. As he deposited a paper bag into the wastebasket labeled "For the Fire," he picked a crumbled piece of paper out of it, smoothed it out, held it up, squinted in critical scrutiny, rotated it into various orientations.

"You happy now, Marsha? No reason not to be."

"I just don't think you need to rewrite all the rules. Freedom is one thing, but people need to treat one another with some common decency."

"Before we obey the rules we need to understand them. We need to explore the reasons behind them. We obey the rules not because we have to, but because we choose to. Blind obedience is not the way to go."

Fred found a thumbtack and pinned the smoothed-out piece of paper to a prominent place on a housepole.

"Wow," Oakley said. "That's cool. What is it?"

"Marsha's artwork," Fred said. "She draws in a sketchbook, then tears out the pages and throws them away."

"It's not abstract art, you know," Marsha said. "That was supposed to be a—"

"I don't care what it was supposed to be. I can see what it is."

She sat down at the picnic bench, elbows on the table, head in her hands, shaking her head. "Sometimes I think I'm missing the boat here."

Fred smiled warmly at her. "How can you miss the boat when you *are* the boat?"

"God damn it, that's what I mean!" She slammed a fist on the table. "Comments like that. 'How can you miss the fucking boat when you *are* the fucking boat?' It sounds so clever and so true. But what the fuck does it *mean*?"

"It has something to do with being free."

"It that what it's all about? Is that what we're doing here?"

"You're free to be anything, anywhere, everything, everywhere."

"I don't want to be everything everywhere! I just want to be something somewhere."

"Nothing wrong with that. Except for the danger of being nothing nowhere."

"Stop it, Fred! I don't want to hear it now. It's just a bunch of word games."

"Exactly! Games to sharpen your wits and polish your soul. Games to cleanse the doors of perception. Games to set you free."

"Right now I want to be set free from you. Free from all your stupid Zen riddles."

Marsha stood abruptly and started for the trail, but Fred grabbed her by the elbow and turned her around. She fought to free herself from his grip.

"You think I'm talking about Zen?" he asked. "You're right, it's just a bunch of word games. I'm talking about an awareness, a way of living that lets you control your own destiny. Completely create your own reality. But you don't want that much freedom or power. You just want a little bit. Equal rights for women."

"That wouldn't be bad, for starters."

She pulled away again, and he let her go.

"Women's rights, civil rights, gay rights, they're all just little slices of the pie. Zen takes the whole pie, and throws it in your face."

"That sounds very cosmic, but I don't know what it means and I can't use it. Sometimes you remind me of Werner Earhard."

She walked off onto the trail, toward the beach.

"Isn't she great?" Fred asked Oakley.

"Sure."

"She's a lot closer than you are."

"Closer to what?"

"You know what I'm talking about."

## THE ROAD TO HANALEI

On Friday morning I sleep in, curtains drawn against the blue outside. I'm not hung over. I drank a lot of water. Solution to pollution: dilution. Up at eight, I make coffee, eat some leftover fruit and a couple of pretzels, drink a bottle of juice, then go out to check the surf. The swell is down but the crowd is up. I leave the board locked up in the room, then walk back down to the beach for a swim. Near the hotel is a shore break, small waves I can catch bodysurfing. Without a board to float on, I'm more in the water, tasting more of it, more conscious of the white foam patterns left behind by the breaking waves.

I check out at 10:30. I have the desk clerk page Miles.

"Thanks for the board and everything."

"You want to take it with you? You can, you know."

"No, that's all right."

"Please, take it. Nobody's using it."

"I don't have a rack."

"Try get it inside. If you can't, I'll help you tie it down."

"How will I get it back to you?"

"You flying Aloha or Hawaiian?"

"Hawaiian."

"Leave it at the counter when you check in, tell them to keep it for Wayne Takahashi. He works there."

I write the name down. "Any surf on the north shore?"

"Not today. But you never know."

Outside the lobby, we shake hands. Miles hands me a small envelope.

"Something to bring back the old days."

In my car, the surfboard a tight fit inserted diagonally from the front passenger seat into the back behind me, I open the envelope. Inside are three fat joints.

Back in Lihue, at Okamura's Okazu-Ya on Rice Street, Pualani meets me for lunch as promised. She's wearing jeans again, this time with a sleeveless blouse printed in a hibiscus pattern, and the same purple daypack. I can see her collarbone. Nice. Her neck, too.

"Thanks to you, I was treated like a dignitary."

"A surfing dignitary. Miles was impressed."

"I didn't think I could get back into it so soon. It felt good."

We order noodles.

"What did you think about the website?"

"Archaeologists sound so sure of themselves. But they're just guessing. They could be dead wrong."

"For example?"

"For example everything, from Mesopotamia to Egypt to China. How can we really know?"

"I mean the Taylor Camp thing."

"OK, worst thing is their across-the-board attitude about behavior. They dig up a sardine tin, they say something like 'the inhabitants of Taylor Camp depended upon canned fish, meats, and other foods.' But what if a hundred people were living there or passing through at that particular time, that level of the dig, and only six of them ever ate canned food of any kind?"

"Good answer, even if it ends with a question."

"The conclusions they made about Taylor Camp were maybe half right, tops, according to my experience."

We talk some more: about the B&B I'm going to in Hanalei, a block from the beach on the bay. I tell her the name and she knows it. The food arrives and we stop talking to eat. But after a while I realize, it's now or never.

"I was wondering. If you want to visit me in Hanalei sometime over the weekend. We could surf or snorkel or hike or something."

Trying to be casual about it.

"That's a long bike ride."

"You don't have a car?"

She shakes her head.

*Now or never.* "Then come with me today."

She's quiet for a moment. Then: "Why are you coming on to me?"

"For no reason that should make you upset. I like you. I'd like to spend more time with you."

She takes in a big breath, slowly lets it out.

"And I like your collarbone," I add during her exhale.

Another sigh.

"I like you, too, I guess. Even though I've never seen *your* collarbone."

I pull down the neck of my T-shirt to show it to her. She laughs.

"So we'll drop your bike off at your house, then head for Hanalei."

"Not a good idea. Think about it, Oakley. You have things to do there, you need to be alone. You want me to spend the night with you, but what about the day? You want me hanging around all day long?"

"I wouldn't mind."

"Believe me, you would."

I smile at her. "Then the obvious course of action is for you to spend the night with me and get lost before dawn."

She laughs. "You are one smart-ass haole."

"Come on."

"Forget about it."

"You really want me to?"

"Are you married?"

"Separated. Almost divorced."

"Is this a line?"

"No. The papers are probably waiting for my signature as we speak."

"What happened?"

"She left."

"Why?"

"Another guy, but it's not all her fault."

"Who's fault is it?"

I look away. "Long story."

"Did you cheat on her?"

"Nope. Vice-versa."

"Either way, you're on the rebound."

"Can't deny that. What difference does it make?"

"Maybe you're too desperate to know what you're doing."

"That's possible in other aspects of my life, but not this one."

"I appreciate you being open and truthful with me, if that's what you're doing. Will you do me a favor?"

"Sure."

"If you're lying to me in any way, will you please tell me now?"

My turn to sigh. "I can't vouch for my emotions, because right now they're all over the place. But the facts are true. My marriage is over, except on paper."

"Then thank you for telling me. That's the best part."

"So you're coming with me?"

Another smile. "No way."


In a souvenir shop I buy an opaque plastic sports water bottle encircled with cartoonlike bands of plumeria and the words "I ♥ The Garden Isle." In the car, I fill it with vodka and fruit juice—one for the road—and suck it through the attached straw.

The sign at the north end of town says it's thirty miles to Hanalei. In memory, it was a lot farther. I light up one of Miles's joints and watch the sights go by. Wal-Mart, new. Coco Palms Hotel, not.

Outside of Kapaa, heading up the island's east side on Kuhio Highway, I see evidence of new development—fancy signs advertising residential "estates" for sale—but they're invisible from the road, which runs a mile or two inland, and the open spaces are still there, the rolling ranchlands and empty green foothills. It looks a little like parts of central California.

Past the Princeville Airport, things begin to change. Princeville looks massive, with a gated security entrance, a golf course, and a streetfront shopping center. The first views of Hanalei Bay are the way I remember them—vast, fairy-tale beautiful—and the crossing into Hanalei town at the bottom of the hill is still a one-lane bridge, cars taking turns, waiting for gaps in the stream of approaching traffic. At the bottom of the valley the road runs beside the river, then takes a left turn away from it, into the little town of Hanalei. Which is a lot bigger now.

The Ching Young Store has evolved into "Ching Young Village"— a conglomeration of souvenir shops, restaurants, art galleries, and a food market. Across the street, the classic old Hawaiian-style building I remember as Hanalei School is now a mini-mall containing, among other establishments, a gourmet deli and a shop called Tropical Tantrum.

I pull into the "Village" lot, get out of my air-conditioned capsule for the first time in an hour, and step into a steambath. Low gray clouds, no breeze. Dead, wet, sticky air. Sweat pours from my armpits, crotch, forehead, and temples. On the back of my head, my hair's wet.

I walk along the main street, in the middle of which, thirty years ago, a dog was sleeping. Today, in a minute, that dog would be a wall poster.

A sign outside "Sushi Blues" restaurant advertises "live music and dancing on weekends." A sports shop with a kayak on the roof promotes a variety of activities, listed large in the windows: horseback riding, helicopter tours, luaus, Na Pali boats, kids tours, scuba lessons, snorkel gear, kayak rentals, dive tours, fishing, windsurfing, massages.

I can't check into the B&B for another hour. I find a restaurant with a bar and take a stool. It's not air-conditioned but the windows are open, the ceiling fans are turning, and it's shady. There's a baseball game on TV. More oldies on the stereo: "We Gotta Get Out of This Place," "Ninety-Six Tears," "Dancing in the Streets," "Norwegian Wood," "Don't You Want Somebody To Love?" Is this island locked into a time warp?

I'm the only one at the bar. It's between lunch and dinner, and all but two or three of the tables are empty. The bartender wears a tank top bearing the words "Kayak Hawaii" and an illustration of a mermaid holding a paddle, riding on the back of a sea turtle. Suspended from the rafters is a long red outrigger canoe with a yellow pontoon. On the walls are dozens of turtle images.

"Any surf nearby?"

"Not yet," the bartender says, mixing me a vodka tonic.

"What's with the turtles?"

"This is Honu's. Honu means turtle in Hawaiian."

" I don't remember seeing any turtles when I was here before."

"When was that?"

"Nineteen-seventy."

"There you go. That was before the law was passed protecting them. They made a comeback, big-time."

"Where can I see them?"

"Lots of places. But you know Tunnels?"

"Yeah."

"That's the best place, as long as there's no swell running."

"Close to shore?"

"Out at the oceanside edge of the reef. What you want to do is rent a kayak and paddle out there. There's a turtle house. You'll see dozens of 'em."

"I'll give it a try."

"Get there early. Otherwise there's no place to park."

"How early?"

"No later than nine."

I pay the tab. "Ever heard of Taylor Camp?"

"Before my time. But keep asking. You'll find people."

Strolling around the "Village," I shop at Big Save. It's cool inside, which might explain why it's so crowded. The food is high-priced, but for some reason the alcohol isn't. I buy a bottle of Absolut and some ingredients for a B&B in-room dinner: cheese, French bread, salami, sliced smoked turkey, small jars of mustard and mayonnaise, wine, bottled water.

I check out the sport shop and rent a hunk of molded gray plastic called a Cobra. It comes with paddle, strap-on seat and racks for the car. The opens early enough for me to get to Tunnels before nine, so I tell the man I'll pick up the gear in the morning.

Pulling out onto the road, I stop with the other cars as a large black dog ambles lazily across the street.

At the B&B, a three-story house, I get my key from a lock box using the combination on my email printout. I have a top-floor corner room. The bathroom is outside the door, but it's mine alone. The room has no air conditioning. The corner windows are supposed to compensate, but not today. Fortunately, there's a ceiling fan above the bed.

By the time I'm settled, I'm no longer up for a drive to the state park previously known as Taylor Camp. Instead, I collect an armful of guidebooks from the library in the communal living room downstairs, bring them up to my room, mix myself another Hawaiian vodka cocktail, settle on the bed and read.

From 101 Things To Do: Kauaʻi
*"64. Spend Some Time At Kaʻu. Take a short walk back towards Haʻena along the beach from Kaʻu for a panoramic view of the Na Pali coast, and keep hiking along the coast for a look at where Kauaʻi's most noted hippie commune, Taylor Camp, once stood near the mouth of Limahuli Stream.*
*"74. Take A Day Trip In The Kalalau. Baseball fans' trading cards can't match the enthusiasm with which repeat visitors to Kauaʻi's wild Na Pali Coast swap stories. 'Did you hear the one about the trust-fund hippies who came to the coast in the 1960s and loved it so much they had their waterbeds flown in?'"*

From Beaches of Kauaʻi and Niʻihau, John R. K. Clark
*"Haʻena State Park consists of 230 acres of beachfront lands situated between Limahuli Stream to the east and Na Pali Coast State Park to the west…Despite the park's rich pre-contact archaeological resources, it is probably best known for a modern settlement within its boundaries that*

*was called Taylor Camp…associated with the hippie movement of the late 1960s and early 1970s.*

*"The fame of this Taylor Camp spread, attracting a steady flow of 'flower children.'…As with many other hippie communities, however, the return to the land at Taylor Camp was itself superficial and only marginally successful at best…*

*"In 1972 the state began condemnation proceedings to acquire the land as part of Ha'ena State Park. Taylor and the camp residents protested. Nevertheless, the court ruled in favor of the state, but with the proviso that the evicted campers be given relocation assistance. The state finally took over in 1977…*

*"The channel cut through the reef by Limahuli Stream was called Poholokeiki. This was also the name of the shoreline area where Taylor Camp was located."*

Poholokeiki is a name new to me.

*Keiki* are children and, according to the Hawaiian dictionary, poholo means "to sink, slip into easily, plunge out of sight, vanish." Would that make Taylor Camp a land of lost children? A repository for the disappearing dreams of youth?

From Lonely Planet Guide Hawai'i

*In the late 1960s, a little village of tents and tree houses sprang up on property owned by actress Elizabeth Taylor's brother. Reports of drugs, orgies and pipe organ music in the middle of the night eventually prompted the authorities to crack down on the camp. When state officials tried to evict everyone on public health grounds, the campers challenged them in court, claiming squatters' rights. The 'squatters' eventually lost, and the property was condemned and incorporated into the state park system. Taylor Camp remains part of North Shore folklore, though there's nothing left to see.*

Guess I missed out on the orgies. And the pipe organ.

Is there really nothing left to see?

Outside my window, the clouds turn pink. I walk to the beach, past the Hanalei Bay Pavilion, where people gather to watch the sunset: guitar and ukulele pickers, groups cooking on hibachis, couples strolling, runners running. I walk along the curved bay, the sun behind me, taking in the views, listening to the soft wash of tiny waves. The houses are set far back from the beach. High above, the cliffs that cup the waters of the bay are grooved, like forest-green corduroy.

At the pier I turn back and watch the sun sink beyond the tip of the bay, into the water. Maybe a hundred people watch, in scattered groups or pairs or alone like me. A woman sitting on a beach chair speaks into a cell phone, looking self-conscious as I pass. A teenager wearing headphones squats on a mound of sand near the water's edge.

As twilight fades, reluctant-looking people leave the beach, headed for whatever they're reluctant about. I wait a little longer and walk home in the dark.

Back in my room I make a salami and cheese sandwich and try to watch TV. It's all shit. I take a couple of hits from one of Miles's joints, then get into bed and read.

What am I doing here? I really don't know. Escape? Everything comes along with me. Desire? For what? A goal, a purpose? What?

But tomorrow will be a full day. I turn off the light.

## HIPPIE DREAM GONE BAD

I got flower power
        E    A E
Good vibrations too
      E    A E
Got a God's eye and a mantra
                     A E
But they just won't work on you
        E7
I think it's obvious
         A
That peace and love was just a fad
                         E A E
           37
And the blues ain't nothin but the hippie dream gone bad.
                                     A                   E

The rich are getting richer
The poor are just as poor
Politicians are still lying
And the world is still at war
I think we're losin' it
'Cause everybody's getting mad
And the blues ain't nothin but the hippie dream gone bad.

Got my brown rice
Got my herbal tea
Got my macrobiotic diet
Now the air is killing me
I know I'm breathing it
The way they poison us is sad
And the blues ain't nothin but the hippie dream gone bad.

We ate magic mushrooms
We followed gurus
We saw the light
But we didn't see you
I think I'm out of it
This is the strangest trip I ever had
And the blues ain't nothin but the hippie dream gone bad.

## THE TRUE MEANING OF "HAOLE"

Oakley was hitchhiking to Hanalei, walking on the ocean side of the road, hauling a plastic trash bag filled with soiled clothing, towels, and bedsheets to wash at Ching Young's laundromat. Ten minutes before, he had left Taylor Camp in morning sunshine. Five minutes later, clouds had appeared and it had started to drizzle. He was slowly getting soaked, but was used to it.

An approaching pickup truck swerved onto the shoulder, dousing Oakley with muddy water, forcing him to jump into a small ditch. The truck pulled to a stop. A large man leaned out of the passenger-side window, wielding a pair of scissors, closing and opening its blades with both hands.

"Eh, hippie haole," he said. "How 'bout one hair*cut?*"

Oakley didn't answer. The man got back into the truck. Oakley heard laughter as the driver peeled out. He got up, brushed off his laundry bag and headed back toward Taylor Camp. His laundry could wait for another day.

Later in the morning, he mentioned the incident to Norm. The sun was back out, the sky clear and cool, and they were in the garden. Norm pulled weeds and watered the lettuces and vegetables. Oakley was the waterboy, filling plastic one-gallon jugs at the nearby stream, two at a time, hauling them up to the garden, and exchanging them for two empties.

"Back in the states," Oakley said, "it's no big deal anymore. Even rednecks have long hair."

"On the Mainland."

"What?"

"Not 'back in the states.' Hawaii *is* a state."

"I guess it doesn't feel that way to me."

"That's what I like about it. A tropical island in the middle of nowhere, but you don't need a passport."

"It's not just the long hair, it's the whole thing. The locals don't like us."

"Can you blame 'em? Two hundred years ago, the first haoles come over here and tell everybody to put on some clothes and get down to business. Work, work, work. No time for surfing. No lascivious hula dancing. Worship the right God. Now a new bunch of haoles comes over and preaches about what everybody should do next: Get naked, get back to nature, live off the land, dance and play. And oh yes, by the way, God is dead. Wouldn't that piss you off?"

After a while they switched jobs, Oakley tending to the plants and Norm fetching water. The greens seemed to be doing the best: the tough collards and the small, soft heads of Manoa lettuce. The tomatoes were struggling: something kept eating them as soon as they began to turn red.

The garden was a series of experiments, many of which failed. But it didn't matter because most of the camp's residents had enough money to buy what they needed from the market in Hanalei. Other food was growing all around them, free for the taking, in the mountains and rainforests and even by the side of the road: coconuts, bananas, mangos, guavas, avocados, macadamia nuts. And then there was the ocean with its bounty of fish, crabs, lobsters, and edible seaweeds. Hardly a day went by without someone bringing some kind of food into Taylor Camp—big chunks of fresh Marlin, ripe papayas or mountain apples, a burlap bag filled with macadamia nuts in the shell—and handing it out to anyone who wanted some.

"You know what 'haole' means?" Norm asked.

"A white person? A Caucasian?"

"There's this friend of Fred's, supposedly a kahuna, a holy man. He told me that haole means a person without a soul."

"That's a nice sentiment."

"But somebody else told me that was wrong, all it means is 'foreigner.' So I went to the library in Lihue and asked the librarian. She isn't Hawaiian, she's Japanese, but was born on Kauai and lived here all her life. She said, 'ha' is the name for some kind of Hawaiian religious breathing exercise, like yoga. And 'ole' is a negative. So the foreigners were called haoles because they didn't get up at sunrise to do the Hawaiian yoga."

"I like that better than the soulless one."

"But then it gets more complicated because 'ha' also means breath, or breath of life. So then haole could also mean 'without breath' or 'without life'."

"So how do you know which particular meaning is intended at any given time?"

"You look in their eyes. And you listen for subtle modifiers, like this." Norm shouted "*Fock*-ing haole!" then added, calmly, "When you hear that, you don't want to hang around."

## IDENTITY MAKEOVER

It was nighttime at Fred's treehouse. Insects were singing. Mosquitoes were buzzing. The kitchen area was lighted with several large candles and a couple of Coleman lanterns. Oakley, shirtless, sat on a wooden crate. Sandy checked out his back.

"Everything healed up pretty well," she told him. "Does it feel OK?"

"Feels fine."

"You were lucky. You could have broken your neck."

"Can I put my shirt back on now? I'm getting bit."

Sandy, wearing a tube top and cutoff jeans, was oblivious to the mosquitoes. Oakley put on his T-shirt and stood up to stretch.

"Could you do me another favor? Cut my hair?"

She looked at him. "Fred got to you, too."

"You ever cut hair?"

Sandy pulled on his hair, next to his ears and in the back.

"Long or short?"

"Short."

"Joining the Zen club?"

"I'm just tired of being treated like a freak. Can you?"

"Let's do it professionally."

She fetched a pair of scissors, a comb and a beach towel. She wrapped the towel around Oakley barber-style and proceeded to cut his hair in a in a rapid, haphazard manner. She stood close. She smelled good. No mosquito lotion. Did black people smell different? Better? Worse? Oakley didn't have any close black friends. All he knew was that Sandy smelled good.

"Tell me about Fred," Oakley said. "Where does he come from? Why's he living here?"

"He came here about a year ago with Marsha. They used to live in San Francisco, but I didn't know them until I met them here. They sort of took me in when I was at the end of my rope."

"What happened to you?"

"Not now."

"OK. But what about Fred and Marsha?"

"Who knows? They almost never talk about themselves, or the past. And they never answered my questions about them, so after a while I stopped asking. From what I can gather, Fred was either a bomber pilot or a cab driver...or both. Then something happened to him— you know, satori. But it was only after it happened that he picked up on Zen. He says it's the best explanation for what happened, given the fact that it can't be explained. Anyway, he was connected with Esalen and the human potential movement. That's where he met Marsha— and when they heard about Taylor Camp, they took off for Hawaii. I think they're living on her money. Her parents are rich, supposedly. I think they own a record company."

"Fred was a bomber pilot?"

"Pick the story you like best. What about you, Oakley? What did you do before you came over here?"

"I was an English teacher."

"I thought teachers got draft deferments."

"They did. They do. I lost mine because I must have fucked up some bureaucratic detail in the paperwork, or else they just misplaced my file. So I went into the lottery and all of a sudden I was drafted."

"Couldn't you straighten out the mistake?"

"I might have been able to, but everything happened pretty fast, and I was getting more and more pissed off about the war, and I wanted to get as far away as I possibly could, as fast as I possibly could, so I came over here."

"That's how I got here, too. As far away as I possibly could. I didn't even know if there were any brothers or sisters here."

"I haven't seen many. Maybe in Honolulu."

"There! All done!"

Oakley patted his head, worried. "Already?"

"Sure. Duck soup. Wanna see it?"

"Yes, please."

Oakley tried to get a feel for his new haircut as Sandy searched for the mirror. She found it—a jagged fragment—and handed it to him. His tried to suppress his shock.

"Good! Now I don't look like a hippie anymore."

Fred walked in from the trail. "Now you look like a prisoner of war." He took a large tin from a shelf, opened it, and pulled out a couple of Hostess Twinkies. "Anybody want one?"

Sandy and Oakley weren't interested. Oakley got up from the barber stool, removed the towel, and brushed the hair from his shoulders.

"I think I'll go make myself some dinner. Uh, want to join me, Sandy?"

"Oh! No, I can't. I mean, Fred's cooking something special tonight. That is, if he doesn't spoil his appetite! Thanks, anyway."

Fred spotted Norm on the trail and called out to him. "Hey, Norm! How about a Twinkie?"

Norm joined the group. "Did I show up at the right time or what?" He accepted a Twinkie and produced a joint. "And I happen to have with me the perfect Twinkie companion!" He took in Oakley's new look. "Wow—cutting your back to ribbons wasn't enough, eh? You had to do the same thing to your hair!"

Norm toasted Fred with the Twinkie, lighted the joint and began consuming them both.

Oakley said, "Nah, it looks OK."

"Don't worry, Oakley," Sandy said. "Don't make no difference to me what this creep says about my work."

Fred gave Oakley the eye. "The patient is making remarkable progress."

"You let *her* cut your hair?" Norm asked. "You deserve what you got."

Oakley got up to leave. "Later. Dinner time."

"Have it with us," Fred said. "Unless you prefer collard greens and brown rice to steak and potatoes."

"You got steak?"

"T-bones from Lihue, in the cooler. We'll grill 'em on the fire, wrap the potatoes in foil and bake 'em in the coals, Sandy will make a big salad, and we'll all have a feast. Plenty for all."

Marsha climbed down her ladder, walked over to Fred and hugged him.

"Does this mean I'm not a bastard anymore?" he asked.

"No. You're still a bastard. But I love you anyway."

Danny, who had been hovering for a moment on the trail, joined the group.

"Some people just keep coming back for more," Norm said.

"Fuck you. Got another Twinkie, Fred?"

"All gone!" Fred said, finishing his last bite. "Sorry."

"That shit's bad for your system, anyway."

"I don't have a system. I just let things happen."

"How about a hit on that joint?"

"I think it's interesting," Norm said, passing Danny the joint, "that you have no qualms about bumming everybody else's smoke, but you won't share your psychedelics with anyone."

"Forget about it. There's only enough for me. Acid doesn't grow on trees like this stuff."

Danny took a hit, offered the joint to Fred. Without taking a hit, Fred passed it to Sandy. She didn't take a hit either, passing it to Marsha, who took it, hit on it, and passed it back to Norm.

"What's the story on the weird haircut?" Danny asked Oakley.

"Oakley's a seeker," Fred said. "He's looking for the right hairstyle."

"A serious and meaningful quest," Norm said. "It's my theory that Oakley is a latent businessman, afraid to come out of the closet."

"He's just old-fashioned, like the boys I used to know in Iowa," Sandy said.

"You're really from *Iowa?*" Marsha asked.

"He thinks we're all here to escape reality," Norm said.

"Hey," Oakley said. "I'm right here. Why is everybody talking about me in the third person?"

Marsha was massaging Fred's neck. "What the hell are you doing here, Oakley? You should be back in the thick of things, taking care of business."

"Like you, Marsha," Fred said.

"Yeah. Maybe."

"The thick of things," Fred said, tapping on his temple, "is in your thick head."

"Fuck you, Fred. I know you can't hide from yourself and all that shit, but if Oakley wants to be where the action is, I think we'll all agree that Hawaii is maybe not the best place to be. The action is somewhere else, like back in LA. Or New York or San Francisco. Even Chicago. Oakley's right; this place is unreal."

"Maybe Kauai's unreal," Danny said, "but Oahu's real. Honolulu is a real city."

"Are you kidding?" Marsha asked. "You don't know shit about Honolulu. Just because it's urban doesn't mean it's real."

"Marsha's right," Norm said. "Honolulu is just pretending to be a real city. They have freeways, but nobody drives over fifty on them. And whenever it begins to rain, even if it's just a drizzle, all the cars slow down to twenty. The television stations run five or ten minutes behind schedule every day, but nobody cares! And Good Friday is a state holiday!"

"That's unconstitutional." Oakley said.

"They don't care!" Norm said.

"People live and die in Hawaii," Sandy said. "You don't call that real?"

"That's not what we're talking about," Marsha said.

"Nothing's real anymore, man," Norm said. "When you look up close, everything that seems to be real is coming apart. Nobody's putting things together now, they're taking things apart. The reality of American life is dissolving—with the help of lysergic acid. Then we'll bring it all back together again, recreate the reality. But this time around we'll do it right. Here at Taylor Camp, we're an important part of that phenomenon. We're helping to melt down the doors of perception. You got any acid, Danny?"

"You're so full of shit, Norm." Danny spit into the fire pit. "This place is nowhere."

"The place is here, the time is now," Fred said. "Take our young friend Danny, hiding out in the jungle. He feels so sorry for himself, holed up in...nowhere, his life in limbo. A person can't be expected to face up to the here-and-now when he's in limbo! Can he, Danny?"

"Leave him alone, Fred," Marsha said, bored.

Fred did not. "'If I could just clear up this deserter business,' he whines, 'Then everything would be OK' But if it cleared up today, do you think Danny would change? Not a chance in hell. He'd just find another reason to blame his miserable life on something else, another excuse not to be free. Am I right, Danny, or am I right?"

"You're full of shit. Maybe I'm a deserter, but you scuzbags are on R&R from your sanity!" He stared at Oakley for a couple of seconds. Then he ran out.

"Once again," Marsha said, "Danny misses the point by a mile."

"Nobody's illusions are safe around here," Norm said. "Anybody wanna go shovel some compost?"

"Is that dinner invitation still good, Oakley?" Sandy asked.

"Sure." He was thinking about Danny, that look. What did Danny want from him?

"Will you do the salad, Marsha?"

"Take off."

## LONG TIME PASSING

Barking dogs, manic birds, and grinding car ignitions wake me up on Saturday morning. There's just an inch of Absolut left in the bottle, so I take a pull and finish it off. Bracing.

Downstairs, I introduce myself to a woman in the kitchen making breakfast. Turns out she's the owner. She's in her fifties, stocky, strong, and healthy-looking, eyes shining with either long-held new-age visions or genuine wisdom, it's hard to tell which. I compliment her on the facilities, she thanks me, tells me coffee's outside, help yourself, smiling politely, her tone telling me she's too busy right now for small talk. On the lanai, I sit at a round glass-topped table.

Two other couples are already there, at tables nearby, drinking coffee. Both seem eager to chat, but I don't want to linger. We introduce ourselves and I offer a few brief replies to their questions. When breakfast is served, I eat quickly and bow out with a nod and a mumble.

On schedule, still early enough for a head-start on the throngs, kayak strapped to the foam-rubber-cylinder rack on the Neon, surfboard safely stashed in my room, I head for Tunnels.

At the west end of Hanalei Bay, the left tip of the horseshoe, I pull over at a scenic lookout. Visible across the bay near the other tip is what must be the Princeville hotel, not more than four stories high but sticking out conspicuously, a gigantic white layer cake against the green wall of the seacliff.

Back on the road to Haena, I drive past expensive-looking homes, several for sale, some offered for vacation rental. The stilt-homes I remember are still here, more elaborate now. Post-hurricane fortified architecture.

The short, narrow dirt road to Tunnels is lined with parked cars. Across the street, a boy sits on a folding chair in his driveway beside a sign, "Tunnels Beach Parking $5." Further down the road, past several "no parking" signs, I come to a well-remembered part of the road where it dips and a shallow stream runs across it. They haven't built a bridge, so the road probably still gets washed out in heavy rains. Just past the stream on the left is the big cave, where every tourist pulls over for a short look inside, and on the right Haena Beach Park, with its campground and parking lot, which is only half full. The park looks the same as it did back then, when we used to stop here, check out the surf, and walk up the beach a quarter mile to paddle in.

I figure I can launch the kayak from the shore right beside the lot, and reach the reef in five or ten minutes. Taylor Camp is just down the road, but I've got plenty of time, and I want to get my kayaking done before the wind starts blowing.

The morning blues of the sea and sky are sharp and saturated. The ocean is calm, cobalt-colored, waveless, scattered with swimmers and snorkelers. Outside I can see the bobbing flags of scuba divers and the flashing of kayak paddles. Some kayakers are floating in the center of the bay, pole-fishing.

My gray plastic rental kayak is bulky but not heavy, and steady in the water. I rest my back against the nylon sling seat and push off from the shore, feeling the pull of the paddle. I can see the bottom all the way out into the deep water. When I get out to the reef, where the waves break when there's a swell, no one else is around. It's near high tide and the reef is completely submerged. I find its edge, where the celadon shallows end, plunging into depths of royal blue. I stop paddling and look around.

I see something floating on the surface, round like a coconut. Then it disappears. I see another: a head popping up? The top of a shell? I slip up slowly, not paddling for the last few yards. A turtle is floating on the surface, head underwater. Its shell is at least two feet long. As

I pull up beside it, it lifts its head to get a look at me. Then, with an indignant snort and a startled splash, it disappears. I keep trying, but the turtles never stick around. They're too shy and skittish.

I sit in the kayak, enjoying the view of the cliffs from offshore, rising bright green into the sky. Around me, the surface of the water is as smooth as mirror glass. The morning sun illuminates the reefs with a blue-green glow. Calm and quiet, I wait.

In time my patience is rewarded. Another big one floats up for a look at me, as if wondering, Who is this creature attached to a long gray shell? It glides back and forth under the kayak, so gracefully it looks like it's flying. When it surfaces I can hear it breathe, in loud snorts.

After a few minutes, five or six of them surround me, floating suspended beside the kayak or swimming slowly beside it, some of them coming close enough to touch. I laugh out loud. Beautiful creatures, winglike front flippers curved and pointed, and sectioned like a reptile's skin. Their back flippers are broad and flat, like ducks' feet. Their top shells are patterned in hexagonal sections, each containing a tiny amber circle from which green, brown and yellow rays emanate like sunbeams. They look like shields made of seashells.

A breeze ripples the surface of the water, and the sun's rays superimpose additional patterns, in broad streaks of light, to the turtles' backs.

When the wind jacks up another notch, I call it a morning. I paddle in, drive back to Hanalei, rent the kayak for another day, and leave it in the B&B's garage.

After lunch I head back to Ke'e. The lot at Haena Beach Park is full, and cars line the roadsides, some with parking tickets on their windshields. Beyond the park, the road narrows as the mountains come up close and the jungle closes in. On the mountain side I see something new, some kind of botanical garden. The sign reads "Limahuli Gardens, National Tropical Botanical Garden, Admission By Appointment Only," and a phone number. I remember reading about this place, where a mountain-climbing botanist discovered a new species of plant growing on the side of a vertical cliff.

Just past Lumahai, a sign on the ocean side of the road: "Haena State Park." Nothing that looks like a park; all jungle. I pass a dirt clearing where cars are parked, but it's not the old Taylor Camp lot, I can tell. I must have already passed that, because I'm suddenly at Ke'e, the end of the road. The place is packed with parked cars, at least a hundred, with a dozen drivers looking for parking spots, slowly negotiating the turnaround. I turn the car around and park in the spillover lot. It's a quarter mile back to Ke'e, past the road-level wet cave, past the trail to the wet cave on the hillside, past a sign that says "No camping in park."

Ke'e is bustling. Hundreds of people on the beach, dozens more headed in or out of the Kalalau trail along the Na Pali cliffs. Restroom and shower facilities have been installed, as well as a kiosk with trail information. Beside the restroom, six different signs warn swimmers against various dangers: strong currents, rip currents, high surf, waves breaking on the ledge, the sudden drop-off, and slippery rocks.

I decide to approach from the beach, walking back along the strip of sand in the direction of Hanalei. I sit in the sand to check out the surf, but there is none. The tide is high, so I can't see the reef. The surf is flat, so I can't locate the spot we called "Impossibles."

Likewise, on land I recognize no Taylor Camp landmarks. The jungle is overgrown, a tangled organic wall, its interior darkness a stark contrast to the harsh afternoon sunlight on the sand and water.

When I cross the mouth of a stream, a flash of recognition: Limahuli Stream, the camp's main waterway. At the ocean's edge the stream is broad and shallow; as it curves into the jungle it deepens and narrows, its banks rising two or three feet. Eventually it disappears into darkness.

Limahuli was the only one of three streams running through Taylor Camp that had a name. It was our designated community bath. The first thing we told newcomers was, "This big stream is for bathing, this other one for washing clothes and dishes, and the little one is where we get our drinking water. Follow these rules and nobody gets sick."

Most of the treehouses were on the Ke'e side of the stream, so that's where I head into the jungle. A sand and dirt road runs parallel to the shoreline just behind a beachfront phalanx of ironwoods, shedding their thin needles and gumball-sized cones. The road wasn't here before. Beyond it, the undergrowth is dense and unwelcoming; beneath a canopy of sixty-foot kamani trees is a tangle of tree roots, crawling vines, spider webs, staghorn ferns, fallen leaves, decaying logs, and broken branches. Big kamani seeds are everywhere, looking like miniature versions of the pods from *The Invasion of the Body Snatchers*. I remember how I used to stick my pocket knife into the seeds, then twist them around the blade and break them open to get to the edible nuts inside.

Something's missing. What happened to the guava trees? They used to be everywhere, their yellow-skinned, red-meated fruits decaying on the jungle floor, devoured by roaches, worms, and clouds of fruit flies. Now I can't find a single one, can't smell the sharp stench of rotting guavas. I remember that I would always cut them in half before biting into them, to make sure there were no worms inside. An old song comes to mind, with a new lyric: *Where have all the guavas gone, long time passing?*

Unseen birds chatter in the trees; wild chickens scurry through the brush. I try to maintain my orientation: the beach at my back, Limahuli Stream on my left. I trudge around randomly, looking for signs of previous habitation. I follow what I think is a trail until it disappears into nothing. I'm wearing only shorts and a tank top, low-cut hiking shoes and socks, but the heat is oppressive and I'm dripping sweat from my forehead. I forgot to bring mosquito repellent, so I swat and scratch.

I find another trail and again it leads nowhere. I try to force my way through the jungle to the road, but soon lose my sense of direction and don't know where I'm going or where I came from. I turn in a direction I hope is back, thinking that it's closer to the beach than the road. Eventually I get back to the beach, frustrated and tired.

Back in my room, after dark, I sit at my tiny desk, a converted antique wood-topped sewing machine, the chair back so close to the bed that I have to straddle it to sit down. I try to write but I can't. So I stretch out on the bed and let my mind wander.

Why am I going to all this trouble? What exactly do I hope to find? I don't really know. But here I am, wandering through "Ha'ena State Park," nothing but wilderness, the tropical, impenetrable kind, which is all right with me but not preferable to what it replaced. For nothing beyond decorum, the state destroyed a working alternative community. Tomorrow I'll go back to look for it again.

I flip through another book I found in the B&B library, Carlos Castaneda's *The Teachings of Don Juan: A Yaqui Way of Knowledge*. I remember when I first read it, at Taylor Camp. Fred the Zen loaned it to me. What a coincidence that it's here again, waiting for me.

"Helloooo. Alternate-O, are you there?"

No answer. I open the book at random.

I chance upon the part where Don Juan leaves Carlos Castaneda alone for a night, in a cabin in Mexico, to find his "spot" on the porch, the "spot" being a place where a person feels strong and happy. Carlos doesn't have the slightest clue how to go about it, but unless he finds his spot, Don Juan will have nothing more to say to him and he will have to go home. And also, if Carlos doesn't find his spot, he'll be in danger.

The next page I flip to describes four enemies on the path to becoming a man of knowledge. First fear. Then clarity, because when you have conquered fear you see clearly and think you know everything. Overcome this second enemy with its false sense of power and the impatience that comes with it, and you achieve true power. But power is the third enemy, if you don't hold it in check.

The final enemy is old age. You grow tired, you want to rest, to stop learning and changing. Give in to this enemy, and your life is over before you get the prize.

You become a diminished thing.

"I'm on to you, Alternate-O," I say to the sky above. "I know why you did this."

But there's no answer.

## POISONING THE WELL

"Hello there?" A stranger's voice called from the trail.

Norm, Fred, Soundtrack, and Oakley were hanging out at Fred's treehouse, sitting on the stools and benches, shooting the shit and smoking some, too. Norm snuffed the doobie and stashed it in his bag.

Two men walked in—untanned, in cheap aloha shirts, Bermuda shorts, black shoes and socks, shirts were stained with sweat, hair slick, panting and suffering in the hot wet air.

"Can we come in?" the taller of the two asked with a plastered-on smile.

"You're already in," Fred said. "May we help you?"

The shorter one, eyes darting around, taking it all in, said, "Yeah, we're looking for somebody. Thought you might be able to help us find him."

"Gee," Fred said, "I wonder what you guys do for a living."

The tall one says, "Don't get uptight, my friend. Peace. Love. You wouldn't like us to go digging through your kitchen, would you? Never know what we might turn up. Maybe something could put you away for a long time. I'll bet your friends here have some great shit right in their pockets!"

"I don't partake in illegal drugs," Norm said.

"Me neither," Oakley said.

"My ass," the short one said.

"Sure smells like pot," the tall one said.

"This is my home," Fred said. "If you want to look around, I'd like to see some identification and a search warrant."

"We don't need a warrant to bust an old faggot shacking up in an illegal structure in the jungle with underage males and females," the short one said. "I'll bet you're growing a crop right out back."

Taking the cue, shifting into a lisp, Fred said, "I *so* would like to see some identification."

"Sure," the tall one said, pulled out his wallet, flashed a card and repocketed it.

"I barely got a glimpse," Fred protested. "May I please see it again?"

"You wouldn't understand it anyway, old man," the tall one said. "Let's just say we're with a classified branch of the military police. We're looking for a guy name of Dawson. David Dawson. Know where we might find him?"

Still lisping, Fred said, "No such person in these parts. Listen, if you're military police, you have no authority over civ—"

"Shut the fuck up," the short one said. He asked Norm, "What about you?"

"Never heard the name. Got a photo?"

"Fuck photos. Cut the bullshit. We know all about him. He's camping out somewhere around here. Where is it?"

"We told you," Fred said, "we never heard of him." He turned to Norm. "Darling, why do we even bother with Jehovah's Witnesses? They never listen, they just talk."

"I told you to shut up, you old queen," the short one said.

"How about you?" the tall one asked Oakley. "You got a friend named David, or Dave?"

"Never heard of anybody called Dave."

The tall one turned to Soundtrack. Soundtrack shook his head.

"Are you freaked out on angel dust, or did your old wife here rip out your tongue?"

Soundtrack did not respond.

"He's fulfilling a vow of silence," Oakley said. "This guy Dave was a soldier?"

"He *is* a soldier," the short one said. "Look, we know that somebody who fits his description is hiding out somewhere in this shithole. He's 22, blond hair, good build, smokes two packs a day, has a bad attitude toward authority. You must have seen him."

"Surely you can give us a better description that that, officer," Fred said, still lisping. "Are his lips thick or thin? Are his limbs supple? Give us a hint, Dick Tracy. Did you do a dick tracing? How long is it?"

"I'll give you a hint of brain damage," the short one said.

"Easy," his partner said. "They say they don't know. Maybe they do, maybe they don't. We'll just have to take their word for it."

"By any chance," the short one said, indicating Soundtrack, "is this guy related to the Manson family?"

"Not by blood," Norm said.

"Not by blood!" Fred screeched, gently slapping his knee. "That's so precious!"

"Maybe we'll take a walk down the trail," the tall one said. "Maybe we'll find something. In which case, we'll come back to take you away for harboring a fugitive."

"This Dave guy is AWOL?" Oakley asked.

"A deserter," the tall one said. "He's in deep shit."

"I gotta take a pee," his partner said, addressing Norm. "Which way to your water supply?"

"Three miles up the mountain," Norm said.

The cops left. Nobody spoke.

Norm broke the silence: "They'll never find Danny's tent. I just hope they don't piss in the stream." He dug out the joint and relighted it.

Fred untied a bunch of bananas hanging from a rafter, and offered them around.

"Move over, Maui Wowie," Norm said, taking a hit, "here comes Kow-eye Wow-eye." He offered the joint to Fred, who was busy wolfing down bananas and refused. Soundtrack took a hit and passed it to Oakley. Oakley took a hit and passed it back to Norm.

A scream came from above, followed by a series of sharp thuds from the far side of the plank ceiling.

"Son of a bitch!"

"Marsha!" Fred yelled. "You're gonna bring down the house!"

"Ugh! Fucking monster!"

Something fell from the opening at the top of the ladder. Norm checked it out.

"Big one. Five inches. Still not quite dead."

Marsha descended the ladder in a skimpy red two-piece. Fred gave Oakley a lascivious wink. She pounded the writhing centipede with the heel of a sandal.

"It's dead, the bastard," Marsha said. "Curled up inside the sheets. Scared the shit out of me." She kicked the thing into the jungle. "I wonder how those MPs know Danny's here?"

"He wants to get caught," Fred said. "For him it's the only way out of limbo."

Norm re-lighted the joint, took a drag, passed it to Marsha. She took a whiff before toking on it.

"Smells like incense."

"Intensely aromatic," Norm agreed. "Superior to even the finest pipe tobaccos."

Danny appeared, not from the trail but materializing out of the dense jungle behind the banyan tree. He was wearing blue jeans, a sleeveless T-shirt and hiking boots. He was smoking a cigarette.

"Hey, Danny," Norm said. "Or is it Dave? Better lay low. The man's looking for you."

Danny tossed the butt and stamped it out.

"You think I don't know that? I've been tracking those assholes for an hour. They didn't even look for my tent. They left right after they talked to you. I loved that homo routine, Fred. You really shook 'em up with that one!"

"I wish you wouldn't sneak around the underbrush and spy on people all the time," Norm said. "You're giving everybody the creeps. We're not in 'Nam, you know."

"Yeah, I know. We're in America where it's a free country and I can do anything I want."

"Did the short one piss in the stream?" Oakley asked.

"The tall one talked him out of it."

"Let's put Danny's military training to good use, Norm," Fred said. "Let's recruit him for latrine duty."

"Fuck you," Danny said. "I'm busy."

"Try some of this man, mellow out." Norm offered the joint.

"No thanks."

"Danny-Dave Detour-Dawson turns down free dope," Norm said. "It's a first."

"I dropped some mescaline. I'm starting to come on."

"Good thinking, Danny," Marsha said. "Don't adulterate that first psychedelic rush."

"Can you switch tracks?" Fred asked.

"What does that mean?"

"Can you change horses?"

"Too late now," Danny said. He gave Oakley a quick glance.

"If you get caught," Fred said, "You can always uncatch yourself."

"Don't worry 'bout me, pops. I'm just havin' some fun."

"Remember what I said."

"I already forgot." Danny's attention was diverted by something he saw on the ground.

"When we, the pioneers, took hallucinogenic drugs," Norm said, "we did it to open our minds and explore our souls and ponder the meaning of life. Now Danny does it for kicks. That could mean anything from beating his meat to skinning a mongoose."

"Don't worry," Danny said, "I won't bother you. I won't murder anybody, either, like they do in 'Nam, snuffin' commie gooks for Uncle Sam!" He let out a maniacal laugh, then again became absorbed in whatever he saw at his feet.

"I just invented my true calling," Norm said. "Owner and operator of Earth's first psychedelic travel agency! I could come up with different itineraries for a bunch of pre-packaged consciousness-expanding trips. Then people like Danny, who have no idea of the true potential of LSD, would come to me. And I would customize a package for them, based on a preliminary interview, and be the guide on their individualized trip sequences."

"What do you mean?" Oakley asked. "Like a menu of things to experience? Music, food, a phone call to your ex-wife?"

"Yeah," Norm said. "Whatever."

"There's your first customer." Oakley indicated Danny, who was now on hands and knees, studying the dirt floor of Fred's kitchen. "Hey, Danny!"

"Shhh!" Danny hissed.

"Danny doesn't need you, Norm," Marsha said. "He can entertain himself."

"Due to their educational value," Norm said, "my trips would be tax-deductible. Night school for life skills."

"What's in Danny's sequence?" Oakley asked.

"I would instruct him to dig foxholes and fill them back up, like they do in the Army. But instead of a drill sergeant hollering orders at him, it would be me standing there, reading him the Myth of Sisyphus."

"I read that in school," Marsha said. "What a downer."

"No way," Norm said. "It's hope for mankind. The idea that we can find affirmation in absurdity. What a concept!"

"Norm's right," Oakley said. "Deeply felt, fully involved participation in the meaningless, repetitive, fruitless activities of life is a triumph of the spirit."

"When you put it that way," Norm said, "it gives me second thoughts."

"These bugs are frickin' fantastic!" Danny said. He crawled off into the jungle.

"I see Danny's future," Fred said, "in entomology."

## DOWN WITH PRECONCEPTIONS

Oakley was hired to teach at Woodknoll Preparatory Academy, a small private high school in Santa Monica. Class size was limited to fifteen students, and he was allowed to determine the content of his own courses—syllabi, reading lists, writing assignments, tests, everything. Another bonus: The school was only a ten-minute drive from his Venice apartment, so he could slip in a dawn-patrol surf session before school began, as long as he didn't drive too far to find waves. He began teaching in the fall of 1967.

He didn't like standing in front of his students, the "him vs. them" scenario it set up, them seated in rows before him, him separated by his big gunmetal desk, him turning his back on them to write on the blackboard, him standing, them sitting, him giving, them receiving, him spouting words of wisdom, them writing it all down.

Also he didn't like standing in front of his students because, after about fifteen minutes, his left leg would go numb.

He went to see a doctor to find out what was wrong. It turned out that he had scoliosis, a lateral curvature of the spine. The doctor told him that, because his left leg was half a centimeter shorter than his right, and because his muscles were more developed on the right side of his back (to the point where he had a visible hump of muscle mass on that side), he had probably had this condition since childhood. He had either been born with it or might have suffered a slight and undetectable case of polio.

There was little to be done about the numb leg, which was probably caused by the physical asymmetry resulting from his scoliosis. If he were female, the doctor told him, it would be a problem. Women, especially if they got pregnant and put more pressure on their pelvises, tended to have more severe symptoms of scoliosis that could require prolonged and painful procedures to straighten their spines. But Oakley's scoliosis was minor and would probably not cause any additional trouble—although, the doctor said, it would probably disqualify him from military service. He gave Oakley a booklet containing recommended exercises.

In his classroom, Oakley rearranged the rows of desk chairs into a circle. He sat at one of the chairs and conducted discussions in lieu of lectures.

It was Joe's idea to see Krishnamurti when he spoke at the Santa Monica Civic Auditorium. The Civic was where Oakley used to see surf movies, narrated live by the filmmakers—Bruce Brown, John Severson, Bud Browne—while bleach-blond gremlins, with snaps of their fingers, flipped bottle caps through the air and hooted.

They arrived late. The auditorium was almost full, and the only seats left were up high and way back. Krishnamurti appeared as a tiny figure, alone on the stage hundreds of yards away from Joe and Oakley, the stage bare except for the chair he was sitting on and a table beside it which held a glass of water. He spoke without notes. He spoke so softly that Oakley could barely hear him. Little noises, people rustling in their seats, were irritating. He strained to make out what Krishnamurti was saying.

Then something happened. All the distractions in the auditorium suddenly faded away, and all Oakley could hear was Krishnamurti, every word he spoke, crisp and clear. He could also see Krishnamurti's face, every expression, as if he, Oakley, were sitting on the stage directly in front of the man. The universe was reduced to two beings, Krishnamurti and Oakley.

Krishnamurti told Oakley: Our perception of life is shaped by the concepts already established in our minds. We can't look at a tree because our botanical knowledge prevents it. We can't look at a friend because our preconceived image of that friend prevents it.

He told Oakley: Don't condemn, explain away, justify. Observe without comparing, analyzing, judging. The explanation, the description, is not the thing.

When you become aware of the movement of your own thoughts, he said, you will see the division between the thinker and thought, the observer and the observed, the experiencer and the experience. You will discover that this division is an illusion.

If you want to know the purpose of your life, he said, first free your mind from its own conditioning and then ask the question. And perhaps you will find that when your mind is free, that very freedom itself is the purpose of life.

When Krishnamurti left the stage, the sounds of the world around Oakley resumed. He felt as if he were coming out of a trance. As he left the auditorium, he described his experience to Joe.

Joe said, "That is really *weird*. The same thing happened to me."

## HANGING WITH HONU

Up at dawn on Sunday, I skip the B&B breakfast, strap the kayak on the car, put a mesh bag full of additional gear in the trunk, and get coffee and a bagel at a convenience store.

I'm back at Tunnels early. Less than a dozen cars are in the lot. Paddling out in the clear water, the color of malachite, I can make out the hooked shape of the reef. Inside the hook's curve is the lagoon. Out at the edge, there are still no waves, not even a swell to bob the kayak. I'm calmly floating on an undulating mirror reflecting the sky and clouds. I paddle to a spot about a quarter mile from shore. I can see people walking on the beach.

Today I know what to do: Paddle gently and glide, then sit still and wait. And I'm better equipped. In my bag are a face mask, snorkel, fins and thirty feet of yellow nylon rope.

The turtles show up, curious, hovering, circling, slowly writing figure eights beneath the hull, cruising from side to side. I tie one end of the rope to the bow ring on the kayak, the other to the strap of my right fin, and slip in to join them.

Tolerant or indifferent, they let me get up close. Time must be different to these creatures, suspended in silent blue liquid, serenely winging along or lounging on the reef, munching seaweed.

I read in a booklet at the kayak rental shop that turtles haven't evolved much in 150 million years. I also read that it's illegal to approach as close to them as I am. But there's only me, and they don't seem to mind. I know I'm anthropomorphizing, but hey look wise, imperturbable. Watching them, I feel like I'm meditating.

I stay in the water more than an hour, tied to my kayak, diving and staying down as long as I can, then kicking up fast, gasping for air, my ears squeaking, then flipping down again, getting up close but never touching them, and sometimes just floating on the surface, watching.

Turtles aren't the only things out here. I see a cloud of skinny fish, synchronized swimmers with electric yellow fins. A school of white fish with black stripes, tiny undersea zebras. I follow some kind of manta ray with spots on its back, heading out beyond the edge of the reef, where it drops off into deep blue nothingness. And out there, in the watery distance, appears a vague shape of something large and familiar.

My heart leaps but I keep my head. I don't panic, splash frantically, attract attention, show it I'm scared…just calmly get the fuck out of there. I'm consciously trying not to influence or create the reality that will make me shark bait. Maybe it's too far away to have spotted me. Maybe it has and doesn't care. I know that sharks eat turtles and, therefore, if there are turtles around, I should be OK. But then I look back down at the reef. The turtles are gone.

I flip to the surface and over to the kayak, trying to move fast without splashing too much. I pull myself out of the water. Relief. I take off the fins and mask, looking around, trying to spot the shark. Nothing. It could be a half-mile away by now, on some pelagic highway to a distant shore. Sharks rarely attack people. Still, why take a chance?

Enough turtle-watching. It's time to return the equipment and get back to Taylor Camp for another round of exploration.

As I untie the rope from my swim fin and start to haul it in, it gets jerked out of my hands and disappears over the side. Immediately I feel a sickening lurch as the rope pulls taut in front of the bow ring and yanks the kayak into motion. The paddle falls over the side, but it's attached by a coiled leash and I retrieve it. As the kayak gets pulled out to sea, the bow begins to dip into the water, so I get down on my belly, grab the rope and pull. It's angling into the water at about forty-five-degrees. The shark—or whatever it is that's got hold of the rope—is heading for deep water. I figure I can ride it out until the thing gets tired and lets go. Still on my belly, I keep trying to pull the rope free, but the pressure is too strong.

The kayak noses under, launching me and my equipment into the water. I let go of the rope, afraid of being dragged under or hit on the head by the hull. I fetch my fins and mask, floating nearby, and put them back on. I'm alone in the water, dog-paddling and turning in circles, far now from the reef, maybe a half mile from shore, with no one else in sight. The kayak is gone.

I'm frightened because I'm so exposed. It's hard not to panic. I swim quickly but calmly and deliberately for shore, thankful for the fins. On a last look back out to sea, I spot the kayak floating there, inert, about a hundred yards away.

For a moment I can't figure out what to do. Swim for shore and forget about the kayak, paying the rental company whatever it costs for a replacement? Or go back for it, assuming that the shark isn't hanging around, waiting for me, using the kayak like bait? I decide to abandon it: better to lose a couple of hundred dollars than my life.

But then, about halfway to shore, I see another kayaker and flag him down. He agrees to take me back out. We find the kayak floating upright, undamaged, the paddle still attached but in the water, the seat and deck dry in the morning sun. All that's missing is the mesh bag. I get into the kayak and pull in the rope, checking it for teeth marks, finding none. The kayaker wishes me well and pushes off with a look that suggests I might want to keep my shark story to myself.

# SECOND SURFIN' SATORI

In the dark, he heard a call.

"Rise and shine, Oakley! Get your board! Let's go!"

His awakening consciousness identified the voice.

"Where?"

No answer.

Oakley never had a problem getting up, especially with the anticipation of riding the day's first waves. Trunks, T-shirt, rubber slippers, towel, surfboard, and flashlight. The only sounds on the trail were the crunching of his own footsteps, and the slapping of rubber against the soles of his feet.

On the rack of Fred's station wagon was a ten-foot relic from the early sixties. They strapped Oakley's short board on top of it.

"Where?"

"Tunnels."

"Didn't know you surfed."

"I have a surfboard, don't I?"

"That log? It's a museum piece. Looks like nobody's ridden it for ten years."

With an expression of pity, Fred pulled out onto the unilluminated road. The big Buick's left headlight was burned out, but one was enough. Fred drove like a navigator on a ship leaving harbor, with focused awareness, holding the speedometer between five and ten m.p.h.

"Think you can get us there before noon?" Oakley asked.

"One was enough," Fred said.

"One what?"

"How's your back? All healed? Sometimes those coral cuts never go away."

"I'm OK. One *what* was enough?"

"The day your hurt yourself."

Oakley figured it out.

"Getting tubed like that doesn't happen all the time. I wanted to make it happen again."

"You stopped surfing, started showing off."

"I wasn't showing off!"

Fred's eyes widened in mock amazement.

"If I can get an emotion like that out of you, if you get defensive, if I've hurt your feelings, then you've got some hang-ups to get rid of."

"You don't have any?"

"Doesn't everybody? But we're talking about you."

"You brought up the subject, not me."

"Then let's talk about—oh, I don't know…*surfing*. OK?"

Oakley looked away, not eager to play the game.

"A wave gives you a gift, the gift of its energy and form. Your obligation is to receive it properly. How do you do that, Oakley?"

To Oakley, it was a fair question. Why not go with it, a pseudo-Socratic dialogue with Fred?

"I do my best to ride the wave well."

"Can you be more specific? How do you ride a wave 'well'?"

"With skill and style."

"Still too abstract. What are 'skill' and 'style'?"

"OK: Using the energy and shape of the wave in the best possible manner."

"And how is that done?"

"You use a minimum amount of your own energy. And you're in the best location of the wave."

"Where is that?"

"Deep."

"Voila!" Fred shouted, triumphant. "That's your hangup, Oakley, you don't ride deep enough."

Oakley felt a flash of pressure pushing out from the insides of his face. Caught again.

"You can't avoid danger," Fred said. "You need to be in the middle of it, precisely where the wave is most threatening, as close as you can get, doing your dance on the edge, maneuvering in and out of danger. Agreed?"

"If you put it that way, sure."

"I've seen you surf, Oakley. You're too timid. You turn too soon. You ride too far out on the shoulder. You put yourself in a place where you're not getting the most out of the wave."

"I'm having a hard time getting used to Hawaiian waves."

"Surfing is living. Everything is everything. You're living too safe. You're not taking enough chances."

Oakley noted the way Fred maneuvered from one topic to another.

"I'm a draft evader and I'm not taking enough chances?"

"Not the one you need to take. Go home and face the consequences. Then you can either go to Vietnam or stay put and refuse to obey. In either case, your life would be progressing."

"What makes you think it's not progressing now?"

"You've got 'limbo' written all over you. You and Danny. That's why he feels a connection with you."

"You see that?"

"You've got a lot to learn, Oakley."

"This is why you got me up in the dark? To lecture me?"

"No. It's time for a surfing lesson."

Fred pulled over at the Haena Beach Park campground lot, engine running. In the pre-dawn they could barely make out the swells forming up off the point. It looked good, but Oakley couldn't estimate the size because no one was out riding, there was no perspective. It could have been three feet or eight feet.

Two hundred yards down the road, Fred turned left onto a wide dirt path, the closest public access to the shortest paddle out. From the beach park it was a long walk. Here it was a few steps from their car, the first of the day parked at the end of the road where the packed dirt gives way to soft sand.

"You're going to give *me* a surfing lesson?"

Fred didn't answer.

"I admit, I'm a little too cautious in the way I surf."

"Not anymore."

"Since when?"

"Since the first wave you caught that day at Impossibles. You made it. Suspended your trepidation. Took a chance. It's easy from now on. You know how it's done."

This was one of the ways Fred always surprised Oakley, with his quick changes from criticism to praise.

"Usually you fail before you succeed. You're telling me I succeeded on the first wave, then failed on the second. It happened in reverse order."

"Who says things happen in one particular order? As soon as you turn the valve, even a little, the whole universe opens up. God and the Devil, everybody's there. There's a point where you get beyond the idea of degrees, and all of a sudden it's all or nothing. You could be there if you wanted to."

"Not sure I want to be there," Oakley said. "I kinda like certain aspects of limbo."

"Too bad for you. Continue on that path and you're condemned to a sad life of compromise and regret."

Fred and Oakley waxed their boards and walked down to the water. No one else was on the beach or paddling out.

"You're sure you want to do this?" Oakley asked. "Tunnels is not a good wave for longboards."

"We could think up excuses, or we could go out and catch some rides."

"Let's go."

It was an absolutely beautiful dawn. The strengthening light revealed a sky free of clouds. The water was smooth and slick, unrippled by the tradewinds that would come up in an hour or two.

The breaking waves were five feet high from crest to trough, full of energy but not threatening. The ocean welcomed the visitors, making it easy for them to paddle out through the deep channel adjacent to the churning curls hitting the shallow reef. The rising sun illuminated the advancing walls of water.

Although they pushed off from shore at the same time, Fred quickly moved many yards ahead, paddling with deep, quick strokes. Oakley couldn't catch up. By the time they reached the lineup, he was already riding his first wave.

Oakley watched Fred, quick and agile, too old to be so flexible, stand on his antique platform in an upright posture of control, relaxed and confident, not the stance of a fifty-year-old man. He swung the long, heavy plank smoothly to the right, just in front of the wave's cascading lip.

At that point, if Oakley had been riding the wave, he would have crouched and waited until he popped out from under the curl, then maybe carved out an off-the-lip cutback, slapped the top of the wave as it broke, then descended quickly to the bottom for another snap-turn.

Instead, in the style of the sixties, appropriate for the board he was riding, Fred calmly walked forward, not shuffling but raising one foot slowly off the deck in front of the other so that, most of the time, he appeared to be balancing on only one foot.

As he moved, the entire platform rose to a point just beneath the wave's forming curl. At his final destination, with the toes of both feet curling down over the nose of the board, he stood straight and still, arms undramatically draped at his sides, completely synchronized with the motion of the wave.

Oakley watched in bug-eyed disbelief. Fred moved as he had never moved before, at least in Oakley's presence, merging with the wave, riding in the most critical spot, calmly balancing and trimming the long plank across the waveface, wasting none of his own energy, letting the wave supply it. Oakley paddled up the waveface a couple of yards in front of Fred, getting a close-up of his facial expression, one of utter calm and total attention. Fred changed his path slightly, aiming at Oakley, barely missing him as he passed by with a wink and a grin.

Out in the lineup, before Oakley could catch his first wave, Fred got his second with a no-paddle take-off after sitting and waiting for the swell to come to him, swinging his board around to face the shore, tilting it down the slope, giving it a push into the wave, then smoothly standing and sliding into the wave's shoreward motion. Oakley had never seen anyone catch a wave with so little effort.

For the next half hour, Oakley and Fred had the waves to themselves, Oakley doing all right, Fred surfing with the confidence and agility of a twenty-year-old pro. As soon as someone else paddled out, Fred was gone. Oakley caught a final wave and joined him onshore.

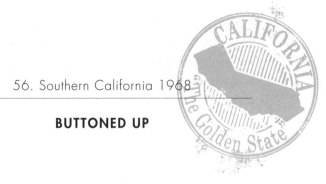

## BUTTONED UP

Early June, school out. Oakley began his three months of freedom by camping out for two nights at Big Bear Lake, a two-hour, hundred-mile drive east of Los Angeles.

Along with camping equipment, food and drink, he brought a bag of peyote buttons, a gift from Crystal and Dylan, who had just returned from their annual pilgrimage to Mexico loaded with the stuff. Its source was a woolly cactus that grew all over the northern desert plateau, not hard to find if you knew what you were looking for, and they did.

For the trip, the hippie pair had cut their hair and disguised themselves as straight people, wearing civilian clothing, coming across as gringo tourists taking advantage of Mexico's cheap hotels and food, the strength of the dollar versus the peso.

In three days, driving across hundreds of miles of desert that the Yaqui Indians historically trekked on foot during their ceremonial peyote hunts, Dylan and Crystal had collected hundreds of mescal buttons, plucking off the dried tops of the cacti, and smuggled their booty across the border sewn into goose down sleeping bags.

Oakley had never tried peyote before, but Dylan raved about it—"totally organic, nothing artificial or manufactured, a pure and smooth and natural trip"—and had briefed him with careful instructions for its preparation and consumption.

Oakley also did some research at the Powell Library, to which he still had access as a member of the UCLA Alumni Association. He learned that the woolly cactus, botanical name *Lophophora williamsii*, grew only in northern Mexico and south Texas. For possibly more than three thousand years, it had been used for its vision-inducing properties, medicinal qualities, and what one book had described as "beautiful intoxication."

When the Spanish arrived and conquered the territory, they had condemned peyote because of its "diabolic fantasies" and "satanic trickery." But the indigenous people, who imbibed it regularly, claimed that it sustained them, freed them from fear and hunger and thirst, gave them strength and courage, and induced fantastic hallucinations.

Arriving in the early afternoon, Oakley found a campsite on the lake that rented rowboats. After pitching his tent, he ventured out onto the lake. The afternoon was sunny but cool. A breeze rippled the water's surface. Turkey vultures cruised high above.

Rowing beside the shore, within an hour he found what he was looking for: a rock outcropping in an unpopulated place, a private spot where no one would bother him.

He rowed back to the campsite and cooked himself dinner on his Coleman stove, brown rice with chunks of canned tuna, cut-up carrots, zucchini, spinach, garlic, and onions. Inside his tent he smoked a joint and read, by lantern light, Graham Greene's *A Burnt-Out Case*.

Shortly after dawn on the next morning, skipping breakfast, Oakley set out. He was carrying food, water, and the baggie of peyote buttons. The morning air was chilly, the lake glassy and peaceful, populated by only a few fishermen.

He roped his rowboat to a rock at the water's edge and climbed with his supplies up the small promontory, about twenty feet above the water, looking out over the lake and backed by a thick pine wood. On top of the rock was a flat area, about fifteen feet wide and thirty feet deep, covered with grass and a few small trees.

Dylan had warned Oakley to take care when he prepared the buttons. He had to scrape off all the white hair on them, which contained strychnine. Oakley had eight buttons, which Dylan felt was the ideal amount for a decent trip. Sometimes Dylan and Crystal had consumed up to a dozen, and they had friends who claimed to have eaten thirty in a single night.

One after another, Oakley ate the buttons. They tasted bitter, but he chewed them thoroughly before swallowing, as Dylan had instructed.

When he was done he sat at the edge of the rock, looking out over the lake, waiting. The sun was shining, the day was warming and white clouds were reflected on the lake waters.

After about twenty minutes, Oakley's stomach began to feel upset. Dylan had prepared him for this: "You're going to throw up. But it's all right. It actually feels good. That's the beauty of it. You purge your system, get rid of the bad stuff, and all that's left is the good stuff."

Dylan was right. When Oakley upchucked, it didn't feel anything like when he had had too much alcohol. There was no retching or heaving. He simply opened his mouth and, without effort or resistance, it came. It was a smooth, natural motion, a purging that was the reverse of swallowing. It was over in less than a minute, and his stomach was calm again.

He rinsed out his mouth, drank some water from his canteen, and poured a little over the pool of vomit to dilute it as it sank into the ground.

He felt light and clean and clear. His stomach was empty but he wasn't hungry.

"When the stomach pain disappears," Dylan had told him, "you'll feel like you've been set free from your body. And then you'll spend the next eight hours feeling very content, very comfortable, and unlike on some kinds of acid, very unagitated. And all the while you'll be having amazing thoughts and feelings and visions."

Right again, Dylan. Oakley felt such an overwhelming sense of well-being that it brought a smile to his face. He laughed out loud, a shout of a laugh. He lay on his back and looked at the sky, light blue interspersed with pillows of clouds.

He had read that native Americans who used peyote regarded it as a "divine messenger" that let them communicate with God without the medium of priests. But whoever wrote that was wrong, he thought, to use the word "God" and even the word "priest." What tribe believed in God, one God, and had priests? Better words would be "the Creators" and "shamans."

Never mind. Oakley was alone, away from everything, content and fearless—even as the world around him shifted into another reality. He saw things in the clouds: faces, breasts, castles, dragons, ships, cartoon characters. For a moment the sky looked like a thin veil with something behind it, something he could not make out.

He felt supremely grateful to be where he was, *who* he was, outside in a beautiful place, surrounded by things natural rather than artificial. The colors of sky, jewel-faceted water, rock, dirt, grass, tree branches and leaves were rich and kaleidoscopic, gleaming in infinite vibrant hues.

He wondered what messages the messenger was delivering to him. His mind wandered.

*Who am I?*

*Why am I here?*

*RFK assassinated two days ago. Martin Luther King assassinated two months ago. What the fuck is going on? Nothing I can influence or control. All I can do is focus on the immediate sphere, my personal reality, my social milieu. Everything else is beyond by reach. Work on myself, do what I can, and that will project outward to influence whatever it can. Otherwise, it's useless.*

The fact that reality is only consensual made it disappear. Oakley, in a dissociative mode, understood that nothing was what he had been led to believe it was. This was a cause not for terror but for bliss. The sky was not made of air, the water was not water, the rock he sat on was not solid. He stood and thought about diving from the non-existent rock into the non-existent water. What a thrill it would be.

He stripped to his swimming trunks, taking off his hiking boots, socks, blue jeans, flannel shirt, and t-shirt. He stood on the edge of the rock and prepared to dive. But something held him back: a vision of a skull-splitting impact on a rock two feet beneath the water.

Barefoot, he climbed back down to the water's edge, waded over mossy stones into the shallows and dove into the water. It was cold but not uncomfortable. It was invigorating. The liquid ran over his body in a pleasurable way.

He swam out a couple of yards, looking up at the overhang where he would attempt his dive. He figured he couldn't launch himself outward more than couple of yards. In position of his estimated landing, he swam for the bottom. He touched it about ten feet down. It would be enough for a dive, if he pulled out soon enough.

He climbed back to the promontory, his skin warming up in the morning sun. He positioned himself at the edge of the rock. He dove.

During the freefall he hallucinated.

He envisioned stars, the earth from outer space, a musical crescendo visible on the surface of the sea. He understood the infinite. He felt terror and bliss simultaneously.

He fell through the air and hit the water, slicing through in a clean dive. He altered his impetus as quickly as he could, arcing away from his downward thrust into a horizontal momentum.

Stroking underwater, he looked at the green world before him. He surfaced, sucking in fresh air, gasping in need and exultation. He swam out from shore, then dove under again, eyes closed, feeling the liquid flow across his skin. He turned on his back and opened his eyes, looking at the sunlight filtering through the water, flickering and glittering. He stopped stroking and hung suspended, slowly floating to the surface through viscous fluid, surrounded by millions of microorganisms.

He swam to shore, climbed back up to the promontory and stretched out on the grass. The sun was high in the sky, warm on his bare stomach and legs. He rolled onto his stomach, breathing in the rich aromas of grass and soil. The patch of grass stretched into the distance and became an infinite jungle.

A breeze came up, rustled in the trees, and raised goose bumps on his skin. He marveled at his flesh, the bumps rising, set in motion by the breeze just like the pine needles in the trees. His skin was not solid, a barrier that separated his body from the air. It was all just molecules. The idea of his body, his self, separated from the world around him, was an illusion.

He shivered, stood, and put his clothes back on, then lay down on his back and closed his eyes. Behind his eyelids, colors danced and shapes floated.

*He threw his surfboard from the deck of a ship and jumped in after it. He caught and rode the ship's wake. He accelerated so much that he was lifted into the air. The surfboard changed into a large, light paddle that he held above his head like a sail. It occurred to him that it would be hard to find the ship again, but for some reason he was unconcerned.*

*He was flying, looking down on the green earth below, a full, round sphere. Above him, the sun appeared from behind a cloud, revealing that it was not dry land below, but wetlands—rice paddies. A wet fabric. No one could walk on that green blanket. It was not solid. Its earthiness was an illusion.*

*Then the paddies gave way to brown flatlands and low, round hills. Scattered everywhere were round buildings that looked like little pointed hats—hundreds of them, in clusters or standing alone, on hilltops, on the flatlands, beside rivers. The ones on the hilltops had steps leading up to them from four sides. The buildings were topped with golden spires.*

*A fantastic creature flew up beside him. It had the head of a lion, the body of a dragon, the wings of a bat, the tusks of an elephant, and the legs of a deer. It spoke to him.*

*"Don't you have something to ask me?"*

*"Who are you?"*

*"Wrong question."*

*"Who am I?"*

*"You are here."*

*"Why am I here?"*

*"Because you are who you are."*

*"What am I supposed to do?"*

*"Polish your soul."*

*The creature veered off and flew away. He tried to follow it but it was too fast for him, and was soon out of sight.*

When Oakley woke up, the sun was lower in the sky. He ate an apple and some trail mix, then climbed down the rock to his boat. As he rowed back to the campsite, he recalled the details of his dream—

the rice paddies, the round buildings that must have been temples or pagodas, the strange creature that flew beside him. It hadn't felt like a dream, but as if he had been there.

## IN THE CLUTCHES OF DEATH

Nighttime at Fred's treehouse. A single lantern illuminated the kitchen and its inhabitants. Oakley was stretched out naked on the picnic table, on his stomach, a towel over his buttocks, eyes shut. Scantily-clad, voluminously freckled, ivory-skinned Marsha was giving him a full-body massage, working from the neck and shoulders down to the calves.

"Now turn over." He turned, quickly moving the towel to cover his midsection.

"Why so shy? It's not like I haven't seen your dick before. I've had it in my *mouth*, for God's sake."

Oakley couldn't think of a reply, but he felt the beginnings of an erection. Marsha deftly massaged his feet, pushing the thumbs of both hands against the sole of one, and then the other.

"That feels good."

"People say you can massage a person's whole body without ever leaving the feet."

"I believe it."

"It's all connected." She worked up to his toes, massaged each one individually, then left her fingertips touching the tips of his toes for a moment before releasing them. "There. Don't move yet. Just relax. Keep your eyes closed."

Oakley heard a shuffling, then felt the touch of new hands on his feet, larger hands. He opened his eyes. It was Fred.

"Massage, part two. You heard the lady. Close your eyes." Fred pressed his thumbs against Oakley's instep.

"That's OK, Fred, Marsha did enough." He started to get up.

"Come on, relax. I'm not going to grab your dick or anything. Unless you want me to."

"No thanks." Oakley gave in. Fred knew what he was doing, as usual. His hands were stronger and his massage went deeper. He worked in the opposite direction that Marsha did, moving from Oakley's feet to his ankles, shins, kneecaps, and thighs. Then he reached around under the towel to massage the sides of Oakley's buttocks. Again, Oakley felt a twinge of an erection.

"Whoa!" Fred said. "Somebody's getting interested. Sure you don't want a hand job?"

"No, thanks. I'm not into men." Oakley, nervous, opened his eyes and propped himself up on an elbow.

"That's not what your cock seems to be saying."

"It's a natural reaction to touch. Like being tickled."

"You've got an answer for everything. Get back down. I'm not going to molest you."

Oakley lay back down, closed his eyes as Fred massaged his ribs, chest, underarms, and shoulders.

"If you weren't so uptight, you would have twice as many potential partners in the world for sex and love."

"What are you trying to do, turn me into a bisexual?"

"You're missing the point. It's about being free."

"I thought being free included freedom from desire and the distractions of the flesh."

"Be realistic. That only happens when you die. Or get yourself castrated."

"Then being free means becoming a bisexual?"

"How about an omnisexual? A mouth is a mouth, a hole is a hole. Free yourself from all preconceptions about the nature of love and sex."

"So I guess fucking mules and sheep is OK, too."

"Open the door and you let everything in. All the possibilities. Nothing is forbidden. No more good and bad, right and wrong. God is there, and so is Satan. Angels and devils, and you have to deal with all of them. You can't have just part of it. You get all of it, and then you take whatever you want."

"OK, you accept it all. But you don't have to do everything. You don't have to fuck sheep. You're free to make that decision."

"When you accept everything, you see the world for what it is: everything. Everything is possible unless you decide it's not. You might not want to eat an insect, but you'd soon change your mind if you were starving in the jungle."

"I happen to like women. I'm not sexually attracted to men. So what's the point I'm missing?"

"Just relax." Fred was massaging Oakley's scalp now, his temples, reaching around to the back of his neck, lifting his head gently. "The point is not sexual. The point is that we let our minds set the boundaries of our experience. In all ways. Out of fear, social taboo or whatever. We tell ourselves what's real and what's not, what's right and wrong, what's true and false. Wouldn't it be nice to be free of all that, to be in a place where anything is possible? Don't answer. This is the last part. Relax and let go. Marsha's going to help."

Fred massaged Oakley's face: eyebrows, cheekbones, ears, nose, jaw. Marsha got up on the table, sat on Oakley's legs and massaged both arms, moving from his shoulders down to his elbows.

"Life is the greatest gift," Fred said. "The only gift. We have nothing if we can't appreciate the simple fact of being alive. On the other hand, if we can appreciate it, truly appreciate it with our heart and soul, we have everything."

Fred massaged Oakley's collarbone, Marsha his wrists and fingers.

"Somebody as smart as you should have understood, but you didn't. While you were developing your mind, you lost touch with your heart and soul. You could have had it all—infinity. But instead you let your mind put you into a little box. To the eternal deities you have been ungrateful and ungraceful. And now it's too late. Goodbye, Oakley."

Marsha gripped Oakley's wrists. Fred held Oakley's head against the table with one hand on his forehead, while the other gently pressed fingers against his throat. Oakley struggled, but he was pinned.

He tried to shout or scream, but it was too late. The last thing he remembered was looking with horror at the smiles on the faces of Fred and Marsha.

## 58. Kauai 2001

## REVISITATION REVELATION

Sunday afternoon. After a burger and a beer at a Hanalei restaurant I head back to Keʻe across the seven skinny one-lane bridges that keep tour buses out, but not rental cars, driving slowly, taking in the details, conjuring up three-decade-old memories.

The bridges look the same, the first three paved with asphalt. After number three is the lookout where I can see the hotel defacing the view across the bay. The road goes uphill to the Lumahai Beach trail, the shoulder filled with parked cars. Bridge number four is wooden and crosses to Wainiha, a tiny town once destroyed by a tsunami. Two more wooden bridges past Wainiha, one after the other, a short turnoff between them. Past the Hanalei Colony Resort, the only vacation condominium that was there before, yet another bridge, this one longer and two-lane.

Beyond the last bridge are the stilt homes, the spires of mountains, the stream across the road, the dry cave, and Haena Beach Park.

Past the "Haena State Park" sign, I park in the Keʻe Beach auxiliary lot again. This time I remember mosquito repellent. Down the road a trail leads up to the first wet cave, a short climb to a ridge, then a quick descent down a rocky slope into the cave mouth, a hundred feet across, with a band of packed-soil beach in front of the dark, cool pool. The water smells of mold, and the slightest sound is amplified in the cavern. Behind me, an oval of green trees, sky, and clouds.

Back down the road, I find a sign I missed before—faded, almost illegible, probably posted in 1977 when they tore down the camp.

## STATE PROPERTY
Park to be constructed on this site.
No dumping, camping or residing on this property.
Violators will be prosecuted.
Department of Land and Natural Resources

Behind the sign, I suddenly realize, is the old Taylor Camp parking area. I walked right past it yesterday, missed it because the old turnoff is gone, overgrown with tall grasses. I leave the road to explore it. I find a rusted old chassis, springs, and a wheel with the tire still on it—remnants of a camp dweller's car? A large piece of corrugated tin—an old treehouse roof? The handle of a coffee mug. I can't find the walking trail into the camp, but there's a broad dirt path I don't remember from before, wide enough to accommodate a compact truck. I follow it into the jungle.

It's hot and still, quiet except for the calling of birds and the buzzing of mosquitoes around my head. Beneath the canopy of trees, the pod-like kamani seeds litter the ground in various stages of decomposition: first green and smooth, then brown and dry, then black with rot, then gray and shriveled in dead skeletal remains. The trees' roots rise from the ground like small, tapered walls, and the tendrils of crawling vines hang down from their branches. Again, I find no guava trees, wonder how they disappeared. I remind myself to jot down the Lumahai Gardens phone number. Maybe they can fill me in.

Tramping through the stubborn vegetation, I wish I had a machete. I worry about centipedes. The path penetrates deep into the jungle, past old Hawaiian rock walls still upright and solid, but no evidence of Taylor Camp. I give up and turn back in what I hope is the direction of the beach, eventually hearing the ocean again, then seeing the diffused light, the sky emerging not above but straight ahead. The path widens and the dirt mixes with beach sand. It moves up a rise, past a sign that reads "Please don't drive on the sand. Respect the land." I reach the windbreaking row of ironwoods that fronts the beach above the west bank of Limahuli Stream, looking down to its delta at the sea. I stop at a place that feels familiar, a low promontory. I remember how I used to sit here, alone at the edge of the jungle, the ocean breeze evaporating my jungle sweat, reading or just cooling off, gazing at the horizon.

I walk down to the beach and again try to orient myself, to conjure up the ghosts of treehouses and the hidden trajectory of overgrown trails. Sharp spires of mountains rise up from behind the jungle, green and black.

I re-enter for one last search. I don't want to leave Taylor Camp until I find something.

I'm thinking about Don Juan and how Carlos found his spot on the porch. So I'm calmer, more deliberate about it. I wander around, taking my time, trying to feel the residual energy, until something tells me to stop. I close my eyes, breathe deeply, still my expectations. Then I walk away from the spot, slowly, in an expanding spiral, scanning only the area directly in front of me.

And sure enough, in time, I find something: the banyan tree where Fred the Zen built his treehouse. It has to be the one; there was only one. I search the undergrowth at its base. Almost instantly I discover a cluster of round river rocks cemented together, a man-made boulder about two feet in diameter, with a hole in the middle wide enough to secure a thick pole. It's the crudely but solidly manufactured base for one bamboo cornerpost of Fred the Zen's treehouse.

A pun comes to mind: "concrete evidence." But evidence of what? Something I already know? It doesn't matter. Whatever I have been looking for, this is what I have found. I feel exhilarated. Strong and happy, like Carlos when he found his spot.

I cross the stream to the east side to search for the site of my treehouse. Can't find it. Too far gone, destroyed long before the rest of Taylor Camp, right after I left, when the residents agreed with the authorities to evacuate and tear down all of the structures east of Limahuli Stream, because they were outside the boundaries of Howard Taylor's land.

Down the beach at Ke'e, the end of the road where the tourists are concentrated, more than a hundred rental cars are parked in the muddy lot: Neons, Prizms, Cavaliers, Luminas, Malibus, Corollas, Maximas, Escorts, Mustangs, Intrepids, PT Cruisers. A massive traffic jam blocks the turnaround, with cars waiting for spaces, other cars honking at them, others attempting to back out of the jam, chickens on the road.

On my way back to the auxiliary lot, I pass the second wet cave, the one beside the road. At the entrance, a sign warns "Leptospirosis— Fresh water streams and mud possibly polluted with bacteria." People are swimming in the cave pool.

On the way back to Hanalei, I stop at Lumahai Gardens and speak to a botanist. He tells me that the guava trees were displaced by another invader, the *schefflera* or Octopus Tree.

The invaders from the Mainland, the Taylor Camp residents, were forced out and replaced by tourists. An improvement?

"Not to judge," I am reminded by Alternate-O. "Just to observe."

"Thank you."

## 59. Kauai 1970

## REBIRTH

When Oakley regained consciousness he was where he had been, on his back on top of Fred's picnic table. Marsha was gone. Fred had a thumb on Oakley's wrist. He struggled to rise.

"Take it easy. You're OK. Welcome back to the land of the living."

For some reason Oakley felt no anger. He was calm and relaxed. And very glad to be alive.

"How do you feel?"

"Fine. Kind of light-headed." He looked around Fred's kitchen in the lantern-light. "Everything looks so intense, so brilliant."

"That's the way things always look when you're truly in the moment."

"What did you do to me?"

"Just shut you down for a minute. It's a trick I learned in the war."

"Which war would that be?"

"The war against ingratitude. The war against habit."

"So this is my lesson for today?"

"It's a lesson for your whole life, if you could only remember it. But you won't. Pretty soon all the bright colors will go away, and you'll go back to taking your precious life for granted, grousing and grumbling, yearning for yesterday or waiting for tomorrow."

"I hope not."

"Just like the visions and insights you get from drugs. Flashes of instant enlightenment. But when you come down, you don't take them with you. They're like dreams you forget as soon as you wake up and get on with your daily life. So you don't even try to let them change you. You just enjoy them while they last, then forget them."

"But what can you do to remember them?"

"Stop taking drugs. Anywhere you can go with drugs you can go without them. And if you get there by your own effort, you won't forget what you see when you reach your destination."

## CANADIAN SURPRISE

With his teaching deferment, Oakley was in no danger of being drafted. The war was an ugly presence, creating confrontations and sit-ins and random violence, but after Century City Oakley was no longer participating in the protest movement. He had seen enough. He was trying to do his part in a different way, in another arena—Woodknoll.

He wasn't earning as much as he would be teaching at a public school, but the intimate class sizes and academic freedom more than made up for it. He didn't need a lot of money. The rent at the Venice apartment was cheap, his car was paid for, he and Joe ate at home most of the time, sharing cooking and clean-up chores, and he had no expensive habits. Pot was cheap and he didn't spend a lot of money on alcohol. He did his own oil changes on his VW Beetle. In his spare time he surfed, read books and went to the movies. Life was good.

He was teaching eleventh and twelfth grade English. His students were smart and, with a few exceptions, motivated and disciplined. He devised a course, an elective for seniors, which he titled "Contemporary Media"—allowing him to include in the curriculum not only books but television shows, movies, magazines and newspapers.

They read Marshall McLuhan's *The Mechanical Bride: Folklore of Industrial Man*, Paul Goodman's *Growing Up Absurd*, S.I. Hayakawa's *Language in Thought and Action*, Alexis de Tocqueville's *Democracy in America*, Terry Southern's *The Magic Christian*, and Nathanael West's *The Day of the Locust* and *Miss Lonelyhearts*.

They went on a field trip to see *The Graduate*, a matinee, Oakley pointing out that the first line of the movie contained an allusion to

Dante's "Inferno" and all other journey-to-hell literature: "We are now beginning our descent into Los Angeles."

They saw *The Sand Pebbles*, in which the name of Steve McQueen's character, Oakley noted, had an allegorical significance, as revealed by a whore in a bar: "Jake Holman? Ahh...so! Whole man! You *whole man*, no?"

They went to see Antonioni's *Red Desert*, in which Monica Vitti's character said, "I cannot look at the sea for more than a moment without losing interest in what happens on the land."

They listened to music in the classroom, including a song by Jesse Hill titled "Ooh Pooh Pah Doo," in which he sang, "I won't stop trying 'til I create a disturbance in your mind."

Oakley assigned bad television shows as homework, encouraging his students to, in the words of Marshall McLuhan, "dislocate into meaning by inspection." He asked them to:

1) Watch TV with the picture on, volume off. Phase two: add their own soundtrack by playing an LP.
2) Listen to TV with the picture off.
3) Watch an old TV series now syndicated and shown nightly on a local station repeatedly until they were able to see beyond the plot to the form and mechanics.

As an example of number three, Oakley observed that *Lost in Space* had an interesting substructure which shifted the roles of some of the characters. Dr. Smith was really a little boy, the Robinson boy was a robot, and the robot was merely a toy for Dr. Smith. Oakley directed his students to watch, with a similar eye for subtext, *The Flying Nun*, *Adam-12*, *The Beverly Hillbillies* and *Mod Squad*.

In June of 1969 Oakley taught summer session and went surfing with Joe and Norm. He spent less time on campus than during the regular semesters, when he would meet often with students and faculty, and when he was assistant coach of the varsity basketball team. He had tried to make surfing an official school sport, but everyone, administration and faculty and students alike, laughed at the idea.

Summer school was a half-day commitment, which allowed him to surf in the morning, teach, and surf again in the afternoon. In the evening he would read his students' essays. He didn't watch much television, except for the shows he assigned his students. He didn't have a girlfriend but it didn't seem to matter.

One Tuesday afternoon in mid-August, without forewarning, Fleur knocked on his door. She was not alone. Nevertheless, he immediately felt glad to see her. She looked great, flushed with excitement..

She introduced him to her companion. Ian. He was there to attend film school at UCLA. They had suitcases and backpacks. They were moving to Los Angeles.

Fleur asked if they could spend the night at Oakley's apartment, maybe crash there for a while—just until they could find a place of their own.

Oakley consulted with Joe, who reluctantly agreed as long as they were out of there as soon as possible. Joe still didn't cotton to Fleur.

Feeling strange about the gesture, Oakley gave up his bed to Fleur and Ian and slept on the couch. In the morning, up before everyone, he phoned Norm and asked him if he happened to have any vacant cottages for rent.

It turned out that Norm did have a vacancy. And it turned out to be not the only service he provided.

On Wednesday morning, Oakley drove Fleur and Ian to the Santa Monica cottages on Montana Avenue where Norm worked for the owner, renting and managing and supervising maintenance.

Oakley introduced them. Ian didn't notice but Oakley, apparently still attuned to Fleur's subtleties of expression, saw flashes of instant approval in her eyes as she appraised Norm. Her quickly rearranged smile, adjusted from inward to outward, her sudden shift of posture, her general demeanor.

Oakley wanted out of there, and Norm, perhaps sensing Oakley's discomfort, offered to set him free. He knew about Oakley and Fleur. So he told her and Ian that he would show them the cottage and then drive them around Santa Monica, Venice, Malibu, and West LA. After the tour, he would drop them off at Oakley's pad. A done deal.

Fleur and Ian rented the vacant cottage. Within two weeks, Fleur had moved in with Norm. Ian was incensed and threatened violence, but he never went through with it. He was short, small, and wiry, and although he seemed to have a short fuse, he never exploded. He was all bark and no bite. He was a dud. He didn't even move out of the cottages. Watching him made Oakley think he should have fought harder for Fleur. Fought at all instead of just giving up.

Norm and Fleur hit it off famously. Oakley did not enjoy watching them moon and paw at each other. He stayed away from them all— the newly enamored couple, the lonely and desperate Ian. He didn't want to be anywhere near them.

In early December, after the first quarter at UCLA film school had ended, Ian went back to Canada to visit his family. Norm quit his job managing the apartments, and he and Fleur took off for Hawaii.

Before they left, Norm told Oakley that they were going to a place they had heard of where you could live for free, build your own house in the jungle, grow your own food, and do nothing but enjoy life. On the beach. On Kauai, the northernmost of the inhabited Hawaiian Islands. In a place where the cops wouldn't harass you. Where the sun always shone and high-quality surf was everywhere.

Norm was excited about the prospect. He seemed to be trying to sell Oakley on it, inviting him to join them. Oakley didn't take the bait. He told Norm he had to stay around for Christmas with his parents.

Oakley did not spend Christmas with his parents.

## 61. Kauai 1970

## A HEROIN EXPERIENCE

Oakley and Norm had been hauling water. It was November, but the heavy winter rains hadn't begun and the garden was dry. They sat on large rocks at the edge of the stream, taking a break, sharing a joint. There was a north swell running, and onshore winds had infused the air with a salty haze.

"You ever shoot smack?" Norm asked.

"No way."

"I tried it once."

"Jesus. I didn't think that was possible. Just once."

"That was all it took to satisfy my curiosity. I never went back. I never got hooked."

"Why did you do it in the first place?"

"I'm an equal-opportunity druggie. Give everything a chance. But the only two I really like are this stuff and booze."

Oakley splashed his sticky face with cool stream water, then wet his head and neck.

"What was it like?"

"Like nothing. It didn't open up my mind, it shut it down. It reduced all my desires right down to zero. My body felt like a car engine in neutral. I shot up in Berkeley with a friend. We sat in his apartment living room doing nothing. We listened to the radio because it was on. He went to the bathroom, threw up, and came back. We sat there listening to soul music. I wasn't hungry, or thirsty, or frightened, or horny, or anything. Later on, we walked to the supermarket and bought some orange juice."

"So why bother?"

"That's what I thought. Though I can understand how some dude up in Harlem, freezing in the wintertime, starving, rats nibbling on his toes, might really enjoy a spoonful. When you've got less than nothing, getting to zero is moving up in the world."

"But here we are in paradise, warm and comfortable and free."

"Living in a beautiful place. Building our own shelters. Growing our own food. I'm living on fifteen dollars a week, and most of that goes into beer and wine."

They filled four plastic gallon jugs with stream water and carried them, one in each hand, along the short trail back to the garden. Away from the stream, the air smelled like salt.

"Don't you ever feel like going back?" Oakley asked. "Don't you want to *do* something?"

"What are you talking about? I'm doing something every day—working in the garden, building a shower and a super-outhouse, adding on to our treehouse, working on the car. What kind of something do you want to do, change the world? Make a million?"

"I don't know. I'm just worried that, if all the really bright people drop out, then who's left to run the world?"

"You want to run the world?"

"No. But there must be some way to make a bigger contribution. None of us are doing anything positive, we're all just running away from the things we don't like—cities, people, responsibilities. Right?"

"Speak for yourself, brother," Norm said. "Don't lay your Protestant Ethic anxieties on me. I come from a different tradition."

Oakley and Norm walked the parallel rows of lettuce and vegetables, pouring water into furrows. It was quiet, except for mynahs high up in the trees.

Oakley said, "I just wonder sometimes: Who's going to participate if we don't? Right now the country's being run by assholes like Richard Nixon and Ronald Reagan."

"If that's how you feel, why aren't you trying to do something about it?"

"I don't know," Oakley said.

"You know what they say: If you're not part of the solution, you're part of the problem."

"I never believed that. Somebody else telling me to be part of their solution."

"I know what you mean."

"I'm not sure what matters anymore. This seems to be a place where nothing matters, and anything goes, and you make up your own rules, and nobody tries to tell you what to do. And that's a pretty good thing."

Finished in the garden, Norm and Oakley took a swim to wash off and cool down. The waves out at the reef were small, the wind blowing white sheets of spray off their curling tops.

"Where were you yesterday afternoon?" Norm asked.

"On the trail. Just to Hanakapiai."

"We looked for you. A bunch of us went to Pine Trees for a picnic. Fred, Marsha, Sandy, Fleur, and me. You missed it. Chicken on the hibachi and Fred's potato salad."

Oakley was floating on his back, looking at the blue-and-white sky, little waves washing over his face.

"Fred brought his banged-up old tanker," Norm said. "You should have seen him trying to surf."

"Trying?" Oakley changed to a dog paddle, looking at Norm.

"That old fart may be in good shape, but he can't surf for shit."

"Wait a minute. I went out with him last week. He's good."

"Are you kidding? He's totally uncoordinated. He tried to cover it up by clowning around, making it look like he was fucking up on purpose, for laughs."

"Norm, he *was* fucking up on purpose. He really can surf."

"No fucking way."

Oakley told Norm about the morning at Tunnels, how Fred had been surfing like a young kid, all energy, looking so light and agile, doing all the radical maneuvers.

Norm said, "We're not talking about Fred here."

"Yes we are."

"No way."

"Yes way."

## 62. Kauai 2001

# CAMERA VU

Monday. I begin my last full day in Hawaii with a morning hike along the Kalalau trail. I assume that if I set off early enough I'll have the trail pretty much to myself. Wrong. When I pull in to the parking area about a half hour after sunrise, a dozen other cars are already there, with no people in sight. I apply mosquito repellent to my neck, shoulders and arms, hands, legs, and feet, toe by toe. I take a bottle of water but leave my camera in the trunk. I haven't taken any pictures with it yet. Haven't felt like it.

As I hike up the first rise, I encounter several backpackers on their way out, looking muddy and grimy from what might have been several nights' camping out. The trail is deeply rutted, packed hard and smooth by the trodding of countless shoes. The popularity of the trail is understandable: After just a few minutes' climb, the views are incredible.

The cliffs stretch out ahead, rising vertically from the ocean, and behind me the reef at Ke'e, the Taylor Camp jungle canopy with ironwoods sticking up through it, a groove in the green where the Limahuli Stream cuts through, and up the coast all the way to Tunnels. The ocean is light blue and infinite. The sky is speckled with puffy white clouds. The air smells like flowers and mud.

The trail follows the jagged contours of the pleated cliffs, disappearing into their folds, then turning and emerging at small promontories before reversing back again. Even at this hour of morning it's hot and I'm dripping sweat. I linger at the view points, sitting on rocks, feeling a slight cool breeze on my face, fresh from the sea, smelling of salt. Negative ions. Supposedly good for you.

Ferns cover the cliff faces like wallpaper, pandanus trees jut into the air with their tooth-edged leaves bent in the middle like flex straws. Finally I come across one of my missing trees, a guava, growing out over the cliff beneath the trail. I shimmy a few feet out on a branch overhanging the edge, to grab a yellow fruit. It's sour and seedy, just the way I remember it. Pink inside, like a woman. Like Sage. Like Fleur. Fleur, who once told me that guavas grow on trees and contained shitloads of vitamin C.

As the morning progresses, the trail fills up. People pass me in both directions where I sit: seriously equipped hikers, lean and fit, power-hiking with large packs; nature lovers in safari vests and Tilley hats, taking it slow, adoring the trees, flowers, and birds; overweight, out-of-shape tourists in tank tops, with no equipment, not a daypack or even a bottle of water, breathing heavily but smiling as they pass; families, couples, and lone walkers. Locals. Tourists from the mainland. Tourists from Japan. Tourists from Germany and France. Photographers, using everything from disposable cameras to Nikons on tripods. People who want to be here, people who look like they'd rather be someplace else—on a beach towel, in an air-conditioned car, in front of a TV.

In 1970, you didn't need to go far to get away from the crowd. On twenty-first-century Kauai, you need to get serious: Get a permit, backpack, tent, food; equip yourself properly and go deep into the wilderness.

When I reach the Hanakapiai Valley overlook, two miles in, I see about thirty people on the beach below. Time to turn back.

Couples and trios and families fill the skinny trail, making my return more time-consuming and difficult. Kids run around blind corners. There aren't many places to step off the trail and let people pass. I stand aside, tucking into the nearest groove or shoulder, and let them pass: fat people, thin people, white- and dark-skinned people, carrying cameras and waterbottles and day packs, wearing swim suits, T-shirts, tattoos, logo caps, slippery flip-flops, and overdesigned high-tech trekkers.

Back at the trailhead, I rinse off at the public shower and dry out standing in the sun at the edge of the sand. The surf looks higher than it did at dawn. It's just after 10 am, but the beach is filling up with bodies, like the trail. I feel lucky to have spent so much time at this place before it became so popular.

Approaching my car, I can see that the trunk has been popped. The lid is open, suspended an inch above the latch. I lift it. My camera's gone. I let out a laugh.

*Déjà vu. Been there done that. Use it or lose it. Poetic justice.*

I decide not to report the theft. I'm not going to waste precious hours of my last day in Hawaii waiting for, and dealing with, the police. I don't care that the camera's gone. The trunk still latches and the key still works in the gored lock.

What I want to do is tell Pualani. Get her reaction. Later. Now it's time to catch some waves.

In Hanalei, I have a fish sandwich and a beer at Honu's. I hear lots of talk about the approaching swell, supposed to hit six or eight feet by this afternoon. Pure north, wind offshore. Great conditions.

I pack my board and leave everything in my room except for the car key, my driver's license and a towel. Learned my lesson.

Surfers at Honu's were raving about lots of pumping spots: the Bay, Hideaways beneath the Princeville cliffs, the Pinetrees shorebreak, Waikoko, Cannons, and Tunnels. I pick Tunnels because I know it best.

The afternoon parking is brutal. I get lucky when someone pulls out from a spot about a half-mile up the road.

It's worth the walk. The waves are just overhead, six-foot faces, and the tubes are fast and hollow. I paddle, stand, trim, tuck into the curls and speed along the faces.

There's a bit of a crowd, but lots of waves too, and everyone is observing the "don't drop in" rule of etiquette.

Until I screw up, that is. When I'm catching a wave, the offshore-wind-generated spray obscures another surfer taking off deeper. I don't see him until it's too late, I've already dropped in, the tube has formed, and I'm too deep to kick myself and my board out of the wave. I can't get out of his way.

"Fockeen haole bastard!" The voice behind me is loud and angry. But what can I do? I could say, "Sorry, I didn't do it on purpose, really!" But the guy wouldn't hear me. I can't turn around to apologize, because I'm in the middle of a screaming tube, with my pursuer only a couple of feet behind.

I shrug my shoulders and outstretch my arms, a gesture I hope will be interpreted as "Oops! Sorry! But what can I do?"

"Fuckeen asshole son of a bitch!"

"Sorry! Really sorry!" I yell.

At the first opportunity, I make an early exit from the wave. To my relief, my unintended companion continues his ride.

"Fock! Shit! Fockeen haole dropeen in!" The cursing continues until the surfer is out of earshot.

After watching long enough to assume that my new enemy is not coming back to find me and punch me out, I paddle into the lineup. But now I'm anxious, and I grow hesitant. I don't want to leave yet, because he might be onshore waiting.

So I stay in the water, too inhibited to assert myself, not catching many waves, for another half hour. Then I decide it's time to ride one in and call it a day.

Ten seconds into the wave I wipe out and get hurled from my board, spinning in the tunnel. I land flat in the water, on purpose, to avoid the shallow, sharp reef. I don't hit the coral, but it's right there, a foot or two beneath me. I try to swim out of the impact zone, away from the onrushing white water of the next wave and into the calm blue, but the next wave catches me. I can't duck-dive under it because of the reef. I swim directly at the wave and let it hit me.

In the churning foam, I fight to stay on the surface. My leg is tugged by the leash around my ankle as my board is engulfed in the crashing soup. Suddenly the tugging stops. The leash has snapped.

It's a long swim, but that's only the beginning. I can't find my board. It's nowhere to be seen as I swim in. I walk a half mile up and down the beach, but can't find it washed up on the sand. I walk the route again, looking for it floating in the shallows offshore. Finally I spot it and, weary and discouraged, swim back out to retrieve it.

Back at the B&B, I shower and put on clean clothes. I'm too tired to walk to the beach for the sunset, so I watch from my lanai. Mynah birds clamor in the treetops. The air cools palpably as the sun fades. Mosquitoes begin to buzz my head and bite my ankles, so I go back inside.

I call Pualani and tell her about the camera.

"You're kidding."

"Nope."

"You left it in the trunk? Why didn't you take it with you?"

"I didn't feel like taking snapshots. I just wanted to look."

"Well, I guess you weren't supposed to have that camera after all."

"You're not upset?"

"Should I be?"

"I don't know. I know I'm not."

"I can tell."

"I didn't even report it to the police."

"What would be the point?"

"That's what I thought. It's my last day here, the surf is coming up, and I'm stuck waiting for the cops to write a report."

"I heard about the swell. Did you go out?"

"That's another story. Why don't you come up tonight and I'll tell you about it?"

"Yeah, right. Thirty miles on my bike after dark."

"Borrow a car."

"Can't. My brother's at a friend's."

"I'll come in and get you."

"That's silly. It'll take you an hour each way. It'd be too late."

"Not if I don't have to take you back home until tomorrow."

"You are persistent."

"Is that a bad thing?"

"No. Not with you. But…"

"I have plenty of vodka and fruit juice and some little goodies Miles gave me. We'll have fun."

"I don't drink or smoke. I'm no fun."

"Hey, it's not required. We had a good time just talking, didn't we?"

"Yeah, we did. But not tonight, Oakley. I like you, but it's impossible. Anyway, you're leaving tomorrow. I don't like one-night stands. Maybe I'll see you off at the airport."

"Hawaiian Airlines, departs at 11 am for Honolulu. I hope you show up."

"Tell me about the surf up there."

"I was having a good time until I got into trouble."

I decide on dinner at Sushi Blues. I could use some company, and from the outside, with its signage promising dancing and live music, it looks like a happening place. But it's still twilight, way too early. There's no music, no dancing, not much action at the bar. Monday night football is on the TV. Only a handful of tables are occupied by diners.

I eat at the bar, sampling sushi with cold sake, watching the Broncos beat the New York Giants, satellite-delayed so the people of Hawaii can catch the game after work. I hate football, but there's nothing else to do.

## THERE ARE NO ACCIDENTS

Soundtrack and Oakley were back from a long and pleasurable morning session at Tunnels, six feet and glassy, uncrowded, perfect conditions, long tube rides, exhilarating fun. They left only when their arms ached and they were exhausted and hungry.

Back at Oakley's treehouse, he made coffee and cooked them up some oatmeal, adding bananas and honey.

While they were eating, Oakley said, "Sometimes I wish you'd talk to me, but it's no big deal. I respect your vow of silence. But sometimes I think we might mutually benefit from conversation about ourselves, our lives, shit like that."

Soundtrack shrugged.

Oakley said, "Blah, blah, blah."

Soundtrack smiled.

After breakfast, they dropped in at Fred's Banyan Tree Lanai. The only one downstairs was Marsha, sitting in a well-worn wicker chair, drinking coffee, looking at a sketchbook. She was wearing a Los Angeles Dodgers baseball cap and a floral-print bikini that displayed a universe of freckles on her milky white skin.

"Sometimes I feel like there's nothing anybody can do about anything," she said. "But I don't always feel that way. Do you?"

After a look at Oakley and a noncommittal response, Soundtrack shrugged.

"Sometimes. But not always," Oakley said. He wondered what Marsha was talking about.

"What do you think of this? You like it?" She turned the sketchbook towards Oakley and Soundtrack.

Soundtrack nodded enthusiastically.

"Nice work," Oakley said.

"Ah, you're just saying that. I think it looks like shit. What am I doing sketching, anyway? I *hate* sketching. I'm just doing this because I think I should be expressing myself. Well, how's this for self-expression?"

She tore the page out.

"I'm not a goddamn artist. All I am is a *woman*. You know what that means?"

Soundtrack looked at the floor.

"Do you want me to answer?" Oakley asked.

"No. I'm telling you. Right now it means nothing but trouble. You know why? Because I'm still learning how to make it, but I'm already out in the jungle. It's on-the-job training, but it's not a rehearsal or a simulation. It's the real thing. Mistakes are paid for."

Oakley conferred silently with Soundtrack and said, "We would like to know what you're talking about, specifically."

"I'm saying that I couldn't go back if I wanted to. Not that I would ever want to. But sometimes it pisses me off."

Oakley asked, "Back where?"

"Try this: What do you think I'm doing here? Don't answer that! I know what you think. I know what everybody thinks. You think *I'm* with *Fred*, right? *Right?*"

They both nodded.

"Well, you're wrong. Did you ever think that *Fred* might be with *me*? Nobody bothers to think about it that way. He might be older and smarter than me, but other than that we're equal. It was my idea to come to Taylor Camp, not his. And you weren't here yet, but I built this treehouse as much as he did. He doesn't own me and I don't own him. In other words, he fucks around and so do I. And besides, we're living on *my* parents' money! I don't have to draw any damn sketches just to prove my independence!"

She threw the sketchbook beyond the boundary of the dwelling, into the jungle, out of sight. Oakley and Soundtrack stood there, watching her, waiting for the next scene.

"There! That's that," Marsha said. "Don't look at me that way!"

She went to the sink-without-plumbing to wash her coffee cup. She poured water from a plastic jug into the cup, washed it with a sponge, and put it into a drainer. The water direct from the sink drain spilled into a plastic bucket beneath.

"You know what really pisses me off about men?" Marsha eyeballed Oakley and Soundtrack. "They can get away with anything."

She singled out Soundtrack. "Like you, whatever-your-real-name-is. You just decide to drop out of the human race and stop talking for a while, and everybody thinks it's cool. They even give you a nickname that makes it even more cool. But what if I tried something like that? Do you know what would happen?"

Soundtrack shrugged.

"You'd think I was out of my mind. Losing my fragile feminine grip on reality."

Soundtrack stared at the ground.

"You don't have to take it out on him," Oakley said.

"OK, then, what about you?"

"What about me?"

"For starters, you think Sandy's crazy, don't you?"

"No, I don't."

"Be honest."

"I think she believes in certain things that are not good for her psychological health."

"You're so fucking diplomatic. You know want Sandy needs? She doesn't need therapy, she needs guts. She's a gutless wonder. You gotta have the guts to stay sane in a world made by men. And being black just adds to the problem."

"Some people believe that women are the ones who really run the world."

"That's so much bullshit!"

"Men need women. For a lot of reasons."

"But they still call the shots. For example, a man likes sex and he's a stud, a lover. I like sex and I'm a tramp. Fred shacks up with a woman half his age, and he's cool. I shack up with a man twice my age, and people think something's wrong with me. And what if I shacked up with a boy half my age?"

Oakley said, "I don't hear anybody criticizing you for living with Fred."

Marsha turned on Soundtrack.

"You know, it's rude not to talk to people when you can. It's selfish. Why don't you say something, just once? Stop playing your game for a minute."

"Leave him alone. It's not a game."

"Come on, tell me your real name."

Soundtrack shook his head.

"I'll tell you what. Say just one word and I'll give you a blow job."

Soundtrack smiled as he silently declined.

"I gotta hand it to you, Soundtrack," Oakley said. "You've got a lot of fortitude. I just said ten or twelve words, Marsha. What's my prize?"

"Fuck you, Oakley! And fuck you too, Soundtrack. If you want to be like that, go be alone somewhere!"

Soundtrack didn't move.

"I mean it! Get out of here! Go on!"

With a nod to Marsha and a quick look at Oakley, Soundtrack stood up and walked out.

"Jesus, Marsha, leave him alone. He's not hurting anybody."

Oakley was about to follow Soundtrack when Sandy came down her ladder. Marsha picked up a carton of Saloon Pilot crackers, munched on one, and walked to the edge of the jungle, looking into the thick wall of vegetation.

"Hi," Oakley said.

"Hello," Sandy said, but she wasn't interested in him at the moment. She walked over to Marsha and stood before her. Then she said in her soft voice, "I don't like being talked about behind my back. And I don't like being called a 'gutless wonder.'"

Marsha was unapologetic. "I knew you were up there. I knew you would hear me."

Sandy kept calm: "I still don't like it."

"Because it's true?"

"It's not as simple as that."

Marsha flopped back into her chair. "Yes it is, Sandy. Like Fred says, changing yourself is as easy as changing your mind. You just make a decision." She picked up a magazine from the ground and flipped through it.

"What is it I need to decide?" Sandy asked, standing over Marsha, trying to engage her attention.

Marsha looked up from the magazine. "Whatever it takes to get you back into the real world. Like, for starters, stop blaming yourself for your old man's death."

"But it was my fault. It was my anger that—I started the argument. I made *him* angry. I drove him away."

"That may be true. But that doesn't mean it was your fault he ran a stop sign and hit another car." Back to the magazine.

Sandy snatched the magazine from Marsha. "It wouldn't have happened if it weren't for me."

Marsha gave up on the magazine. "You can't believe that."

"I do. I can't help it."

"Bullshit. It was an accident."

"There *are* no accidents. We create our own lives, our own fates. If I stub my toe, it's because I want to hurt myself. I wanted to hurt him, so I did!"

Marsha sighed. "I know what you're saying. It's like your subconscious is influencing your behavior. But your subconscious isn't in control of everything. It can't control other people's behavior."

"Are you serious? People do it all the time."

Marsha gave her a look. "Whatever. But blaming yourself is wrong. It's self-destructive."

"I'm just taking responsibility for my own actions. If everybody did that, there wouldn't be so much murder and pollution in the world."

"You know something, Sandy? You shouldn't be in Hawaii. You should be in India, with the Jains."

"Who?"

"This religious group in India. When they walk around, they always carry these little brooms, and they sweep the path in front of them, so they won't step on any bugs." Marsha got up to demonstrate the walking and sweeping. "They try not to harm any living thing, not even a bug."

"Wow. What if a mosquito is biting you?"

"You can't kill it. You can't even brush it off 'cause you *might* kill it."

"That's going too far."

"Look who's talking. You didn't kill your husband. Even if you wanted to. I mean, if *your* vibes are so powerful, you have to assume that other people's vibes are powerful too. He could have neutralized your vibes with his vibes. It's his fault that he didn't."

Sandy didn't reply for a moment, then asked, "What do they eat?"

"What does *who* eat?"

"The Jains."

"Oh. I don't know. Why?"

"They obviously can't eat meat. But vegetables are alive, too. So is wheat. So is rice. So is tea."

"Jesus, Sandy, that's what I'm *saying*. Once you start thinking like that, life can get pretty difficult. If you want to build a house, you have to kill a tree. If you want to make clothing, you have to kill cotton. If you want to stand up for yourself, you have to get angry once in a while."

"Fred says that being too careful is like being dead."

"You don't need Fred to tell you that. Figure it out for yourself."

"You don't need Fred either. But you're with him."

"As I told these assholes, it's the other way around," Marsha said. "He's with me."

Oakley applauded Marsha. Sandy glared at him.

Marsha said, "The only thing you really need to know, Sandy, is that I'm with him because I want to be, not because I need to be."

## THANKS A LOTTERY

While Oakley was wrapping up the 1969-70 school year, America was breaking apart. The war dragged on, disillusioning an increasing number of Americans and swelling the ranks of the Vietnam opposition.

Notwithstanding, the U.S. Senate rejected a bill that would have repealed the 1964 Gulf of Tonkin Resolution, which virtually gave a president blanket power to wage war without consent of Congress.

President Nixon had been promising to de-escalate and "Vietnamize" the war by replacing U.S. soldiers with South Vietnamese. Yet, on the last day of April, he announced on national television that he had sent twenty-five thousand American troops into Cambodia.

The news of this invasion was greeted with outrage. Response was immediate and violent, especially on college campuses. On the May 4th protest at Kent State University, National Guardsmen shot and killed four students and wounded nine more.

Because young men weren't rushing to enlist in the Armed Forces, it had become necessary to instigate a national lottery. It was set up as a random selection process among registrants born between 1944 and 1950. All birth dates were printed on slips of paper, placed in fat plastic capsules, spun like bingo balls in a glass cylinder, and drawn one by one. The first dates drawn determined the first eligible males to be called for induction. Unlike most games of fortune, if your number was drawn, you lost.

The first lottery, held in December of 1969, was televised nationally. The second, held in early July 1970, was also on the air. Oakley didn't watch either one, but he read the results in the newspapers. In the first drawing, his birthday was number 198. In the second, it was 12. If it weren't for his teaching deferment, he figured, he would probably be drafted.

Oakley taught summer school, six weeks beginning in early June, which left him six weeks of freedom after the session let out. The only problem with teaching summer school was that you tended to get back the students you flunked during the spring semester.

One such student was Jeff Thorn, who just weeks ago had cut class regularly, flunked exams and rarely turned in homework. When he did, it was incomplete, perfunctory, and inadequate.

On the first day of class in the summer session, Oakley spoke to Jeff after class.

"What's the problem?" Oakley asked him. "I know you're not stupid. You can do better than the shit you've been handing me."

Jeff said nothing. He was thin, with blond hair that stuck out in front, but not on top or the sides. His features were sharp and handsome. Oakley figured he had his share of girlfriends.

"Jeff, let's see if we can work together to help you get out of this class. How about it?"

"I hate your fucking meaningless assignments."

Oakley looked at him silently for a moment. The he said, "You know what, Jeff? If they mean nothing to you, don't write the fucking assignments. Write what you want to, and let me read it."

"There's nothing I want to write."

"Come on, what do you do with your life? What about your family?"

"My mother and father are living together but have separate lives. They're never at home. My sister is in college in Massachusetts."

"So, how do you occupy yourself?"

"When I'm at home I steal my parents' pills from their bathroom. I don't even know what I'm taking, I just swallow a pill from every bottle."

"Maybe I'm wrong. Maybe you *are* stupid. If you're going to take drugs, you should know what they are and what they do to you."

"I'll bet you take drugs."

Oakley regarded him again. "I don't deny it, although I'd appreciate it if you kept this nugget of information between you and me. I trust you to do that, OK?"

"Fuck you."

"I take that as an OK. Now, the difference between me taking drugs and you taking drugs is this: I know what I'm swallowing, and I do it for a reason."

"So do I."

"And the reason is…?"

"To get the fuck away from my life."

Oakley sat back into his chair and sighed. "Jeff, I'm not your shrink, I'm your English teacher. So let's get back to the task at hand. I want you to write something for me. Something you can put your heart into. What do you like to do, who do you like to be with, what is your fondest memory? Don't answer now. Close your eyes for a minute and think about it."

To Oakley's surprise, Jeff closed his eyes. For a long time. When he opened them, he looked resentful.

"I thought about something," he said. "My father used to take me duck hunting. Before we lived in this shithole, we lived in Connecticut. I was too young to fire a shotgun, but I loved going out with him. We would get up and leave the house before dawn. My mother and sister didn't get up. Dad would have food all made up and packed for breakfast. It was cold, but I was all bundled up and felt great. And that's the high point of my fucking life."

"Write about it. Five hundred words. Due Friday."

Jeff brought Oakley three hundred and fifty words on Monday. The writing was dreadful.

"Not bad," he told Jeff. "But let's make it better."

"What about the next assignment?"

"There is no next assignment. We work on this paper for six weeks until you get it right."

Week after week, the paper got better and better. Oakley kept asking Jeff to improve every sentence, adding sensory detail. He had Jeff describe his father without judging him—what he looked like, how he behaved. When Jeff said he wanted to write about why he hated his father, Oakley told him to write a detailed description of just what his father had done to offend or alienate him.

The last draft Jeff submitted was, in Oakley's opinion, publishable. He suggested to Jeff that he send it out, just for the experience.

In mid-July, two days after Oakley finished the summer session, he returned from a day on the beach to find a "Selective Service System Notice of Classification" waiting for him, informing him that his "random sequence number" was 012. The letter contained a new draft card with the number on an attached stub, and instructions to carry it with him at all times. He didn't give it a second thought. He assumed it was merely a formality.

To his shock and dismay, in early August Oakley received another letter from the Selective Service, this time an "Order to Report for Armed Forces Physical Examination." He couldn't believe it. It was his draft notice, ordering him to report for his exam the following week in downtown Los Angeles.

He telephoned his local draft board to report the mistake. He told the man who answered the phone that he had a teaching deferment. The man pulled Oakley's file and told him that there was no record of such a deferment.

"There must be some mistake," Oakley said. "I've been teaching school for three years, ever since I got out of graduate school at UCLA."

"We don't have any record of your employment as a teacher," the man said.

"I informed your office three years ago that I was employed full-time as a teacher."

"If you did, somehow that information didn't make it into your file."

"Well, then, how can I set the record straight?"

"Too late for that now. You've received your notice. You're required to report."

Oakley hung up. He felt hopeless and desperate. His safety net was not only gone, it had never been there in the first place. It was all an illusion.

His mind raced. He thought about becoming a conscientious objector like Joe, but it was too late for that. He thought about going to Canada, or back to Europe. One thing he knew: He would not go to Vietnam. Not to that stupid, wrongheaded, disastrous war. It was not his war. It was somebody else's.

Then Oakley remembered what his doctor had said about the scoliosis. It would probably make him ineligible for military service. Immediately he calmed down. That was the solution. He would take his physical exam, flunk it, and be free again.

He obtained the medical information from his doctor, including x-rays and a letter explaining Oakley's condition, his symptoms, the possible causes of the deformity, and his personal recommendation that Oakley be exempted from service in the military.

Relieved, confident, dossier in hand, Oakley showed up for his physical on the appointed day. He was ready to endure this temporary inconvenience and eager to put the whole matter behind him.

# ALL WE NEED IS STRANGE

Love is just a dream but love is real
Love is an opinion that you feel
Love lives in the heart but rules the mind
Love will show the way but love is blind

Love is blind but love will show the way
Love is free but lovers always pay
Love is like a rock but love will change
Love is all we need but love is strange
Love is all we need but love is strange

## 66. Kauai 1970

### STILL CRAZY?

Fresh from his evening bath in the stream, smelling of Dr. Bronner's Peppermint 18-in-1 Castile Soap, Oakley prepared for the nightly arrival of the biting creatures: long pants, long-sleeved shirt, repellent on feet, hands, neck, and face.

His home-cooked dinner: brown rice stir-fried with olive oil, onion, garlic, collard greens, chopped macadamia nuts, and a filet of ahi given to him by one of the camp fishermen, cut up into chunks. For dessert, a Butterfinger.

After dinner he sat on his sofa, looking out at the beach and ocean and approaching sunset, and read another book Fred had loaned him, *The Teachings of Don Juan: A Yaqui Way of Knowledge*, in which a UCLA anthropology student described his encounters with a *brujo*, a sorcerer, named Don Juan, who used marijuana, mescaline, and peyote to guide the student into states of "nonordinary reality."

*The devil's weed is only one of a million paths...All paths are the same: they lead nowhere...Does this path have a heart? If it does, the path is good; if it doesn't, the path is of no use. Both paths lead nowhere, but one has a heart, the other doesn't. One makes for a joyful journey; as long as you follow it, you are one with it. The other will make you curse your life.*

Oakley considered the path he was on. Did it have heart? Yes, because the experience was rich and full—living in paradise, healthy and TV-free, in the company of a sorcerer of sorts, someone he felt he had something to learn from. No, because he was avoiding things. He was a draft evader in limbo.

He spotted Sandy, walking slowly down the beach in the hard sand near the water. He went down to her.

"Mind if I join you?"

She smiled at him but said nothing. They walked together in silence, up the beach, the camp and the sun behind them, a couple of shorebirds skittering before them.

She said, "Let's sit for a while."

They walked to higher ground, dryer sand, and sat facing the setting sun, watching the sky change color, saying nothing.

After a while Sandy said, "You've been sleeping with Marsha."

"Yeah, a couple of times."

"Are you keen on her?"

"Keen? I wouldn't say that. I like her spirit, but for both of us it's just sex. She offered and I accepted. That's all. She's not really my type."

"Who's your type?"

"You are." He looked at her, but her gaze was fixed on the sunset.

"You really want that kind of trouble?"

"Interracial couple? I don't see it as trouble."

"I'm not talking about that."

"Then what?"

"You don't know me."

"So let's get to know each other."

"OK, Oakley," she said, sounding resigned and a little angry. "Let's tell each other our life stories. Me first. My parents had me committed, and I spent three months in a nut house."

"You're not scaring me off, if that's what you're trying to do. Why did your parents do that?"

"It was after Jeff died. I gave up the apartment we were renting and moved back in with them, back into my old room, which was waiting for me, just like it was when I left it to go to college. It was weird, like I was back in high school again."

She dug a hand into the sand. "I guess I really was crazy for a while. Kind of hysterical. One minute I would be crying uncontrollably, then I'd break up laughing. I was obsessive about cleaning up my room, but I let myself go to seed. I would wear the same clothes for days, never bathe, never brush my hair. It freaked everybody out. So they had me put away."

"What was it like?"

"It was horrible. I was locked in a room and they made me take all these pills. I felt like I was down in a hole, a really deep hole. I was paralyzed. I couldn't move. All I could do was cry."

"Jesus."

Sandy laughed. "But it was actually kind of funny. They thought I was crying about Jeff. But I wasn't. I was crying about the hole they put me in. I couldn't get out."

"But you said you were out in three months. What happened?"

"I did what they told me to do, the group therapy, the consultations, and finally they lowered my dosage, and when I wasn't so drugged anymore I made sure to behave properly. There was no way I was going to let them put me down in that hole again."

"So you did good."

"But I was faking it. Underneath, I was still fucking crazy."

The sun was dissolving into the sea. The air was still. The waves broke with a muffled sound.

"In fact," she said, "I'm just as crazy now as I was then. I just know how to hide it better."

## 67. Southern California 1970

# FUCK NIXON

Oakley was downtown at 6:30, a half hour early, having avoided rush hour and secured all-day parking in an open-air lot between two highrises.

In front of the building, a line had formed on the sidewalk that stretched down the block and disappeared around the corner. Hundreds of people—all male, all boys and young men—had arrived before him.

He took his place in line and asked the guy in front of him, "Been here long?"

"Just a couple of minutes. They bussed us over from the hotel."

"You stayed in a hotel?"

"Had to. I'm from Bakersfield." He was tall, muscular, looked about Oakley's age, maybe a couple of years younger. He had short blond hair and a long nose.

"Bakersfield," Oakley said. The line was quickly filling up behind him. "I thought this was just for LA."

"Hell, no. Try Southern California, San Diego to Santa Barbara, past Barstow out to the Nevada state line."

"Holy shit."

"They said they're going to process about twelve hundred draftees today."

The guy behind Oakley in line laughed. "Is that the word they used, 'process'?"

He looked too young, but he had to be at least eighteen or he wouldn't be there. He was skinny, his clothes were dirty, and he smelled bad. His eyes darted side to side like he was watching a tennis match. He wore blue jeans, black work boots and a T-shirt that read "Fuck Nixon."

He laughed again. "Yeah, man, welcome to the cattle call. You and me and the rest of these poor fuckers, we're the livestock, getting ready to be led to the slaughterhouse. Yesterday Woodstock, today livestock, tomorrow dead meat." He spat on the ground, then coughed convulsively. When the spell was over, he lit a cigarette. His eyes shifted.

He offered Oakley his hand. "Name's Jimmy," he said. "From San Bernardino."

They shook hands. Jimmy's hand was sweaty and clammy.

"Oakley, from Venice."

"Really? Venice is cool."

The guy in front of Oakley joined in. "Don, from Bakersfield like I said." More hand shaking.

Don indicated the manila envelope Oakley was holding. "What's that?"

"Medical records."

"You got something that'll get you outa here?"

"I hope so."

"Good luck."

"They're not gonna take me," Jimmy said.

"How come?"

"Heroin. Started shooting up the day I got the call. Never tried it before in my life, except for the past two weeks. Now I'm a full-on junkie, strung out and totally fucked up and ready to flunk this fucking physical."

"Jesus," Oakley said.

"It was either that or cut off a toe or a finger. A friend of mine drank a couple quarts of Robitussin, but that didn't get him off."

"If you don't get booted for the smack," Don said, "you probably won't pass the psychiatric exam."

"Why's that?" Jimmy asked.

"'Cuz you gotta be outa your fuckin' mind to be wearing that T-shirt today."

# CITIZENS FOR SATIRE

(Slow tempo)

The truth about this country [Fm7] [Em]
Is fulfilling our worst fears [Dm7] [Am]
The watch that man is wearing [Dm7] [Em]
Could feed a family for ten years [Dm7] [Am]
There's no use getting angry [F] [G]
We'll only play their game [F]
The best thing we can do is laugh [F] [G]
And bring them down in shame [C] [D]

We're selling off America
We're cutting down the trees
The interest on the deficit
Has brought us to our knees
The infrastructure's crumbling
The poor are getting mad
Our children grow up stupid
Our future's looking sad

[Chorus]

(Force, faster tempo)

Chorus:
It's the Citizens for Satire [A] [D] repeat 2-chord "march"
Who make this country great
The power of the people
To ridicule the state
Invoke your sense of humor
To overcome your grief
Use your right to fight injustice
With a laugh of disbelief [D] [C#m]

No matter what they tell you
You're not completely free
But at least you're free to laugh it off
In the state of irony
While the government is blowing smoke
The world's consumed by fire
It's time for some serious humor
From the Citizens for Satire

[Chorus]

## 69. Kauai 1970

## THE LOST SUPPER

It was Christmas Eve, and a little group was gathered in celebration. Fred, Marsha, and Sandy had invited Oakley, Norm, Fleur, and Soundtrack over for Christmas dinner, and they were just finishing up.

"Anybody want any more spaghetti?" Marsha asked. "More salad?"

Everyone had had enough.

Fred got up from the table, fed some more wood into the fire pit. "What's for dessert?"

"Pineapples and bananas in guava juice," Sandy said, passing a big bowl and spoon.

"This is one Christmas dinner I'll never forget," Oakley said. "Marsha's vegetarian spaghetti, Norm's garden salad, eleven-grain garlic bread, and tropical fruit for dessert."

"And good ol' Red Mountain," Norm said. He grabbed the jug and started to fill Oakley's plastic tumbler. Oakley covered it with his hand, Norm filled his own and passed the jug.

"Sorry we couldn't cook you the traditional Christmas goose," Marsha said. "We don't have an oven."

"I wasn't complaining," Oakley said. "I was just making an observation."

"We could have barbecued a goose on a spit," Norm said. "Or we could have dug a hole and baked it in the ground. If the Hawaiians can do it with a pig, we could have done it with a goose."

"Isn't the goose the Hawaii state bird?" Marsha asked.

"Not that kind of goose," Norm said.

"When you finish," Sandy said, "pass the dish."

"Uh-uh, Sandy," Marsha said. "We cooked. The men are on cleanup. And Fleur."

"Fair enough," Norm said. "Pass 'em over. How 'bout some after-dinner music?"

Soundtrack fetched his guitar and sat on a stool away from the table, picking out Jorma Kaukonen's "Embryonic Journey." Oakley, Fred, and Norm cleared the table except for the wine and tumblers.

Fleur walked to the open edge of the kitchen and stood there, gazing out into the jungle night. Oakley thought she was being unusually quiet, verbally noncombative for a change.

Fred scraped the leftovers into the garbage, put the dirty dishes into a black garbage bag, and headed for the trail.

"You don't need to wash those now," Marsha said. "It's almost dark."

"I like the dark," Fred said. "I like the sound of the stream at night."

"Need any help?" Oakley asked. "Fleur volunteers."

Fleur didn't respond.

"Nope." Fred donned a plastic miner's hat with a built-in flashlight, dumped a bottle of dish detergent and a sponge into the trash bag, and left.

Oakley felt a remembered sensation…an impending acceleration, an anticipatory tingling, as if he were on the edge of an abyss and about to jump. He ran his fingers along his neck beneath his jaw, breathed deeply, sighed, and shrugged it off. He sat back down at the table with Norm, Marsha, and Sandy.

"C'mon, Oakley, have some more wine. It's Jesus' birthday. He would want you to be happy. People came from miles around to witness the miraculous birth."

"Sangre de Christo. Feliz Navidad." He let Norm fill his tumbler. Norm offered the bottle to Sandy, who refused. So did Marsha.

"What's the matter with everybody?" Norm asked. "We're not up to our usual alcoholic consumption." He rolled a joint.

"I don't feel like any more wine," Marsha said. "I feel kinda funny."

"Me too," Sandy said.

"In what way?" Oakley asked.

"A little tingly," Marsha said. "Sort of anxious."

"I feel like my body's getting lighter," Sandy said, "and I'm about to float away."

Oakley realized what was happening. The familiar tightness in the throat, the blood tingling in anticipation.

"It's acid. Somebody spiked our food. Or the wine."

"Oh, shit." Sandy stood, then sat back down.

"It's not the wine," Norm said. "We were all sitting here when I opened it. I wouldn't do that, anyway."

"Shit," Sandy said. "I don't want this!"

Fleur rejoined the group, her face a beatific glow. "I knew it. Nothing else feels like this. I thought I was having a flashback."

"What about the spaghetti sauce?" Norm asked.

"Wait a minute!" Marsha said. "Danny. It must have been Danny. He was in here this afternoon, tasting the sauce and stirring it. I'll bet he did it."

"It's a fuckass thing to do," Sandy said.

Fleur said, "Maybe he did it for revenge, because he wasn't invited."

"He *was* invited!" Marsha looked pissed. "He turned us down."

"Anti-social," Oakley said.

"LSD wouldn't work in spaghetti sauce," Norm said. "The heat breaks it down."

"Maybe it's the mushrooms," Oakley said. "Where'd you get the mushrooms, Marsha?"

"In a tin can! B and B brand." Marsha got up from the table, walked over to a counter and picked up a plastic cruet. "Here we go. I'll bet it's in the salad dressing!"

"That would work," Norm said. "Sunshine in the salad."

"Owsley in the olive oil!" Fleur said.

"You are quick."

"Well," Oakley said, "nothing to do about it now. We're on a trip, phase one."

"How many phases *are* there?" Sandy wailed. "I've never taken acid!"

Oakley looked at Norm. "Seven, if I remember correctly?"

Norm nodded. "Phase one: the ascent. The roller coaster ride up to the first big thrill."

"Blue Cheer in the blue cheese!" Fleur said.

"Phase two:" Oakley said, "expansion. Synapse release, neurons open fire, neurotransmitters flow. Sensory organs ratcheted to maximum receptivity."

"I'll bet he's out there right now, spying on us, hearing every word we say, waiting for us all to freak out," Marsha said. "We'll show him. We'll all have a good time." She ran over to the trail and shouted into the jungle, "Come on in, Danny! We forgive you!"

"Phase three: revelation." Norm's turn. "You have visions."

"No we don't!" Sandy said.

"We don't have visions?" Oakley asked.

"We don't forgive Danny."

"Oh." He paused for a moment. "Phase four: illumination. Truths revealed, many things become clear."

"If it actually was Danny who did the deed," Norm said, "his action is not without precedent. This isn't the first time the military has gotten people stoned on acid without their knowledge."

"Yeah," said Fleur, "they dropped it over San Francisco."

"Phase five: enlightenment." Norm again. "Understanding."

"Phase six, a perennial favorite," Oakley said. "Pleasure. Bodily pleasure, for sure, but also pleasure in the heart, mind, and soul."

"Fun," Marsha said.

"Lucy in the sky with vinegar and oil," Norm said.

Soundtrack picked out the melody to "Lucy in the Sky with Diamonds."

"You all are having a good time," Sandy said, "but I'm scared."

"It's OK, Sandy," Oakley said. "Just don't fight it and nothing bad will happen."

"Yeah, don't resist it, go with the flow," Fleur said.

"Easy for you to say. White folks on acid."

"Remember that night in Paris, Oakley?"

Fleur was looking at him, smiling, but he didn't return her glance. After four years the love, the desire, and the yearning had finally dwindled to nothing. Then he felt a snap in his head, a release, a realization that, no matter how it ended up, they sure had had one hell of a good time in Europe. He looked at her, returned her smile. She had triggered a surge of remembered images, sensations, sounds, and smells.

"Oh, yes," he said. "Walking late at night, after the rain. Wet streets. People singing in the park next to the little church."

"And the spider web. With raindrops on it."

"What about genetic mutations?" Sandy asked.

"That mutation stuff is all bullshit," Norm said. "More lies from the newspapers."

"You'll be OK, Sandy," Oakley said. "We've all done this before. White folks on acid. We'll take care of you."

"The key concept," Norm said, "is set and setting. You're in a positive setting, surrounded by friends. All you need to do is keep a positive mind set. Understand that what's going to happen is a good thing, not a bad thing."

"I hope Fred's all right," Marsha said. "He had three helpings of salad."

"After all that complaining about collard greens." Norm said.

"When he gets back," Oakley said, "we could be in for a very interesting evening."

"Why wait for Fred?" Fleur asked.

"I think we should stay together," Norm said. "No tripping off alone into that dark night."

"I don't think we need to make rules," Marsha said. "What if somebody wants to be alone for a while?"

"Right," Oakley said. "But Sandy should not be alone."

"Fine with me."

"Enjoy yourself. But if you're having a bad time, you need to let somebody know."

"I have a question," Marsha said, pointing at Norm's head. "Are those your real ears?"

"That depends on what you mean by 'real,'" Norm said.

"I'm having a bad time," Sandy said.

"What's the matter?" Oakley asked.

"I'm losing control."

"Sure you are. That's all right, that's the way it feels. When you're coming on like this, like Norm says, it's like taking a roller coaster up the first big climb. But there's no drop, it's more like floating. It's not a question of losing control, but giving it up voluntarily. Just let go. It won't hurt you. Enjoy it. Learn from it."

"You don't look like *you're* enjoying yourself," Sandy said.

"She's right," Norm said. "What's the problem?"

"I'm concerned," Oakley said to Sandy.

"Open the pod bay doors, Hal," Fleur said.

"Where's Fred?" Marsha asked. "Shouldn't he be back by now?"

"He's only been gone for a couple of minutes," Norm said.

"It seems like a couple of hours."

"If acid is so great," Sandy asked Oakley, "how come you stopped taking it?"

"There was nothing new about it anymore. I just got tired of questioning everything, asking the same questions over and over again."

"What questions?" Marsha asked.

"The basic questions. What the fuck am I doing here? What's the purpose of life? How does a human being deal with the chaos of infinity?"

Marsha laughed. "Whoa! Heavy!"

"You know what Jack Kerouac said after taking psilocybin?" Norm asked. "'Walking on water wasn't built in a day.'"

"What I'm trying to say," Oakley said, "is how long is it necessary to ponder the basic questions before you get down to the business of living?"

"Is that what it is?" Fleur asked. "The 'business' of living?"

"A figure of speech."

"Fred calls it the art of living," Sandy said. "He says we're all artists of life, except that we don't behave that way. We all take ourselves too seriously, rather than having fun making our lives into works of art."

Soundtrack played the opening bars to "Purple Haze."

Fleur got up from the table and stretched. Sandy twirled her hair. Norm stared into the fire.

"You know what?" Oakley asked, turning to Sandy. "Let's you and me take a stroll."

"Where?"

"Anywhere you like. How about the beach where we can see the sky and the stars?"

"I don't know. I'd better stay here."

"Well, I need to go. Are you going to be all right?"

"We'll take care of her," Marsha said. "Have fun."

As Oakley stood, bolts of electric color crackled in front of his eyes. He headed out into the night. Behind him, Soundtrack was singing. "Purple haze, all in my brain…"

"Don't deny it. You still love me." Fleur was beside him.

"I flashed on it. But that was all."

"Bring it back."

"Why?"

"Why not?" She squeezed him through his jeans, pushed her breasts against him. He got hard. She unbuttoned him.

"For old time's sake."

"What's the purpose?"

"Nothing but pleasure." She went to her knees and began sucking him, moaning in the process. Did she really enjoy it that much, or was she acting? Oakley didn't care. It felt good.

"Enough of this," she said. She took his hand and guided him to the beach. They stood on the sand just outside of the jungle. "Undress me."

Oakley could think of no reason not to. He slowly removed her clothing, enjoying every new moment of exposed flesh, stroking her smooth skin, kissing it, rubbing his face against her belly, her back, her legs, her neck, tracing the shape of her collarbone with his fingers.

"Oh, God. Thank you, thank you," she said. "Thank you."

"Doesn't Norm do this?"

"It's the novelty. The pleasure of someone new."

"I'm not new."

"Yes you are. Sure you are."

They made a blanket of their clothing. He licked her until she began to squirm. She grabbed his head with both hands and pulled it up to her face.

"Come inside me."

He obliged.

A short time later, maybe a long time later, they put their clothes on. He walked her back toward Fred's place but stopped a short distance away.

"Thanks for the memory," he said.

"If you wanted, the three of us could be together."

"No."

"Have it your way." She kissed him and was gone.

He walked toward the beach, shining his flashlight on the trail before him. The ground heaved gently in the illumination. Tree roots writhed and squirmed like fat snakes. Fallen wet leaves shone like jewels. His nostrils filled with the smell of damp earth, rotting guavas, and salty air.

He was thinking, what was that all about? Fleur, Flora, her, once his, still an object of desire, still desiring him, still pleasing him, him still pleasing her. What to do about it? Nothing.

He was thinking: Feed your head. Break on through to the other side. Take another little piece of my heart. Everybody knows this is nowhere. He stopped and sat, back to a tree, and turned off his flashlight. Small animals rustled in the brush—birds, roaches, rats. Dark shapes drifted and flowed before his eyes.

This was not like before, with Fleur. Two is company. Now he was alone. If he had been in a different mood, or if he had been a different person, he might have been scared shitless. But he was experienced. The first time he dropped acid was in Paris four years ago, the last at Monterey Pop. How many times in all? More than twenty, less than forty. Once a week for a while with the Seven Psychedelic Samurai. He was an acid pro. He was a member of the court during the acid reign. Even though this was an involuntary trip, he could handle it. Enjoy the ride.

When his eyes adjusted to the dark, he resumed his walk to the beach. Better without the flashlight. He passed transparent-walled treehouses, glowing with warm light and the happy sounds of music and partying people. 'Tis the season to be jolly.

Walking slowly, deliberately, Oakley appreciated the machine that was his body, limbs working efficiently, breath fueling the engine, blood pulsing through his veins. He passed from the jungle confinement to the endless vista of beach, ocean, and sky. The wall of infinity.

He sat in the sand, ran it through his fingers, felt the coolness of the slippery grains. Before him the ocean was a vast, black, uninhabited terrain, but the breaking waves near the shore were silver-colored, and a blue haze seemed to float above them.

The moon was new, a weak sliver hanging low over the horizon, but to Oakley's amped-up ocular receptors the sky was filled with light. A million stars throbbed, sparkled, blinked, launched themselves across heaven like fireworks, and disappeared. He stretched out on his back and watched the pyrotechnics.

Now that he was alone, questions rushed into the void. What was this all about? What was he supposed to be doing here? Was there some purpose, or did he need to create his own purpose out of nothingness?

He could understand the Jesus freaks, the ex-druggies who became born-again Christians. Turning to religion, you removed from your lonely self the weighty existential burden of supplying your own meaning, purpose, and morality to life. An order replaced the chaos with no effort or responsibility on your part. A congregation of like-thinking brothers and sisters supported you. The confusion of infinite possibilities was reduced to a manageable handful. You needed rules? Here were the Ten Commandments. Only obey them and you got the grand prize, eternal life.

Oakley stood and stretched, feeling every bone, muscle, sinew, tendon, and ligament in his body. He looked back at the jungle, where the treehouses glowed in the dark foliage like Christmas tree lights. He heard voices behind him and turned to see Patrick and Heather walking on the beach. They were arguing but trying to keep their voices down. He waved but they either didn't see him or chose not to acknowledge his presence. When they were out of sight, he rolled up his jeans and walked down to the water, carrying his sandals. The wash was gentle and the water was warm. He watched his feet disappear in the wet sand.

His life was idling, suspended. In Taylor Camp limbo. Or the bench in a ball game. He thought: *Turn on, tune in, time out. We're pretending we're doing something, that we've created some kind of a safe refuge. Maybe so, but I feel like I'm sitting on the sidelines. Need to get back in the game. But I'm a fugitive. Can't go back. I dropped out, now I can't drop back in.*

If he could, he decided, he would go back into teaching. You could make a difference, even against the odds. You walked into the classroom with a blunderbuss, fired at random, and hoped that, once in a while, you would hit something.

He thought: *If I don't do it, who will? If I don't get back into the game, the other team wins by default. Nixon and Kissinger and Reagan and the all-star assholes.*

He walked along the shore, away from the camp. Suddenly a dark shape washed up in front of him. At first he thought it was a thick tree branch, driftwood. But it started flopping wildly, splashing in the shallow water, kicking up sand.

*It's a fucking shark.* He jumped away with an involuntary shout. The shark flopped some more, then a wave washed in and carried it back into the deep.

Oakley's heart was pounding. A coincidence, for sure, but there were no coincidences on acid. The acid vibe, the blaring neurons, sent out waves of energy that attracted God knows what. He hurried back to Fred's place.

In his absence, the crowd had thinned. Fleur and Norm were gone. Sandy was nowhere in sight. Soundtrack was playing a flamenco tune, and Marsha was dancing. Fred was back, sitting at the picnic table, looking at Oakley.

"It wasn't Danny," he said. "It was me."

"Why?"

"A psychedelic Christmas present," Marsha said.

"The gift of a temporarily expanded consciousness," Fred said.

"I don't mind, but do you think it was a good idea to turn Sandy on like that?"

"I determined that she was ready. And she was."

"Where is she?"

"Upstairs, listening to Vivaldi and thumbing through magazines."

Oakley sat at the table with Fred. "I need a glass of wine. I want to get drunk and pass out like a regular human being." He poured himself a mug, then stared at his hand. "But instead, I am compelled to watch my skin exchange molecules with the atmosphere."

"Attaboy, Oakley," Fred said. "Dissolve the false barriers. Melt and blend with the universe."

"You are so full of shit," Marsha said. Soundtrack having finished the flamenco number, she joined them at the table.

Soundtrack played "Strawberry Fields Forever," singing "Nothing is real, nothing to get hung about…"

"You're all the same, in a way," Fred said. "Soundtrack wants a way without words. Oakley wants to do something meaningful with his life. Marsha wants to be free of male stereotypes. But we're not victims of conditioning, we allow it to happen. If it weren't for that, what power we would have! What a world we would create! But we all reach our limits on the road to freedom. We all take a turnoff when things begin to upset us, and spend the rest of our lives in a Hilton hotel watching television."

"I wish we had a TV here," Marsha said. "I miss TV."

"I gotta get out of here," Oakley said. "Too much input."

Soundtrack sang, "We gotta get out of this place, if it's the last thing we ever do." He stood up to leave.

"You kept it together tonight, Soundtrack," Oakley said. "No problems?"

Soundtrack shook his head and smiled.

"Have a good time?"

He smiled more broadly and nodded.

"Were you ever tempted to talk?"

He shook his head.

"You're right, the night's over," Marsha said, standing.

Soundtrack sat back down and sang, "Take the highway to the end of the night, end of the night, end of the night."

"You know something about that song, Soundtrack?" Oakley asked. "You know the line in it where Morrison sings 'Some are born to sweet delight, some are born to endless night'?"

Soundtrack sang the lines.

"That's it. Well, Morrison stole it from William Blake. Blake, the English poet?"

Soundtrack made claws and growled.

"Yeah, 'Tiger, tiger, burning bright, in the forests of the night.' The stolen lines are in a poem called 'Auguries of Innocence.' If Morrison had been a more optimistic guy, he might have included the next part of the poem: 'God appears and God is light to those poor souls who dwell in night, but does a human form display to those who dwell in realms of day.'"

"You memorized all that?" Marsha asked.

"I was really into Blake. Especially 'The Marriage of Heaven and Hell.' Filled with good advice, like 'The road of excess leads to the palace of wisdom,' and 'He whose face gives no light shall never become a star,' and 'No bird soars too high if he soars with his own wings.'"

"Wow. Cool," Marsha said.

"And, 'The nakedness of woman is the work of God.'"

"A wise man," Fred said. "An enlightened man. But you, Oakley, have too many ideas of others in your head. Make some room for your own."

"Bedtime," said Oakley. With a glance at Fred he said, "Give my best to Sandy."

"We're not sleeping together any more. Not fucking anymore. In case you wanted to know. She called the shots and I concurred."

Oakley said nothing.

"She's waiting for you. Pay her a visit."

Soundtrack sang "Silent Night." Oakley, Fred and Marsha joined in. "All is calm, all is bright
Round yon Virgin Mother and Child
Holy Infant so tender and mild
Sleep in Heavenly peace
Sleep in Heavenly peace."

## 70. Southern California 1970

## PHYSICAL ABUSE

The doors to the examination center opened and the draftees filed in from the street. Immediately inside the building they were directed into three large rooms, dividing alphabetically by last name initials, A to I, J to R, S to Z.

Oakley sat near the back in one of several long rows of freestanding desk chairs. He watched as the room filled, echoing with chatter and the high-pitched squeaks of sliding furniture. He estimated there were at least three hundred people in the room and, not without apprehension, saw that he wasn't the only one holding a manila folder.

On the front wall was a blackboard. Beside it was a brass plaque honoring the center, bearing a picture and signature of Selective Service Director John Hershey. Another wall-hung, framed photo was of President Nixon. Oakley thought about Jimmy in his T-shirt.

A man in uniform, crew-cut, posture erect, entered the room through a side door. The talk subsided. The man glared at the room as if it were a cage filled with stupid animals.

"Stand at attention when I enter!" he shouted.

They're weren't in the Army yet, and the man wasn't even an officer—he wore the three stripes of a sergeant—but on this day, in this place, it made no difference to the luckless lottery losers. Everyone rose, many expressing defiance by taking their time to arrive in a fully upright position.

"That's better," the sergeant said, ignoring the misbehavior. "At ease."

Half of the group sat down, half remained standing.

"Sit down," the sergeant said, shaking his head in disbelief at their collective idiocy. "You better sit while you can, because you're gonna be in this building for at least six hours, and most of the time you'll be waiting in lines. We've got more than a thousand assholes to check today—and I mean that literally."

He paused for laughter. There was none.

"My name is Sergeant Botha," he said. "Welcome to the first step in your induction into the United States Armed Forces. We're a little short on military doctors today, so you will be examined by civilian volunteers, if they decide to show up, along with medics, clerks, and lab assistants. You will comply fully with every instruction you receive. Anyone who makes trouble will find himself in deep shit."

The sergeant paused to scan his audience. Someone a couple of rows ahead of Oakley raised his hand.

"Did I ask for questions?" the sergeant said. No one replied. "You, the asshole who raised his hand. Did I ask for questions?"

"No."

"No, *sir*," Sergeant Botha said. "Did I ask for questions?"

"No, *sir*."

The sergeant nodded. "Thank you."

He looked around again, taking in the full room. "I will dismiss you from this room row by row, beginning at the back and moving forward one row at a time. Your first stop is the locker room. There you will be given a basket. You will strip down to your undershorts and put everything else in the basket. You will exchange the basket for a clipboard and a numbered neckband. In this neckband you will place your valuables. So, if they get stolen, it's your fault, not ours. On the clipboard you will place all the documents you brought."

He looked around the room again, this time with a knowing smile.

"Just for fun, how many of you have letters from your family doctor explaining that you are medically unfit for military service?"

Oakley raised his hand, along with approximately half the room.

"My advice to you," the sergeant said, "is to never give up your dreams." He shook his head, grinning.

The rest of the morning and most of the afternoon Oakley spent filling out forms and waiting in lines, up against the guy in front of him, balls to butt, either in his underwear or buck naked. It was an assembly-line screening, conducted in a series of stations, some in separate rooms but most scattered around the perimeters of large, open floors.

He peed into a specimen vial. A doctor grabbed his balls and instructed him to cough. He bent over and spread his cheeks for a rectal probe.

He did pushups, situps, arm circles and extensions, jumping jacks. He ran in place. He hopped sideways. He walked backwards and forwards like a duck.

They checked his hearing and vision, his heart and his head (The psychiatrist did little more than ask Oakley his name, as if assuming that if Oakley could articulate it, he was sane.)

In the orthopedic station, a small room, a civilian doctor examined Oakley for a minute and a half. Although he wore a suit and tie, the doc was dumpy and disheveled. His posture was nonexistent. He was a lump. His face was wet and pale. He looked sick. A cigarette hung from his lips, almost touching his chin. When they reached critical mass on the dangling tip, the ashes fell to the floor. He coughed without covering his mouth, turning his head or removing the cigarette.

He held a stethoscope to Oakley's chest without speaking and without looking at him.

Oakley handed the doctor his clipboard with the manila folder. He started to speak, but the doctor held up his hand, again without looking at Oakley.

The doctor opened the folder, glanced at the contents, and handed the clipboard back.

"Well?" Oakley asked.

"It's a minor thing," the doctor replied. "You pass."

"The symptoms aren't minor," Oakley said. "My left leg is numb right now. It's been numb for four hours."

"I can't test for numbness."

"So you think I'm lying."

The doctor stubbed his cigarette butt out on the floor. "I didn't say that. I just don't have the equipment here to verify numbness."

"This began because I'm a teacher, and standing up in front of my students —"

"I have seen hundreds of you today, and I have hundreds more to go. I don't have time to listen to your medical history. Please proceed to the next station."

Eventually, Oakley was directed to claim his wire basketful of clothes, dress, and report to Station 17, the last in the line, the checkout counter.

"How long before I know the results?" he asked the soldier at the desk.

"I can tell you right now," the soldier said, flipping through Oakley's forms.

Oakley waited.

"Well," the soldier said, "Looks like we won't be sending you to the front lines." He handed Oakley a final form to sign. "But we'll do our best to get you a desk job in Saigon."

Oakley left the building at 2:45, paid his parking, and drove home. He talked about the situation with Joe. They shared a six pack of Dos Equis and smoked a joint.

"No way I'm going over there," Oakley told Joe. "Even for a desk job. I don't want any part of that fucking war."

"I don't blame you, man, but that means you have to go to Canada. Then you're a fugitive. Think about going to 'Nam. If you're not in danger of getting killed, it might be a positive experience."

"No fucking way."

"Think it over. Don't decide until you get your induction notice. What's the hurry?"

But Oakley *was* in a hurry. He wanted to know what he should do. He thanked Joe for the advice and drove to the beach to watch the sunset.

As he sat on the beach in the cool evening, his eyes smarted and his lungs seized up in the smog, which had been a ring on the horizon the day before, and had been brought to shore by onshore breezes.

He thought about the postcards from Norm, some with a sentence or two from Fleur, urging Oakley to check out the place called Taylor Camp.

Norm wrote, "Beautiful surf, warm ocean, fresh air, clean water, free food, free rent, free love, unmentionables omnipresent."

Fleur wrote, "Take a chance. Launch into the leap of faith."

Norm wrote, "Come join us in this tropical paradox."

Fleur wrote, "Coup de foudre."

## 71. Southern California 1970

## NOTE FROM THE UNDERGROUND

Oakley didn't wait for an induction notice. Within ten days he was gone.

He closed out his savings account, gave Joe some money for the time it took to find a new roommate (also to serve as an untraceable mail drop for Oakley, and look after his car), and bought a round-trip ticket to Hawaii.

He had decided on a one-way ticket, but the round trip was a better deal, and for some reason this guarantee of departure entitled visitors to travel to any outer island for only seven dollars each way. It was actually cheaper to buy the round trip ticket, so he did.

The day he flew away, he sent his parents a letter:

Dear Mom and Dad:

Sorry to drop this bomb. Somehow I lost my teaching deferment, or never even had one. Now I've been drafted. Passed my physical exam in spite of the scoliosis. My induction notice is due any day.

But I won't be here.

And I can't tell you where I'll be because I'm not sure I trust you, and therefore don't know what you would do with the information. Keep it secret, or turn me in? I really don't know what you would do. So I'm going underground.

If you want to write me, send your mail to the Venice apartment where Joe will get it. He knows someone who knows someone who knows how to get correspondence to me. Don't even ask him to help you track me down. Don't do me that dishonor.

Sorry I didn't discuss this with you. I couldn't talk about it because I know what you would say. We're so far apart, it would be like the Century City peace march all over again. We live in and believe in two different realities, with few points of contact or mutuality. Too bad.

I'll try to keep in touch. Don't worry about me. I'm not as dumb as you think.

--Oakley

## WORRIED SICK

On the day after Christmas, on a visit to Hanalei to do laundry and pick up food and supplies at the Ching Young Store, Oakley checked the post office and found a letter from Joe addressed to him at General Delivery. Inside was another letter, sealed. It was from his mother. He sat on a bench outside the post office.

The letter from Joe was little more than a note:

Hey Oakley:

Wow, your Mom is really bugging me to tell her where you are. But don't worry, I'm keeping my promise. Mum's the word. (Whatever "mum" means. I thought it was a flower.) Anyway, I also promised your mother I would make sure you got this letter from her. She said it was really important.

You've missed some good waves at Secos and County Line (Malibu's a zoo, as always), but then I'm sure you're riding much better waves over there. I'd like to hear about it, but I guess you're paranoid about the letter being intercepted or something. I hope you and Norm and Fleur are living it up. I hear there's some good smoke in Hawaii, homegrown. For a guy in exile, you must not be hurting too much.

Why not call me on the phone? I don't think anyone's bugging our line. You know the number.

Oh yeah, one more thing. Your induction notice still hasn't arrived. (I wonder why not?) So technically you're still not a draft evader

Your friend and ex-roomy, Joe

Oakley opened the letter from his mother. Inside was another sealed letter, with the name Amy Bernstein and a return address. Amy was a former student. He read her letter.

To My Favorite Teacher:

Remember me? Amy Bernstein? I was in your eleventh grade English class at Woodknoll Prep in 1968.

I'm writing because I want to thank you. You were a great teacher and I really learned a lot from you.

I'm a sophomore at San Diego State, and so far I haven't had any teachers like you. But—I just decided to be an English major, thanks to you.

I guess I didn't totally appreciate what you were doing when you were doing it. I don't think many of the other kids in our class did, either. Some of them were put off. Some were even pissed off. You came on pretty strong.

Remember when you suggested to us that "school spirit" was just a fake thing that the administration made up to keep us in line and make us do what they wanted? You really touched a nerve with that one! Sue Morton, the cheerleader, was almost in tears. I think she reported you to the headmaster.

And the books you assigned were really, in retrospect, kind of out there. I remember you getting into trouble when some of the parents complained that your book choices weren't "proper" for high school students. *Women In Love* and *Catcher In the Rye* and *Catch 22* I especially remember. And those weird stories by Flannery O'Connor! And once in your briefcase I saw a book you were reading, *Teaching As a Subversive Activity*. You probably could have gotten fired just for having it.

I loved it when you had us read that weird, funny book about the funeral business, *The Loved One*, then took us to see the movie (which wasn't as good as the book, but still pretty weird), and then you took us on a field trip to

Forest Lawn cemetery. I don't know how you ever got school approval for that trip.

Back then I thought you were kind of weird, but now I know that you were just trying to make us think.

So, thanks for the push. It put me in a good place.

Part of me stays outside of myself all the time. This is not true for a lot of my friends, who don't seem to reflect on themselves very much, but I can't change that. I think it's a good thing for me to be able to stand away and look at myself. It's not easy, but it seems to be a good way to stay sane and healthy. I guess you helped me do that. You always told us: The unexamined life is not worth living.

When I contacted Woodknoll, they told me you were no longer teaching there. They don't know where you are, but they gave me your parents' address. I hope you get this letter, wherever you are. And I hope you're still teaching.

Sincerely,

Amy Bernstein

Oakley read the letter from his mother.

My Dear Son:

I hope you receive this letter. I asked all of your friends—the ones I know, anyway—where you are, but they either don't know or won't tell me. Joe wouldn't tell me, either, but he promised he would get this letter to you.

Your father and I are worried sick. We hope you are in a safe place where you have a roof over your head, food to eat, and a job.

The letter you left us explains it all, I guess. I wish you had told us in person, but you were afraid we would try to prevent you from leaving. And we might have.

But we understood your decision to leave. Your father, as you know, was too young to serve in World War I and too old for World War II. He never had to make any decisions about going to war, although I'm sure he would have fought Hitler if he had been called to.

I remember reading somewhere that Leo Tolstoy said it would be the mothers of the world who brought an end to war, tired of sending their sons off to die in foreign lands.
We certainly don't want you to die. On the other hand, we don't want you to go to jail. Maybe you've gone to Canada to stay out of jail. With your education, they would welcome you. But you would never be able to come home.

There is another solution, and I hope you won't be angry with me for pursuing this course of action. A few days after you left, I phoned the draft board and found out that it is possible to challenge the outcome of a military physical examination.

So I obtained medical records detailing your history of scoliosis from Dr. Dixon, and took them to three other doctors at the hospital. They all wrote opinions for me. Then I submitted the documents to the draft board. This was in September.

Yesterday I received a response. Your classification has been officially changed from 1-A to 1-Y. I was told that 1-Y means your physical condition makes you currently undraftable, but that if the war continues and more troops are needed, then the standards for acceptance may be lowered and you could be drafted in the future.

But a friend of your father gave me a different explanation: 1-Y means that you are fit to serve "only in time of war," and because Vietnam is not technically a war (undeclared by Congress), you will not be drafted unless war is actually declared.

I'm a bit confused, but I know that you won't receive an induction notice at this time. And I believe you'll be safe for the rest of this war-that's-not-a-war. However, I was also told that 1-Y is a temporary category, not permanent like 4-F, and that you can be called in for another physical at any time.

Please come home. I know you were upset about the Century City protest march, and our unwillingness to accept your description of what happened. But I didn't realize that you feel you can't talk to us anymore. That makes me very sad.

Another thing that upsets me is that you don't bother to speak with us because you believe you know what we'll say. That's not giving us much credit. We're not that predictable, and we're not that inflexible.

To tell the truth, I don't know what to believe anymore. In case you haven't heard, after more than three years, the task force that Mayor Yorty appointed to investigate the possibility of misconduct by the LAPD at Century City has published its findings—or, that is, their lack of findings. They reached no conclusion. Three years and no conclusion. It does sound suspicious.

Please come home. Or at least phone us (collect) to let us know you're alive and healthy. We won't even ask where you are.

Love,
Mom

Smiling and shaking his head, Oakley folded the letters and stuffed them into his pocket. He looked at the sky and laughed out loud. He stood, did a little dance, and let out a loud hoot, attracting attention from passersby. Then he went to the nearest phone booth.

# GOD IS DEAF

(Depressed)
DOWN

      Em             A
Last night I said a prayer

   Em        A
But nobody was there

       D      C
Does anybody hear me?

       D      C
Does anybody care?

Can I get through or not?

Are you there for me or not?

'Cuz if you're not listening

My whole life is shot

              G       C
(Excited) I figured it out
UP
        G       C
I got a theory

 G         C
God's not dead

      G       C
He's still near me

       G    C
What He is is deaf

       G C        G
He just can't hear me

       (Repeat slow)

All I asked for was money

And a Playboy bunny

I didn't say nothing

'Bout the land of milk and honey

But when I'm in that promised land

I'll do the best I can

When I meet my maker

I'll speak with my hands

(Refrain)

## 74. Kauai 1970

## MISSING IN ACTION

Early evening, two days after Christmas. Black clouds moved from the northern horizon into the dark gray sky. It was about to rain. Heavy surf crashed on the reef. The air was hazy with salt spray, blown into the jungle by the onshore winds.

Oakley had just returned from an afternoon session at Tunnels, carrying a surfboard under each arm. Norm was at Oakley's treehouse, sitting on the sofa with a transistor radio and a long length of rope. He jumped to his feet.

"Where the fuck have you been?"

"What does it look like?"

"There's a serious storm on the way."

"Tell me about it. The surf went from six to twelve feet while I was out there. Have you seen Danny?"

"No, why?"

"He was out there with me, big mistake because he can't surf for shit. We both got nailed by a close-out set. I paddled in and found Danny's board floating inside, but no Danny. I waited with his board on the shore for almost half an hour, but he never showed up. He might have drowned."

"Jesus."

"But he might be back here. Do you know where his tent is?"

"Yeah. I'll go check. But you need to get ready."

"For what?"

"For the fucking *storm*. I brought you this," Norm said, holding up the rope. "You need to lash down your roof."

"It's going to be that bad?"

"Let's listen to the latest." Norm turned on the radio, switching stations until he found what he wanted: "...gusty trade winds up to forty miles per hour. Rain is forecast on all islands for tonight and tomorrow, and a high surf advisory is in effect for the north and west shores of all islands."

"We need a local broadcast," Norm said, changing stations. He passed some music and talk. "Here it is."

The announcer said, "...heavy rains tonight on Kauai with flash flood warnings. You folks watch out in Waimea. And Wailua. And you folks up on the nort' shore, bettah stay tune' to dis station. The weather bureau expects surf up to twenty-five tonight, maybe beegah. Majah nort' swell, yeah? Get high winds, too, sixty miles an ouah. Wooh, Hanalei Bay goin' be beeg tomorrow! Surf 'em!"

Norm switched the radio off. "Fuck tomorrow! I wanna know if we're gonna make it through the night."

"Why so worried?"

"We never had a storm like this." He handed Oakley the rope.

"Is this necessary?"

"It's getting dark and the wind's getting stronger. Do it before it's too late."

"All right."

"Also, you might want to spend the night somewhere else."

"How come?"

"The surf's coming up. You might wind up as a reluctant passenger on a midnight cruise. With a cabin at sea level."

"Are you serious?"

"I don't know. It's not a tsunami, but if the waves get big enough they could wash over the ridge and into your kitchen."

Norm left, taking Danny's surfboard with him. Oakley tied an end of the rope around one of the ironwood stumps his platform rested on, threw the rope over the ridge of the A-frame, then fetched it on the other side and wrapped it around a diagonal stump. He threw the rope over and back until he ran out of it. As he tied down the other end of the rope, Norm returned.

"Danny's not home."

"Shit. What do we do now?"

"Tell me what happened."

"There were about ten of us out there, me and Danny and some locals. The other guys must have known what was happening, because all of a sudden they were gone. Nobody bothered to let me and Danny in on it; maybe they assumed we'd figure it out by ourselves.

"But we didn't, until those fun-and-easy six-foot waves turned into twelve-foot monsters, closing out across the bay. I started paddling for shore, but Danny headed in the opposite direction, out to sea. He was either crazy or suicidal, or both, because the waves just kept coming and they just kept getting bigger. I yelled at him to turn around, but he just yelled back at me about how I was a chickenshit, and kept paddling.

"Meanwhile, I got caught in the impact zone. Wave after wave kept breaking on top of me and holding me under, until I finally got smart enough to take off my leash and let the board go. After maybe half an hour, I made it to shore. But I couldn't find my board. I walked a half mile up and down the beach, and finally found it. And I found Danny's board, too, but no sign of Danny. I think we should call the Coast Guard, or the police."

"I don't know. He wouldn't want us to call anybody. We'd blow his cover."

"So what? Better apprehended than dead."

"Think about it, though. Nobody's going to look for him in this storm. They'd never find him, dead or alive. If he's still out there, he's drowned by now. Maybe a body will wash up in a day or two, maybe not."

"We've still gotta report it. Otherwise he'll just disappear. His family will never know what happened."

"His family will never know, anyway. We don't know where they are."

"Yes we do. They're in Iowa."

"How do you know that?"

"I found a letter at the dump. Danny wrote it to his girlfriend but never mailed it. I think he planted it for me to find. The address was in Des Moines, Iowa. And we know his real name. David Dawson."

"What if he's not dead?" Norm asked.

"Yeah, maybe he's safe on shore and passed out cold."

"No, I mean what if he's trying to fake his own death—you know, to get those MPs off his back?"

"Shit, Norm, if that's what he's doing, he would want us to report him missing, so he could be officially declared dead."

"So you think we should report a missing person, named David Dawson, home address somewhere in Des Moines, Iowa?"

"And a physical description."

"OK. Tell you what, Oakley. I'll make the call. I know a friendly homeowner down the road who'll let me use his phone. Meanwhile, you take care of your roof."

## 75. Kauai 2001

## ROCK AND ROLL

I'm up at seven with a touch of a hangover. Nothing serious, just a presence, a slowing. Nothing I can't deal with. Maybe I should cut down on the vodka. Or the smoke. Or both.

My plan is to take a morning walk on the beach, jump in the ocean, bid farewell to Hanalei Bay a.k.a Bali Hai, have breakfast, pack, load up, and leave for Lihue in time to return the car and the board, check in for my flight and, I hope, see Pualani again.

Nobody's up, but I hear televisions in almost every room. Urgent voices. News. No one's eating breakfast. The food's not even out.

Not many people on the beach, either, which is fine with me. It's a cool, calm morning. Yesterday's swell is gone and small waves wash across my path as I walk along the edge of the sea. I inhale the morning scents of salt, wet sand, and seaweed. I wade into the water, warmer than the morning air, and dive in. When I finish my swim, the trace hangover is gone.

When I return to my room, the woman who runs the B&B is knocking on my door.

"Good morning," I say. We're both standing outside the entrance.

"Oh, there you are," she says. There's a peculiar expression on her face—concern? Consternation?

"Is everything all right?"

"Well, of course not. It's a terrible tragedy. But we all need to think about what's happening here, and make some decisions."

"I don't understand."

"You can stay here tonight, and for as many nights as you need to stay before things get back to normal and you can leave. I'll give you the weekly rate instead of the nightly. I think that's fair."

"But I'm checking out right after breakfast. My flight's at eleven."

She looks surprised. "You don't understand. All flights are *cancelled*. The airport is *closed*. *Indefinitely*. Nobody's leaving today, or tomorrow, probably for the rest of the week."

"Why not?"

"My God, you don't know what's happened, do you?"

"I guess not." I'm a bit irritated.

"Turn on your TV," she says, opening the door to my room, "and get filled in. Then come out for breakfast and we'll talk about it."


I watch the images, over and again, for an hour. The jets crashing into the buildings, people jumping to their deaths, people running from the advancing cloud of dust, people with their faces covered with handkerchiefs and their bodies covered with chalky soot, people swearing, people praying, people crying.

I phone the airline. Busy signal every time. I get through to the rental car company and am told that I can keep the car for as many days as I please. No one's leaving Kauai, but no one's arriving either. Tourist turnover is temporarily suspended. Everything's in limbo.

Same thing at the B&B. My room was reserved for someone else, but now it's available to me until the airports open.

At breakfast, everybody's talking about it, how the world has changed forever. I keep to myself what I'm really feeling: It's payback time, for American arrogance and greed, for our sins against ourselves and the rest of the world.

I phone Pualani, but she's not in. I watch television until I can't take it anymore. Too much hysterical spin.

Another walk on the beach. Everything looks different.

Small but surfable waves break at Pinetrees. My heart's not in it.

I try to phone Pualani again. No luck.

Back to Taylor Camp.

In mid-afternoon I'm in the jungle, under the banyan tree, at the former site of Fred the Zen's treehouse, with my concrete evidence.

The mound of rock and cement is far too heavy to lift, but I can get my arms around it. Surely I can roll it. Like Sisyphus. I give it a shove, a half turn. The newly-exposed earth beneath churns with scattering underbelly-dwelling creatures. Something stabs me on my left foot, right below where a surf bump used to be, and I curse. I don't get a look at what bit me. A red lump appears and proceeds to swell. It itches. I scratch it.

I wipe my forehead and contemplate the journey. Quite a haul. A lot of work. But worth the effort because this is a monument, a sacred totem of a long-lost civilization, to be relocated to a conspicuous place, in honor of the eternal spirit of Taylor Camp. A cornerstone.

Half an hour later, dripping sweat, exhausted, hands blistered, legs scratched and mosquito-bitten, limping on my throbbing, itching, insect-bitten left foot, I emerge from the jungle with my rock, and roll it to my personal promontory up the rise.

I position it at the top of the overlook, considering the view planes. Satisfied, I sit on it, surveying the empty beach, the surf, the sun low in afternoon sky. I recall sitting in this spot one evening, doors of perception cleansed by a dose of acid, looking at the earth, watching it breathe, the ground gently undulating beneath my feet. I stand and walk down the rise to assess my handiwork from a distance.

I don't like it. It doesn't fit. The problem is, cornerstone or not, last remaining icon of a misunderstood community or not, it's the ugliest monument I've ever seen. It looks like a giant macaroon rolled in huge chocolate-covered almonds.

What can I do, bury it? Not without a shovel. I sit on it again, waiting for a better idea.

I come up with a good one: roll it over the edge of the little cliff, into the stream bed, where it will shatter into several smaller pieces and further decompose, eroding in the current.

I give it a shove, but instead of plunging through the air it rolls heavily down the embankment and comes to a halt in the middle of the stream, in a foot of water, in one piece.

What now? I can't leave it there. It still looks hideous. My foot itches. I scratch it. It's getting raw from scratching.

Twenty minutes later I'm sitting at the top of the beach near the mouth of the stream, the thing perched beside me looking like a huge scoop of Rocky Road. No one was there to observe me rolling it down the stream bed, sloshing over slippery rocks, to the beach.

In the west the sky has cleared over the ocean and the sun is falling into it, changing color from yellow to gold to orange to red, suffusing the breaking whitewater with a hue of light pink.

Sitting in the sand, I compose a eulogy, the dedication of my monument, a tribute to Taylor Camp and to the sixties, to all the good things that happened. To the difference we had begun to make, until the Powers That Be put a final and brutal stop to it.

And then, thirty years on, someone strikes back.

To me, the connection is clear and straight and undeniable. In so many ways, we've been asking for it.

I remember the story my parents told me, about the bomber that crashed into the Empire State Building on the day I was born. A handful of deaths then, thousands now. The paranoid press envisioned a Japanese kamikaze pilot, but it was one of our own.

*Praise Earth Days and organic gardeners. Praise clean energy from the sun and wind. Praise consciousness expansion and affirmative action. Praise small cars big on gas mileage.*

*Support the ERA and women's liberation. Burn bras, burn draft cards. Ban bombs and handguns. Protest the war, any war, all wars.*

*Remember the Beatles and Bob Dylan and the chimes of freedom flashing. Remember the liberals whose name is now a dirty word.*

*Save the whales, save the baby harp seals, save the sea turtles, save the reefs, save the wetlands, save the redwoods, save the wilderness.*

*Free Cesar Chávez, free Angela Davis, free Timothy Leary, free the Chicago Seven.*

As the sun sinks beneath the horizon, I position myself behind my big rock. I don't bother to take off my shoes; they've already been soaked in the stream. I roll the stone into the ocean. The cool water feels good on my wounded foot.

*Free David Harris. Free the dolphins. Free Willy. Don't free Sisyphus, he's already there.*

*Free the river rocks. Dissolve their concrete prison in salt water, scatter them in the surf, break them up and grind them down to a million grains of black sand.*

*Free Oakley.*

I push the rock into the shorebreak, rolling it against the slapping waves until it disappears, eventually to be dissolved in the oceanic flow, carried by the tide around the world, dispersed like seeds on distant shores.

*Here's to the memory of my Taylor Camp friends. Here's to Fred the Zen, man of power and pop icon. Here's to Soundtrack the songwriter. Here's to Marsha and her commitment to the cause. Here's to Fleur and Norm wherever they are. Here's to Sandy, wherever you are.*

This would be an opportune moment for Alternate-O to show up with another suggestion. But he's not here, and I'm not even tempted.

Hallelujah.

## ACTUAL SIZE

She's not too small like in a magazine <sup>G</sup> ... <sup>D</sup> <sup>C</sup>
Not too big like on a movie screen <sup>G</sup> ... <sup>D</sup>
Not too weird like in my dreams <sup>G</sup> ... <sup>D</sup> <sup>C</sup>
What she is is what she seems to be <sup>G</sup> ... <sup>D</sup> <sup>C D</sup>

} all open chords

From head to toe, skin to bone <sup>Bm</sup> ... <sup>F#m</sup>
She's actual size if not exactly as shown <sup>Bm</sup> ... <sup>F#m</sup>
Her hands her feet <sup>G</sup>
Her knees her thighs <sup>A</sup>
Front and back <sup>G</sup>
Ears and eyes <sup>A</sup>
Everything's actual size <sup>D</sup> <sup>C</sup> <sup>G</sup>

} all bar chords

That's how she stands it's not a pose

She fits right in to all of her clothes

No need to change her battery

Got her own internal energy

[Chorus]

What you get is what you see

Not retouched photographically

Never been altered digitally

Except by herself and some others and me

[Chorus]

## BLOWN AWAY

It was getting dark. Where the plastic sheeting of his roof flapped in the wind, Oakley staple-gunned it to the ironwood-and-bamboo frame and covered the staples with plastic tape. He untied the rope, pulled the loops tighter, and retied it. He moved his kitchen things from the ground floor up inside the raised platform.

"What are you doing?"

It was Sandy.

"Boy, you sure tread lightly. I'm getting ready. Norm seems to think it's going to be a bad one."

"The wind is really strong."

"Have you seen Danny?"

"No. Why?"

Oakley told her what had happened. "Norm thinks Danny might have left his board on the beach on purpose, to make everybody think he drowned."

"Well, I'm glad you decided to report him missing." Sandy looked at the ominous sky. "It's going to start raining any minute." She walked up the rise to look at the ocean. "Is it me," she asked, "or is the tide higher than usual?"

"It's the surf. Norm thinks it's gonna come all the way up here and wash away my treehouse. Or else the wind's gonna blow it down."

"None of us are safe. What if the wind blows a tree over and it crashes into our treehouse?"

"Anything could happen. But you're pretty far back from the ocean. I think you'll be all right."

Sandy helped Oakley move things inside. She asked him, "Now that you're not a draft evader anymore, what are you going to do?"

Oakley ran a hand through his hair. "I don't know. I might go back home."

"Can I go with you?"

"What?" Oakley had heard her, but needed time to think of a reply.

"I'm ready to get out of here. We could leave together. No obligations, no plans, no commitments."

"OK with me. Do you have a plane ticket?"

"I have the money to buy one."

"Then let's do it."

"You mean it?"

"Sure."

She hugged him. He put his arms around her. They looked at each other, faces almost touching. They kissed. The wind howled and the surf boomed, pounding so hard that they could feel it beneath their feet.

"What was that?" Sandy asked.

"The earth moved."

She laughed and held him tighter. "Make it move again."

"It wasn't me."

"How do you know?"

They kissed again.

Oakley said, "Can I ask a favor?"

"Sure."

"Can I spend the night at your place?"

"Sure."

"I could sleep downstairs on the kitchen table."

"I don't know about that."

"How come?"

"You might get strangled again."

"I don't think so."

"Don't you want to spend the night with me?"

"No, yes, I do, but I...didn't want to be presumptuous."

"Presumptuous!" She put a hand on his chest and pushes. "Big vocabulary man."

"Can I move some stuff over there, too? Just in case?"

"I'll help."

Oakley rolled up his sleeping bag and stuffed it into his backpack, along with his clothes and his rolled-up tent. Sandy filled three cardboard boxes with books, cassettes and food, the Coleman lamp and the tape player. It took several trips to haul it all, along with Oakley's surfboard, over to Fred's treehouse and stash it under the kitchen table. They finished in the dark, and then the downpour began.

It was more than rain. It was a massive overflow from the sky, dumping, dousing, drowning, heavy and relentless. They couldn't avoid cringing with each new wave.

It was cold and wet in Fred's kitchen. Whenever the wind gusted, the rain was blown sideways, drenching the exposed interior. It was noisy, too, in the howling wind and drilling rain.

Oakley and Sandy sat at the kitchen table, trying to ignore the forces of nature, eating soup that Fred and Marsha left for them hanging in a pot over the dying fire. It was a tasty concoction: carrots, celery, onions, garlic, Portuguese sausage, collard greens, and brown rice in chicken broth from a tin can.

They finished dinner and climbed the ladder to Sandy's room, Sandy leading with a flashlight in hand. The room was about ten feet long and five feet wide, furnished with a twin-size mattress with flower-patterned sheets and a thin blanket, wooden crates that stored books and tapes, a small chest of drawers with a mirror, Coleman lantern and cassette player on top, and Indian-print fabric on the walls. Pinned to the fabric were photographs cut from magazines, mostly pictures of people and places in Europe and Africa, and Dylan, Donovan, and Tim Buckley. Sandy lighted the lantern.

"You did a nice job here," Oakley said. "It's comfortable and cozy."

"Thank you."

They sat on the edge of the mattress. Sandy put a Buffalo Springfield tape in the player. Above their heads, rain pounded on the peaked ceiling. She got up and checked for leaks, found none. Gusts of wind pushed against the walls, puffing them inwards.

"It feels like we're in a barrel, going over Niagara Falls," Oakley said.

"Or the inside of a drum."

Neil Young sang, "There you stood on the edge of your feathers, expecting to fly."

Sandy lighted three candles beside the bed and turned off the lantern. They lay on their backs, listening to the music and the rain and wind, watching the flickering light and the heaving walls.

Stephen Stills sang, "Do you think she loves you? Do you think at all?"

After a while they touched and kissed. Oakley pulled off Sandy's T-shirt and shorts. She did the same for him. He was naked, she was in her bra and panties. They kissed and touched some more. He framed the facets of her sculpted face in the palms of his hands. He took off her bra and kissed her nipples. She let out a soft moan. He kissed her ribs, her navel, her thighs, and then her vagina through the panties. When he pulled the fabric aside and licked her naked, she moaned loudly and began to squirm, thrusting her pelvis up into him.

Then something surprising happened. Moaning and pushing upward, she climaxed, and then went limp. Oakley propped himself up on his elbows and looked at her. She had passed out. He watched for a few seconds until she regained consciousness, with a shudder.

"Oh!"

"Wow. You fainted."

"I know. It happens when I have an orgasm."

"Every time?"

"Almost."

She caressed him with her hands, everywhere: his face, his back, his legs, his stomach, his penis. She rose to her knees, leaned over him and caressed his chest with her hair. She leaned back, pulled off her panties, and opened herself to him.

They climaxed at the same time. Again she passed out and, after a few seconds, awakened with a start.

Oakley said, "Amazing."

"Sorry."

"Nothing to be sorry about."

The night passed, storming incessantly. Jarring gusts of wind slammed the walls like hammer blows. At times it sounded as if someone were dumping buckets of water on the roof. Even in the howling wind they could hear the muffled thunder of waves crashing on the reef. They slept fitfully, wakening often in the chaos of the storm, hugging and kissing, until dawn.

## 78. Kauai 1970

## HOMELESS

Oakley woke up, disoriented until he remembered where he was. Sandy was asleep beside him. Sunlight pierced the transparent walls. The rain was down to a drizzle, the wind was down to a breeze. The storm had passed.

He started to dress, trying not to wake Sandy. She stirred, rolled onto her back, opened her eyes, smiled and said, "Morning."

"Morning." He climbed back into bed and they embraced, intimate again, sharing breath, body to body from head to toe.

Oakley said, "Want to go for a walk?"

"Sure."

The first thing they noticed was the silence. No birds, no bugs, only the ocean in the distance, still pounding but calming down. The loudest sounds were the ones they were making, squishing and plopping as they slogged along the muddy trail in their flimsy sandals. They held hands until it was easier not to.

Sandy broke one of her flip-flops, the strap unable to bear the excess mud-weight, its little plug popping through the black rubber sole and tearing it. She left both slippers behind on the edge of the trail. The breeze was warm on their faces, too light to stir the leaves in the trees.

Gray clouds shouldered their way across the sky, exposing the sun and concealing it again, revealing an alternating landscape, now in sunshine, now in shadow.

As soon as they emerged from the jungle onto the beachhead, a pair of dogs ran up to them, sniffed their legs, then ran off. A malachite sea turned into slate. The air was filled with salt spray and fine, light rain.

On the beach, everything was changed. Large chunks of coral littered the shoreline. In the ocean, churning, disorganized waves lurched in several directions at once, smashing up against one another like cymbals.

As the surf had torn coral from the reefs, the wind had stripped leaves from the trees. Some had been felled. They walked over to a row of four beachfront treehouses. Three had been damaged substantially: roofs and walls blown off, ground floors flooded, possessions washed away. The dazed inhabitants walked around, picking up debris, looking for lost items, removing split wood and damaged furniture, preparing to make repairs.

"We should help," Sandy said.

"Let's check out my treehouse first. Then we'll come back."

They headed back into the jungle, along the east bank of Limahuli Stream. As soon as they left the beach, they were transported into an alien landscape.

"Oh my God," Sandy said. "It's beautiful."

The jungle floor was covered with sand that had been pushed up the stream by the storm surf and high tide, overflowed the banks, and spread across the ground for fifty yards in each direction.

They sat on the trunk of a fallen tree. The jungle was still and quiet, clean and cool. Sunlight came and went. The carpet of sand had smoothed out the rough contours of rocks and plants and tree roots, replacing all the greens and browns and reds with a great wash of beige.

"It looks like khaki-colored snow," Oakley said.

"It's the skin of the planet," Sandy said.

The storm had gutted Oakley's treehouse. The frame was intact, but the plastic sheeting had been torn from the stapling, exposing the interior. Shreds of polyethylene rustled in the breeze. Everything he had left behind was drenched. The cloth that had lined the walls was on the floor. Cardboard boxes were soggy and shapeless. The wooden shelves containing his kitchen implements had been overturned, some blown into the brush. He found his mosquito net covering a shrub. His sofa sat, soaked, torn, and overturned, at the entrance to his kitchen, having been carried by the sea and smashed against a wooden pole at the entrance to his covered walkway, collapsing part of the canopy.

"It's not that bad," Sandy said. "Replace the roof, fix the canopy, dry everything out, and you're back in business."

"I don't know." Oakley tilted the sofa upright and pulled the pole into place, trying to stretch the canopy back into place. The pole fell when he let go of it, and the section collapsed again. "Maybe this is a message."

"Meaning?"

"Time to split. I get the letter from my mother, I think about leaving, then my house blows down."

"Ready when you are."

## FLUSH

Driving back to Hanalei in the dark, having achieved some sense of equilibrium and having made peace with my memories of Taylor Camp, I feel lightheaded, strange, cut loose. Wondering what to do next.

Why am I being prevented from leaving Kauai? The foundation upon which reality sits has suddenly shifted. Everybody knows nothing will ever be the same. But this is only a partial accounting for my peculiar mood.

At Big Save I buy a sandwich, a bag of Maui-style potato chips, a banana, and a papaya, and bring it all home to the B&B. I'm about to mix myself a vodka cocktail, but I change my mind.

I take the bottle and the rest of Miles's pot into the bathroom. I empty the booze into the toilet, break open the joints and flake all the weed in after it, and flush it all goodbye.

I assess my situation. No one knows when the airports will be open, and so far the airlines won't let me reschedule my flights home. I might not be there when school starts. I'm in for some hassles.

On the other hand, Kauai's a great place to be stranded. I have a car, a place to stay, and a surfboard. And then there's Pualani.

The phone rings.

It's her. Right on cue. We share some thoughts about the attack.

"So," she says, "I guess you won't be leaving for a while."

"Definitely not."

"Then you have some time on your hands."

"I suppose I do."

"I have a plan."

"I'm all ears."

"Let's go camping."

I'm sure she can sense me smiling.

"I have a ride to Hanalei, I have all the equipment we'll need, and I have a friend who can drop us off at the Kalalau trail head. You can leave your rental car at her house. We can camp on the beach at Hanakapiai, take the loop trail up the valley, keep on to the Hanakoa Shack, go all the way to Kalalau Beach if we want to."

"Sign me up. I've never hiked that far in."

"Just one stipulation."

"Whatever."

"No booze and no pot. It's a drug-free outing all the way."

"What a coincidence. You won't believe what I just did."

## OUT-OF-CONTROL GROUP

Nine in the morning of the last day of the year. The usual gang—Fred, Marsha, Norm, Soundtrack, and Oakley—were sitting in Fred's kitchen. Fleur was on the beach. Sandy was upstairs. Fred had a mug of coffee, Norm sucked on a roach. Marsha made herself a peanut butter and potato chip sandwich on wheat bread. Soundtrack strummed his guitar and sang with new lyrics to the tune of "Down in the Boondocks."

"Out in the boondocks, out in the boondocks, people run us down, hitchin' into town from the boondocks."

Fred said to Marsha, "I'm going into Hanalei today. I need the car keys and your dirty laundry."

"About time," she said, crunching into her sandwich. "Need quarters?"

"Got 'em."

"Can I throw in a couple of things?" Norm asked.

"I have an idea," Fred said. "Why don't you come with me and help?"

"Can't. Fleur and I are taking Oakley and Sandy to the airport, picking up some bananas, and running some errands in Lihue."

"How about you, Marsha? Want to join me?"

"No way! That guy at the laundromat gives me the creeps. He keeps trying to feel me up."

"He thinks you're an advocate of free love," Norm said. "Which reminds me, how come you cut me off so suddenly?"

"We had our fling. Now it's over."

"So *you* decided. But I was never consulted."

"It's not something that requires your approval."

Fred laughed.

"Well, let me know if you change your decision."

"I'll keep you in the back of my mind."

"Sounds like a lonely place."

Fred laughed again.

Norm rolled a joint. Sandy climbed down her ladder, lugging a duffel bag. Oakley got up to help her.

"Morning, everybody," Sandy said.

"You two are really going to do it, aren't you?" Fred asked.

"Yep," Oakley said. "We fly to Honolulu at one, then to San Francisco tonight."

"What a gesture," Marsha said. "Starting out on a new life on New Year's Eve. You're gonna miss a good party tonight. Fred's cooking steak and potatoes."

"Better keep him under surveillance. He might spike the food again."

"Fred never does anything twice."

"You could stay here with us, Oakley," Fred said. "You and Sandy, the lovebirds, living in her room. All you'd need to do is give me all your money."

Oakley laughed. "Thanks for the offer, but it's time to leave. I mean, in one day I almost drown, and then my treehouse is completely destroyed in the storm. I can take a hint."

Norm looked at Fred. "Should we tell him?"

"Why not?" Fred asked.

"Tell me what?"

"You would have had to move out of that treehouse pretty soon, anyway," Norm said.

"Why?"

"It's not on Taylor's land. His land ends at Limahuli Stream. We heard that the County persuaded the guy who owns the land your treehouse is on to kick everyone off."

"No shit?"

"No shit. That would include Danny, too, and Heather and Patrick."

"Another sign from the cosmos," Oakley said.

"You going to stay in San Francisco?" Marsha asked. "It's cold there. Foggy."

"I don't know. We're going to travel around, check out some places, and settle down when we find a place we like."

"I think I want to go to Portland, or Seattle," Sandy said.

"It's even colder there."

Norm was about to light his joint when he heard a sound from the trail. He put it in his pocket along with his pouch. The two plain-clothes MPs appeared from the trail, wearing the same ridiculous outfits they wore on their first visit. Soundtrack played the "Dragnet" theme.

"Hello again," the short one said. "We're back."

"What a pleasant surprise," Fred said, sans lisp. "Do come in. Happy New Year!"

"What can we do for you this time?" Norm asked.

"This time you can tell us the truth," the short one said. "About David Dawson."

"We haven't met anybody by that name since the last time you were here," Fred said.

"Somebody by that name was reported to the police as missing, four days ago," the tall one said. "By a resident of Taylor Camp who declined to give his name."

"Cat still got your tongue, Guitarzan?" the short one asked.

Soundtrack nodded.

"The caller claimed that David Dawson disappeared while surfing at Haena Point on the afternoon of December 27th," the tall one said. "You don't know anything about it?"

"Afraid not," Norm said.

"Somebody in your, uh, neighborhood goes and drowns," the short one said, "but you don't know anything about it? You don't even care?"

"We're not real neighborly here," Marsha said. "We keep to ourselves."

"How about you, or you?" the tall one asked Oakley and Sandy. They both shook their heads.

"Seeing as how there was no body," the tall one said, "we're not convinced he's dead."

"Wish we could help you," Norm said, "but we can't."

"Oh, come on!" the short one said. "You hippie assholes really piss me off. Maybe we oughta have a look around. Maybe we'll find your stash."

"If you're military police, you have no authority over civilians," Fred said. "Besides, a search is against the law without a warrant."

"A lot of things you're doing here are against the law, old man," the short one said. "How come you get to break the law, but we don't? What if I just decided, like you, that I didn't have to obey certain laws? What if I just decided to beat the living shit out of you?"

"I invite your attempt."

"You expect the government to follow all the rules, and you want the law to protect you," the tall one said. "But personally, you think you're exempt. You think you're above the law."

"That's a double fuckin' standard if I ever heard of one," the short one said. He took a step toward Fred. Oakley decided to intervene, but before he could move, in a quick martial arts maneuver Fred threw the MP to the ground. He landed with a thud and a groan. The tall one moved to attack Fred. Oakley, Norm, and Marsha moved to Fred's side. Sandy watched, horrified.

Before anything else could happen, Danny appeared from the underbrush. He was wearing a backpack and carrying his surfboard.

"That's enough," he said. "Leave them alone."

"Well, lookey here," the short one said, standing and dusting himself off. "Can it be Private Dawson?"

"Reporting for duty."

"Reporting for court martial, you mean," the tall one said.

"Don't you have to read him his rights or something?" Sandy asked.

"He doesn't have any rights," the short one said. "He's in the Army. Or was, before he deserted."

"I was just AWOL for a while," Danny said. "Now I'm voluntarily surrendering. And I have witnesses."

"You don't have shit, Dawson."

"Let's get out of here," the tall one said. "This Manson family's giving me the creeps."

"Thanks, Fred," Danny said. "You were right. I gotta get this out of my way."

"Come on, 'Danny boy'," the short one said. "The pipes are calling."

"Oakley, will you give my board to someone who'll use it?" Danny asked. He looked around. "It was great while it lasted. Thanks for the good times."

The two MPs left with Danny between them. Nobody said anything.

Soundtrack sang, "Breaking rocks in the hot sun, I fought the law and the law won."

Norm retrieved his joint and lighted it.

"Taylor Camp is experiencing a sudden and rapid drop in population," Norm said. "Is there some hidden cause for this effect?"

"It's New Year's Eve," Fred said. "A day of change. A day of resolution."

"That's just the cover," Norm said. "There's a conspiracy behind it. I think Oakley has something to do with it. He's definitely in on it. He might even be the prime mover."

"Give me a break," Oakley said.

"Maybe we're all in on it, Norm," Fred said. "Or maybe we're all just ignorant pawns in somebody else's game."

"I don't believe that," Norm said. "Even when I follow their rules, I'm still playing the game my way."

Fred said, "Amen."

"The way I have it figured," Oakley said, "it's like those psychology experiments. I did at UCLA."

"The marijuana experiments?" Norm asked.

"Not just those. After them, I kept signing up for all kinds of experiments in the psychology department. It was fun, and they paid me. No matter what the experiment was about, they always had two groups: the control group and the experimental group. And the control group was just people under normal conditions, used as a reference point for measuring the changes that happened to the people under experimental conditions."

Norm offered the joint. Oakley refused. Marsha took it. "So what's your point?" she asked.

"Well, for some reason I always ended up in the experimental group. And I thought, that's the way I want to go through life. There's all these normal people living normal lives in the control group, and then there's me, always in the experimental group, always doing something new and different."

"Excellent," Fred said. "May you always be in life's experimental group."

A young woman appeared at the trail entrance, pack on her back. She had long brown hair and was dressed in handmade clothes.

"Fred?"

"Heather! Come in!"

"Where's Patrick?" Norm asked.

"He went for a walk," she said, excited. "A long walk, up the beach. He needs to think things over. I told him I was leaving him. And I am—right now! I'm leaving him!"

"At last," Marsha said.

Fred said, "Congratulations."

"I just stopped by to say goodbye and...thank you," Heather said.

"Thank him for what?" Norm asked.

"You're doing the right thing," Fred said. "Don't worry; we'll take care of Patrick. He's not a bad fellow, but he's not for you."

Heather hugged Fred and kissed him. "Thanks for everything!"

"Everything?" Norm looked at Fred suspiciously.

"Goodbye to you, too, Norm. And you, um…?

Norm said, "Oakley. And Marsha. And Sandy. And Soundtrack."

"Where are you going?" Oakley asked.

"To stay with a friend in Kapaa."

"Need a ride?"

"She's picking me up here. She's probably waiting on the road. I'd better go." She smiled and turned back to the trail.

"Aloha," Fred said.

"You horny old bastard!" Norm said.

"She needed me," Fred said. "My therapy doesn't work without intimate contact."

"That makes two women you've lost in a single day," Norm said. "Sandy and Heather. Lucky you still have one left."

"Marsha won't last much longer," Fred said. "She's getting ready to leave any day now. She's had enough of this limbo. Right, Marsha?"

"Fuck you."

"I train them well," Fred said. "You'll knock 'em dead out there."

"The flower children aren't children anymore," Norm said.

"Time to go, Norm," Oakley said. "You ready?"

"We're outa here."

"Is Fleur coming?"

"She doesn't like goodbyes."

Oakley said to Fred, "Thanks for putting me up."

Fred said, "I'm always glad to shelter the homeless. Happy New Year."

Sandy walked over to Fred, stood in front of him, then hugged him hard. "Bye, Fred. Thank you for saving my life."

"You saved yourself."

"Soundtrack," Oakley said, "judging from your song lyrics, if you ever decide to start speaking again, you'll be eloquent. Good luck with your life."

They hugged. Everybody hugged. Oakley, Sandy and Norm left. Soundtrack picked up his guitar.

## TAYLOR CAMP

I'm doing fine at Taylor Camp <sup>A</sup>
I'd send you a letter but it rained on my stamps <sup>D</sup>
What am I gonna do? <sup>E</sup>
Gonna get lost and find myself too <sup>D</sup> <sup>E</sup>
But I need some more money if it's all right with you <sup>D</sup> <sup>E</sup>
I'll be home soon <sup>A</sup> <sup>D D</sup>
      Taylor Camp <sup>A</sup> <sup>D D</sup>
      Taylor Camp <sup>A</sup> E E  E7 E7   E7 E7  (7th Fret)

Wintertime at Taylor Camp

It's never cold but it's always damp

Some of us are staying clean

Some of us are smoking 'til our brains turn green

Some on acid seeing things we never seen

And never wanted to

      Taylor Camp

      Taylor Camp

If you're burned out at Taylor Camp

Come on in and we'll relight your lamp

What you want, you're gonna get

Whether it's total freedom or just some part of it

It really doesn't matter once you learn the art of it

As you will see

      Taylor Camp

      Taylor Camp

You can crash at Taylor Camp

On the freeway of life this is the off ramp

What are we doing here?

Eatin' and shittin' and sleepin' and screwin' here

In fact, nothing much is really new in here

After all

      Taylor Camp

      Taylor Camp

      Taylor Camp

      Taylor Camp <sup>A</sup> D D <sup>A</sup>

## BEYOND THE FIRE

Pualani arrives before noon with the gear, evenly distributed into two backpacks: sleeping bags, ground pads, a pup tent, ponchos, a small stove, pot, pan, plates, utensils, and enough food and water to last us for a five-day hike.

She's wearing shorts, a tank top, a sweatband and hiking boots, looking fit and eager. She gives me a hug and a kiss on the cheek.

I treat us to a big lunch at Honu's, carbo-loading for the hike, and we buy sandwiches, snacks, and fruit for dinner. Her friend drops us off at Ke'e, and we spend the afternoon in the jungle and on the beach, exploring my remembered haunts at Taylor Camp, swimming in the ocean and sunning on the sand. Pua asks me to tell her the whole story of my sojourn here, so I do—from the day she stole my camera to New Year's Eve, 1970.

In the late afternoon, we pitch our tent at the edge of the jungle. Our intention is to get up early in the morning to hit the trail.

As the sun moves low and the day cools, I gather some driftwood to build a fire on the beach. We sit in the sand, dressed for the night and the mosquitoes in jeans and socks and long-sleeved shirts. Pualani wears a green scarf around her neck.

"What happened to all those people? Where did they go after Taylor Camp was shut down?" Pualani asks.

"Where should I start?"

"How about the one you left with?"

"Sandy? We went to San Francisco, and for a while it was great. I loved being half of a mixed couple, and she was so good-looking when she was up. When she was up she stood upright, straight and proud, and we drew a lot of attention. But I couldn't deal with the other side. All slouched over, head down, unable or unwilling to speak anything but words of sadness and despair. Nothing I did ever helped. I told her she needed treatment, but she didn't think it would do any good. I got in touch with her parents in Iowa, but they wanted nothing to do with her. One night I told her we couldn't be together if she didn't get help. The next day, when I came home from the school where I was teaching, she was gone. I tried to find her but she just disappeared. I never saw her again."

We watch the sun approach the horizon. It's cool and quiet except for the sound of the surf.

"Norm and Fleur had a baby. I think they moved to Canada, but not Toronto. Somewhere in BC, maybe Vancouver Island. They sent me a postcard from Nanaimo, but I think they were just passing through. They were married and now he's a Canadian citizen."

"What about Soundtrack? Did you stay in touch with him?"

"No, but I followed his career. I heard about this San Francisco group called Hippie Dream Gone Bad, and I knew he had to be in it. But in the pictures I saw of the band, no one looked like Soundtrack. Then I read an article in the *Chronicle*, and there was a photo of Soundtrack with the band. Identified as Jeremy Mitchell, 'resident songwriter.' He didn't perform but he wrote all their material."

"Like Bernie Taupin and Elton John."

"Or Keith Reid and Procol Harum."

"Never heard of them."

"Procol Harum?"

"No. Hippie Dream Gone Bad."

"They never made it big, but they were a local success. Played all over the Bay Area. One time they opened for Neil Young at the Cow Palace. He must have hooked up with Marsha, because their one album was on her parents' label. Patchouli. After that they broke up."

"What about the horny guru?"

"Fred moved to Los Angeles and struck pay dirt. Traveled all over the country in the eighties conducting seminars and hit the bestseller list with two books. Do you know them? *Ten Times Zen* and *Ten Times Zen Again?*"

"I do. By Ferdinand Zolgotz. I never read them, but I've seen him on TV. That's Fred the Zen?"

"Yep."

"Wow."

"He made a lot of money, but he spent a lot of it on paternity lawsuits."

"Where is he now? I haven't heard anything about him for years."

"Your guess is as good as mine."

"Anybody else?"

"Marsha made a brief splash in the media in the late seventies with the women's movement. She ran for political office, state legislature I think, but didn't win. Then she got married and did a total turnaround. Her kid became a tennis champion. I saw her on TV and she looked like a Stepford wife."

"What about you?"

"I became a schoolteacher. My marriage failed. I came to Kauai to retrieve a stolen camera I didn't care about. I came looking for Taylor Camp and trying to figure out what went wrong. With me and the United States. Then, on the day I was supposed to go home, the world turned upside down. And here I am."

"Here we are."

We watch the waves. I tend the fire, feeding it new wood, pushing and poking around with a long driftwood branch.

I experience a tremendous sense of a very solid reality: sky and ocean and sand and fire. What could be more substantial, more real?

But then something happens. I look through the fire, and behind the heat waves the whole scene shimmers. Beach and sky and ocean flap gently like a sheet on a clothesline. It's like in an old-time movie when the screen ripples just before the guy who gets hit with the blackjack passes out, or when a flashback is about to begin. Or like a TV sci-fi dissolve, trekkers being beamed up. All the solid things suddenly aren't solid anymore.

"Look through the fire," I say.

"That's what I'm doing."

"And?"

"So much for reality."

"The veil of deception wiggles before our very eyes."

She laughs and smiles without looking at me.

"This can also happen," I say, "when you're driving on a highway and there's road heat rising from the asphalt. Through the vapors the cars coming toward you look like they're shimmering and melting."

"I've seen that."

"So it's true that everything we see is an illusion. However, it's also true that illusory cars can run over you and kill you."

"Sure thing."

"But then there's one more truth: The fact that those cars can kill you, doesn't make them any less unreal."

"You just keep going deeper into the rabbit hole."

The sun moves toward the ocean. The air cools and the sounds grow muffled in the early evening calm. I get up to add more driftwood to the fire and poke things around a little, then sit back down with Pualani.

"Thirty years ago," I say, "that was the acid experience. We learned that reality was not as fixed as we were led to believe. Things could change. We could change the world. We *did* change it."

"We can still change it."

"It seems harder now. The odds are against it."

"Maybe. But that's no reason to stop trying."

"America's going backwards. With a lot of momentum."

"It doesn't matter. I do what I can, you do what you can."

Pualani takes a bottle of water and a banana from her pack. We share them as we watch the sky fill with color.

She turns to me. "You know, I really don't care if you smoke pot or drink alcohol. That's up to you. I just wanted us to take this trip straight and clear. Besides, you get high just being here. That's what's happening now. Why try to enhance it?"

I shrug. "No argument."

She smiles again. "The best thing is that you agreed to the conditions, and that made me feel good."

"Wow. I did something right."

She puts an arm around my shoulder and gives it a squeeze. The sun touches the water.

"You ever seen the green flash?" she says.

"Many times, back then, sitting right here."

"Maybe we'll see it tonight."

Suddenly I feel a sensation I haven't felt in a long time. It's physical and emotional at the same time. It's the opposite of a contraction—an expansion, an opening out. The manifestation of possibility. Like the old acid rush.

Who knows what's happening? Who wants to know? Maybe I'll stick around Kauai for a while. Maybe I'll take a sabbatical. Maybe I'll never go home. Maybe I'm already home.